DAY OF ATON

A. Alvarez was born in London in 1929 and educated at Oundle School and Corpus Christi College, Oxford. He has written two other novels, *Hers* and *Hunt*, several books of poetry and literay criticism, and a number of highly praised non-fiction books including *The Savage God*, *Life after Marriage*, *The Biggest Game in Town*, *Offshore* and *Feeding the Rat*. He is married, with three children, and lives in London.

BY THE SAME AUTHOR

General

Under Pressure
The Savage God: A Study of Suicide
Life After Marriage: Scenes from Divorce
The Biggest Game in Town
Offshore: A North Sea Journey
Feeding the Rat: Profile of a Climber

Fiction

Hers
Hunt

Criticism

The Shaping Spirit
The School of Donne
Beyond all this Fiddle
Samuel Beckett

Poetry

Lost
Apparition
Penguin Modern Poets No. 18
Autumn to Autumn and Selected Poems 1953–76

Anthology

The New Poetry

A. Alvarez

DAY OF ATONEMENT

VINTAGE

20 Vauxhall Bridge Road, London SW1V 2SA

London Melbourne Sydney Auckland Johannesburg
and agencies throughout the world

First published by Jonathan Cape Ltd, 1991
Vintage edition 1992

1 3 5 7 9 10 8 6 4 2

Printed and bound in Great Britain by
Cox & Wyman Ltd, Reading

ISBN 0 09 919061 3

FOR TONY AND CINDY HOLDEN

'The desires of the heart are as crooked as corkscrews.'

W.H. Auden

PART 1

JOE

The day Tommy died it was raining. It had been raining, in fact, for a week – steady monotonous rain out of a sodden sky – and there seemed no good reason to think it would ever stop. There also seemed no good reason to think that Tommy would die, aged fifty-one, in his vigorous scheming prime. Tommy Apple, né Applebaum, hairy and overweight, full of good will, appetite and clever deals.

I was late leaving the studio but even so the tube was packed. We were jammed in shoulder to shoulder, belly to belly, back to back, so close that you could smell the depression and harassment, just as you could smell the steaming coats. Unaired office faces, sour breath, body heat. The furious din of the train tunnelling beneath London. I had to stand all the way to Camden Town.

My leg hurt, as it always does when there's rain. A dull subliminal ache, not enough to complain about, just a reminder that nothing lasts for ever, particularly the body. Years ago, on the squash court, I tore all the ligaments in my left ankle and since then I've walked with a slight limp. It is not anything you would notice unless you were looking for it. But I notice. I think of myself as a man with a limp and it makes me touchy. The ache also makes me feel more tired than I should be at my age. Forty-five isn't old, not any more. The world is full of lusty geriatrics, sharp-eyed, spun-steel, driving relentlessly through their eighties. But I feel old.

Even at Camden Town I had to move fast to grab a seat. The relief, when I sat down, began at my ankle and spread slowly up my spine to the base of my skull.

The man sitting next to me was the kind of Jew that used to make my assimilated father anxious: curly sideburns, shovel beard, sloping shoulders, black broadcloth buttoned tight across a noble stomach. His prayer book was open on his lap and his lips were moving, although he made no sound. 'It's hard enough being Jewish without shoving it down everybody's throat,' my father used to say. 'Why make trouble for the rest of us?' The Hasid was a short man but his feet were big and splayed, as though to balance the overhang of his belly. Tucked between his bulging tightly laced shoes was a smart new holdall – beige canvas with pockets and leather trimmings – that seemed out of place with the old-fashioned black suit and beaver hat. As the train pulled out, he turned to me. He had mild myopic eyes and a powerful Brooklyn accent.

'Dis OK for Boint Oak?' His voice was musical and vibrato and it made Burnt Oak sound exotic.

I nodded at the map above the heads of the gloomy passengers opposite. 'One stop before the end of the line.' I gave him a big smile, thinking of my father and his prejudices.

The Hasid looked at me stonily, grunted 'Tanks', and went back to his prayers. Keeping himself to himself, not wanting contact with the impure, communing with his God. God in the underground, in the drowned streets, in the marriage bed. All in all, my godless father had been right.

The man was still praying when I got off at Belsize Park. The rain hit me as I came out of the station and the wind was cold. I huddled into my coat at the crossing, and pulled my hat down over my ears, while the rush hour traffic hissed up the hill, homeward bound.

The light changed and I hurried across the road. The off-licence and the newsagent were still doing business and behind the steamed-up window of the fish-and-chip shop a small queue of people was waiting to be served. The undertaker's, locked and closed at this hour, had a floodlit front and a neon sign, bright and attractive, like a cinema.

I trudged down Glenmore Road, eyes down, head averted, shoulders hunched. The London cringe. Raindrops swirled around the street lights so wildly that the lights themselves seemed to be swaying like trees. I could see my house framed at the end of the road, big and square and red-brick, its windows lit against the curtains of rain. My parents' house, now mine, an abiding presence in my life, like my wife, like this childless marriage we both work so hard to keep sweet.

Judy must have been lurking in the kitchen, for she was in the hall as soon as I opened the door. Her face was paler than usual and she shook her head before I even said hello.

'Someone to see you,' she said.

Judy is from Aberdeen, a rich and orderly city, and after fifteen years she still believes the streets of London are swarming with muggers and rapists. She distrusts unexpected callers, night visitors, salesmen, Jehovah's Witnesses, even the messenger boys who bring me colour prints from the lab. Every morning she scans the paper for items about urban violence to confirm her suspicions.

'We should hang up a sign, "By invitation only".' I took off my dripping coat and hat. 'What's he selling?'

Judy shook her head again. 'A Mr Riley,' she said. Then she smiled quickly, as if I needed cheering up. She has beautiful teeth and when she smiles she sheds years. As always, her easy smile, the jeans tight over her shapely tail made me forget the ache in my leg and the foul weather outside. I kissed her cheek and said, 'What time do we eat?'

She rolled her eyes at the closed living-room door: 'Whenever.' Then she went back to the kitchen. The smell of her scent mingled with the warm pleasant smell of cooking. Outside on the street, the wind gusted suddenly, the rain rattled against the front door.

Mr Riley was sitting on the edge of the low sofa, a shabby briefcase on the floor beside him. Pinched body and pinched face under a cap of grey curls. Scrubbed cheeks, pouting mouth, sharp nose. The eyes, behind his glasses, were watery. His fingers were stained with nicotine. He got up when I came in, bending hesitantly forward like a long-legged water-bird. He thrust a business card at me.

'It's about Tommy Apple.'

'Haven't seen him for weeks.'

Mr Riley smiled and sat down again, hands hanging limply between his knees.

'The thing is.' He pulled out a handkerchief and dabbed the pointed end of his nose. 'We have a problem.'

The smell of cooking crept under the door. 'A problem?' I glanced at the card: Ramon Fernandez & Company. Importers.

'A business transaction with Mr Apple.' He blew his nose vehemently. 'Some goods have gone missing.'

'Then ask him. I'm his friend, not his business partner.'

'Unfortunately, Mr Apple is no longer available.'

The telephone rang. I started towards it but Judy picked it up in the kitchen.

'Then wait till he gets back to town.'

'That's not really possible.' He hunched forward, clutching his handkerchief.

I could hear Judy's voice from the kitchen. Low-pitched and grave, the rhythm broken. The voice of someone hearing bad news.

'Why come to me?'

Mr Riley plied his handkerchief and blinked as if he were having trouble seeing me through his cold. 'Your name came up. We thought you could help.'

I listened to Judy's murmuring, upset voice, trying to pick out the words. Mr Riley sniffed loudly.

'You've made a mistake. I'm a photographer, not a businessman. You're mixing me up with someone else.'

Mr Riley shook his head, holding his handkerchief to his sharp nose. 'There are loose ends. Wherever we look we find your name. He was a man you saw a lot of.'

'Socially. He's an old friend.'

'You did deals together.'

'It's none of your business.'

The lights on the telephone went out. Footsteps in the hall. Judy opened the living-room door and stood there slightly crooked, as though her side hurt, one hand on the doorframe.

'Joe,' she said. 'Oh, Joe.'

I put my arms around her, murmuring, 'What's up, darling? What's up?'

She leaned her head on my shoulder and wept. All she said was, 'Oh, Joe.'

Mr Riley was watching us, his ferret face bright with interest.

'Out,' I said. 'This isn't the moment.' I gave him his wet mac and shabby umbrella and hustled him out into the rain. As I closed the door, I called after him, 'Tell your people they've got the wrong man.'

Judy had gone back into the kitchen. She stood at the stove, prodding a saucepan full of spinach with a wooden spoon, while the tears ran down her face.

'It's Tommy,' she said. 'He's had a heart attack.'

'Not possible.'

'This afternoon. Keeled over in his office. He's dead, darling. Just like that.'

I held her while she sobbed, her hot wet face against my shirt. The stew cooled on the kitchen table, the rain pattered against the window. I knew I should be crying like her, but all I felt was outrage. Somehow Mr Riley and his streaming cold made it worse. Mr Riley saying, 'Mr Apple is no longer available.' As though he had known all along.

'It's our youth,' Judy said. 'Our oldest friend.'

She pulled away from me, fumbled in her handbag for a tissue, then went to the sink and dabbed her face with cold water.

'How did you hear?'

'Louise.'

'I'd better phone her,' I said.

But the line was busy and it stayed busy all evening. Even at the best of times, Louise could never resist the telephone.

We drank some wine, picked at the food in silence. I washed the plates and glasses, scrubbed the saucepan vigorously, making it shine. I checked the windows, the taps on the oven, the back door and the front door. The everyday rituals seemed suddenly important.

Upstairs, in bed, Judy began sobbing again, her arms round my neck, her face burrowed into my chest. 'It's so sad,' she kept saying. 'So sad.'

'It could have been any of us.' I slid my hands under her lovely tail and held her close. 'Seize the day,' I said.

She shook her head, clung, shivered and went on crying.

A word about my wife. My third wife, to be precise, although the first two only lasted four years, seven months and three days between them when we were all very young. Third time lucky. Judy and I have been married for twelve years – which in itself seems a kind of miracle. It was Tommy who introduced us and then took a proprietorial interest in keeping us together. Whenever we drifted apart in the couple of years before we finally married, Tommy saw to it that the stand-ins got a rough ride. 'How's Judy?' he'd ask, moments after I'd introduced him to my latest discovery. Then he would turn to the girl and ask, all innocence, 'You know Judy Macdonald? Pretty as a picture, smart as a whip. Old friend of Joe. I'm surprised he hasn't told you about her.' Judy's men got the same treatment, so at least he was impartial. When we married he insisted on being best man. 'It's all my fault,' he said. 'The least I can do is be in at the kill.'

Tommy did not get on with either of my former wives, nor they with him. First time around I married a Dan Air stewardess, God knows why. My second wife worked in the print department at Sotheby's and knew all there is to know about eighteenth-century etchings. Two rigorous young women with unreliable tempers and parents who lived in the country and wore green gumboots. Judy is dark-haired, quick-witted and full-souled, a resolute woman with a forgiving temperament. She was also a free agent when we met, unencumbered by previous marriages or living relatives, the only child of two only children, both deceased. Her father was an Aberdeen lawyer with a passion for malt whisky who died just before the oil business came to town and made all his colleagues rich. Six years later her mother followed him into the neat cemetery behind the granite walls and rhododendrons on the road to Braemar. By that time Judy was settled in London, sporadically sharing my bed. She had come south to study design at the Royal College of Art and when I met her she was working in the graphics department of an advertising agency in Covent Garden. The money from her parents' house bought her two large rooms on the lower slopes of Hampstead where she set up her slanted drawing board, installed strip lights and filing cabinets, trestle tables and coffee-maker, and went into business as SIGNS UNLIMITED, designing everything from letter-heads to books. She had a talent for it, a feel for shape and space and colour, as well as a lot of friends from her days in advertising, and she did rather well. Bent over her drawing board, making precise graceful marks on the great sheets of white paper, she is self-contained and at peace. I envy her absorption, her gift for silence, a gift she does not share with other women I have known.

Judy and my mother were very close. My mother's lifelong conviction that the world's problems could be solved if only people would eat properly dazzled Judy who had been brought up in a house where Glenmorangie ruled and eating was an unpleasant duty to be negotiated with a minimum of fuss. My mother believed there was no point in cooking one meal when you could as easily cook two; if the oven was on to roast a chicken, she might as well roast a leg of lamb at the same time. Maybe someone didn't like chicken. Maybe someone unexpected would turn up. How could you ever tell? It was a style of innocent generosity that enchanted Judy and she began to put on weight out of sheer politeness and an unwillingness to disappoint. She was the dutiful appreciative child my mother had never had. So when I told the old lady we were going to get married I assumed she would be overjoyed. Instead, there was a moment's silence. She watched me out of the corners of her eyes, amused, sceptical. Her old-fashioned look. All she said was, 'Well, dear, since you don't seem able to marry money, at least this time you're marrying earning power.'

My mother, alas, is dead and gone but that comforting layer of subcutaneous fat that Judy put on to please her is still in place. The taut belly and tauter backside are softer now and more expansive, though no less shapely or attractive. My wife is middle-aged, I am middle-aged. We no longer flirt in public with other people, we try not to argue unnecessarily, we sleep longer, more gratefully, than we used to, and wake with more difficulty and fewer expectations, knowing the next day will be much like the last. It seemed to have happened absurdly fast and without either of us noticing it. That is, until Tommy Apple died.

When we were younger Tommy and I saw a great deal of each other. We drank together, chased girls together, played cards together and squash. We met, in fact, on the squash court. Tommy was six years older than me, round and heavy even then, but he tore around the court as though his feet were on fire and made up in energy what he lacked in skill. 'All those drop shots and lobs,' he said afterwards in the shower. 'You think there's some kind of art in this game? Not by my book there isn't. All you've gotta do is be in the right place at the right time. Like everything else in this life.'

'I won, didn't I? Don't knock the arts.'

'Wait till next time, buster. I've got your number.'

He lathered his hairy torso, then tipped his face back to the cascading water and gargled ferociously.

Later, in the bar, he started talking about a deal he'd been offered that afternoon: five thousand V-neck pullovers that he could get, he said, for three and a half thousand pounds.

'Why so cheap?' I asked.

'Made in Hungary. Not that you could ever tell.'

'What would you do with five thousand V-neck pullovers?'

'Keep 'em in their plastic bags and wait for the price to go up. It's not a style that's going to go out of fashion. Double your money in a year.'

I was between wives at the time and both my exes had remarried, so the money I had was my own. Three beers later we had agreed to go partners. The next day I was at his office, looking at samples and papers, signing a cheque. I went away with two pullovers in my briefcase – one black, one pillar-box red – a receipt typed by his secretary and a handshake. Nothing else.

Naturally, I thought I was being hustled. But I went on playing squash with Tommy every week and ten months later he presented me with a cheque for £3,500, just as he had predicted. 'I've deducted all the bits and pieces,' he said. 'We did better than I expected.'

'How come there's so much money in pullovers?'

Tommy looked sideways at me and grinned, as if I'd made a joke. 'Don't ask,' he said. 'Take and be glad. Maybe you'll do me a favour some time.'

'I'd like that.'

A quick glance. Dark clever eyes sizing me up.

'Want to invest in New Zealand honey?' he asked. 'Your two thou'll get you four.'

And it did. At the time I wondered why he asked me. It couldn't have been that he needed the money; in all the years I knew him, Tommy was never short of cash. He must simply have decided he liked me. He always acted on impulse and if he was on to something good he liked to spread it around. Whence his four marriages and unending string of girls. When he finally called in his bets I was anxious to oblige.

Once, in my adolescence, I asked my father what kind of Jews we were. I was doing time at a great British public school where being Jewish was not part of any acceptable solution, so the question was more urgent than I made it sound. 'English,' he replied. 'A weird bunch. But not altogether assimilated. The kind that don't eat bacon for breakfast on the Day of Atonement.' Tommy was much nearer the source than we were. His grandparents had emigrated from Eastern Europe to Whitechapel at the turn of the century, gone into the rag trade and progressed rapidly to the suburbs of north-west London. In their old age they still spoke together in Yiddish, while their grandson Tommy went to Highgate School where he learned how to play squash and be a gentleman. But he kept their energy and their appetites, which spared him from ever quite making it as an English gent. I liked him, among other reasons, because he was free of all the apologies and proprieties I had been brought up to. The English Jews, those lawyers and professors and heads of city livery companies, with their Savile Row suits and bench-made shoes and furled umbrellas, like paintings by Magritte and equally odd, tiptoed through this life as through a minefield, endlessly careful, endlessly correct. In comparison, noisy brash Tommy was a free spirit.

LOUISE phoned the next morning. She and Judy wept together for twenty straight minutes before she asked to speak to me. More weeping. Then she said, 'There's a letter for you.'

'What does it say?'

'I haven't opened it, of course.' She sounded indignant. 'It was in his handkerchief drawer. There's going to be an inquest. Should I give it to the police?'

'Let me see it first. When can I come over?'

'Oh, soon, please soon.' She was crying again. 'You were his closest friend.'

This was probably not true but it made her feel better. Tommy still cut me in on imaginative deals but eighteen months ago he had called in his bets, just once, and after that we drifted apart a little. Maybe it would have happened anyway because age and a good marriage have narrowed my world. I love my wife – whatever that means – but, more important, I like her: I enjoy her company, I find her interesting, we make each other laugh. Since the only time we have together is in the evenings, after work, we seem to have less and less energy to spare for other people. That, too, is part of middle age. You don't run out of interest, you just run out of time.

'Come with me,' I said to Judy when I rang off. 'It's going to be a difficult hour.'

'Poor bitch,' said Judy. 'Her great love. His too, according to her.'

'Don't put money on that.'

Louise is a tiny woman with wild black hair, lovely breasts and a knowing face that makes her look older than she is: pouches under her eyes, deep lines from her nostrils to her vivid sullen mouth. She looks like someone who knows all the variations and has strong personal preferences. This gives her an authority, a sultry gypsy glamour at odds with her stature and her otherwise gossipy nature. That morning the pouches were darker, the lines deeper, her eyes red and swollen from weeping. She fell into Judy's arms and wept, then wept again when I hugged her. 'He was a lovely man,' she sobbed. 'Generous, give you anything. Who'd want to hurt a man like that?'

I couldn't see what that had to do with a heart attack but she was right, of course. Tommy bought and sold things, made deals and read the fine print with care. Presumably he trod on other people's toes on his way to the bank, but good-naturedly, not meaning any harm. His only natural enemy was the tax man.

'What do you mean, hurt him?' I asked.

'They say someone broke in. The office was turned upside down. Papers everywhere.' When she dabbed her swollen eyes her mascara left dark marks on the tissue. 'I had to go down to the morgue at the Royal Free and identify him. Lying there under a plastic sheet, his face all twisted, like he'd died of fright.'

'Sweet God,' murmured Judy.

I said nothing. All those appetites. All that good humour. My old, dear friend. Né Applebaum.

Eventually, Louise gave me the letter. I read it while she and Judy were in the kitchen brewing coffee. The envelope was stamped and addressed and ready to send, and the date was the previous week.

Dear Joe,

I've been a bit of a bloody fool as usual and I may have got myself in too deep, as the bishop said to the actress.

The truth is, the company I'm keeping these days is not as kosher as I'm used to and I may need to go away for a while. Like fifty years. Please God it won't be necessary but you never know.

So if the worst comes to the worst, keep an eye on Louise for me, will you, and calm her down. And phone a girl I know – and Louise doesn't. Helen Donovan – 794-5929.

Why I should bother you with all this I don't rightly know. Old times' sake, perhaps.

Take it easy, old friend, and look after your lovely girl. I always fancied her but she never let me near her. You're a lucky sod.

Love you both,

Tommy.

And Louise doesn't. Dear Tommy, fifty-one years old and still unable to pay attention to just one woman, however inventive, at a time. 'Back up', he called it, and 'operating from a position of strength'. How did Tommy, with his fancy footwork, end up on a slab in the morgue of the Royal Free looking as if he'd died of fright?

I'm too old for this, I thought.

Then there was Helen. A name I didn't want to remember. How many Helens were there in Tommy's life?

Tommy and his women and his deals.

What was I going to do without him?

'What did the letter say?' Judy asked when we finally got outside The rain had stopped for the moment and the sun was out. Bu southward, over the city, the clouds were massing again, grea spotlit mountains building and crumbling against an iron-grey overcover.

'All the things you'd expect it to say: he was up to his neck and running scared; he had another woman going. You know Tommy. A man of affairs in the true sense.'

'Shouldn't you pass it on to someone? The police or the coroner or whoever it is.'

'What in God's name have the police got to do with it? Might as well send it to the Inland Revenue. Tommy hated the lot of them, regardless of race, colour or creed. He was the last of the buccaneers. He didn't believe in police, doctors or taxation. It's none of their bloody business.'

'Even so,' said Judy.

We were walking down Fitzjohn's Avenue from Tommy's overstuffed flat in Reddington Road. The Tchechikoffs on the walls, the chintzy furniture from Maples, the Miele appliances and polished copper pans in the kitchen. Judy took my hand and held it firmly.

'What kind of creeps break into offices?' I said. 'What do they hope to find?'

'The same kind of creeps who are roaming about loose all over London. Read the newspapers. Old age pensioners murdered for the small change in their handbags, for their rented television sets.'

'You worry too much. You and your imagination of disaster.'

'I've been proved right, haven't I?'

When I was young Fitzjohn's Avenue was a challenge to boy racers. A long sweeping hill with a curve at each end. The police set speed traps, hiding behind trees with their stop-watches, signalling to each other with handkerchiefs. Now the traffic is nose to tail from 7.30 in the morning until after midnight.

'Tommy wasn't the type to be frightened to death,' I said. 'Anger might have made him burst a blood vessel. Anger or indignation, not fear. Maybe it wasn't a creep who broke in, just an outraged husband. I could believe that, given Tommy's habits.'

Judy smiled for the first time that day. 'He must have picked the wrong wife to act stupid with.'

'Or an argument about business. A difference of opinion among gentlemen and he flew off the handle.'

'Tommy and his everlasting deals. See where they got him.'

'He's come a long way from the rag trade, poor sod.'

'Not far enough,' said Judy.

We walked on in silence. Most of the big Edwardian merchants' houses on Fitzjohn's Avenue are divided up into flats but a couple of them are schools, their gardens asphalted over and turned into playgrounds. It was 11.15, breaktime, and the confused excited voices of children drifted over the houses and the noise of the traffic.

'We should have had kids,' said Judy.

I squeezed her hand. 'No one could ever say we haven't tried, sweetheart.'

She shook her head. 'We could drop dead just like that. And

that would be it. Nothing left. Not a trace. Like poor Tommy.'

'Tommy was overweight, hot-tempered, impulsive. He smoked too much.'

'So do you.'

'He was a wheeler-dealer, always on the go.'

'That's another thing.' She let go my hand and quickened her pace. 'Those deals you did with Tommy,' she said. Her head was down and her face was turned away.

'He cut me in out of the kindness of his heart. Because he knew things were tough and he wanted to help us.'

'They weren't straight, were they?'

'If they weren't, he never told me. I suppose it depends how you define straight.'

'Don't give me double-talk, Joe. The man's dead.'

'I don't know the answer. I never asked.'

She stopped in her tracks and turned to me. She was crying but her face was stiff with anger. 'You've no right to be so bloody simple-minded. No right at all. Why did you never ask?'

'I couldn't afford to,' I said.

Two policemen were walking up the hill towards us. When they came abreast of us they paused and looked at her enquiringly. She shook her head at them and went on crying. 'You're such a loser, Joe. You and the quick buck.'

I took her hand and squeezed it hard. 'It's all right, darling. I loved the guy, too. He was my friend as well as yours.'

She took her hand away. 'That's not an answer.'

'You're not being fair. You already know the bloody answer. It's not easy to make a living as a photographer and I'm no David Bailey. What more do you want me to say? That he felt sorry for me? Tommy helped me out from time to time because he was fond of us, fond of us both. I may not have asked enough questions but you chose to pretend it wasn't happening.'

She walked on, head down, saying nothing.

'Remember his wedding present?' I asked.

'A dinner service, a Royal Doulton dinner service from Harrods. Of course I remember. We've been eating off it ever since.'

'That was the easy part. The real present was the little slum property near Paddington. Don't you remember that? A twenty-five-year lease he'd picked up for four thousand quid. "Go shares with me in it, Joe," he said. "You won't regret it." Two years later we were told the area was being torn down to make room for the Westway. When the compulsory purchase order came Tommy took us to the Ritz to celebrate. You were there. How can you forget?'

'You never told me what was going on.'

'What should I have told you? That he knew the planning officer and the guy who did the official valuations? *That's* what we've been eating off ever since.'

She shook her head. 'That was between you and him. I never asked about that stuff.'

'That makes two of us then.'

We walked to her studio without exchanging another word. When I left her all she said was, 'We should have had him to dinner more often.'

TOMMY and his deals.

The edges of the studio were full of shadows. In the middle was a circle of hard light, glaring, like the light in the dusty street outside. A skinny youth sat on the edge of the bed, naked except for his Y-fronts, knobbly hands hanging loose between his knees. The ring of spotlights picked out the blemishes on his skin, the curling straggly hairs on his chest, a question-mark scar on his shoulder.

'A small favour,' Tommy had said. 'A few hours of your time. Plus some of that professional know-how.'

'Just tell me what you want.'

'I'm setting this up for a pal, you understand. For someone I do business with. It's a one-off job.'

'The favours you've done for me, how could I refuse?'

'That's what worries me. It's not your style, Joe. Not mine either. But I owe the guy.'

'Never apologise, never explain. You owe him, I owe you.'

'You're going to be on location in Tunisia next month,' Tommy said. 'I can fix a studio for you there, no problem. That way there's no awkward questions from the wife. You go in, you take the pictures, you catch the next plane out and no one's any the wiser.'

'Don't worry about it. Anything to help you out.'

'I don't want to take advantage.'

There were two girls, both young. One was oriental, broad-faced, maybe Korean, but with features so delicate as hardly to be features at all. Tiny breasts, slim hips, a body smoothed down like a pebble in a stream. The other was American, blonde-haired, blue-eyed, small-town innocent. The oriental girl was precise and matter-of-fact, doing a job she'd been paid for. The American was vague, drifting, high on something that seemed to transform what was happening into a delicious secret joke.

'My name's Helen,' she said. 'I launch ships.'

She laughed when the youth took off his Y-fronts and she saw the disproportionate size of his member. A young laugh, a ripple of freshness in the heat and glare. 'Gee willikins.'

I moved around the bed photographing tangled limbs, busy mouths, slippery private parts. They stopped when I told them to stop, combined, recombined, stopped again, as though this were nothing more involving than grandmother's footsteps.

There was a fridgeful of beer in the corner and they drank between takes. The oriental girl wiped her mouth with the back of her hand, but delicately, as if this were the proper thing to do, something she'd been taught. The American put the glistening can between her breasts, shivered and giggled. The heat from the lights and the heat from the violent Tunisian sun outside made them sweat more than the sexual acrobatics. It produced light effects I didn't like and I made them towel themselves down every few minutes.

I photographed them in all the possible combinations: in pairs, as a trio, alone. Seven sets of pictures in the clinging heat. When it was over the girls disappeared, the rest of us sat around drinking beer, our T-shirts soaked with sweat. Outside a wind had got up and the air was gritty with blown sand. When I got back to the hotel, I took a long bath and ate on my own in the pretentious restaurant downstairs. I wanted to get home to Judy but a sandstorm was blowing the next day and the flights were delayed.

I told myself it was a favour to a friend, a clinical operation, curiously unrousing, not much different from the advertising shots I'd been taking on location. A young girl on a beach, jeans and no top. The same attention to light and composition and physical detail. Pornography by any other name.

But secretly, I was afraid. Afraid it would catch up on me, afraid I'd set some obscure machinery in motion that would destroy my marriage, afraid Judy would find out. I put it down to native guilt, something in the genes that had no bearing on the world out there. Even so, a veil came down between Judy and myself. We had always made a point of not intruding on each other. It was part of our intimacy. She had her work, I had mine and we took it on trust that neither of us had anything to hide in our separate lives. All that changed after Tunis. I became sly for no reason at all. I kept things hidden and explained myself unnecessarily. Before Tunis, we used to joke about the models. I pretended to be more attracted to them than I was, she pretended to be jealous. It was a way of flattering each other, of adding an edge to our love-making. Now I avoided mentioning them. I fussed over Judy, bought her flowers, watched for signs of irritation or discontent, ready to placate, smooth over, make good. Only Tommy and I knew about the pornographic pictures and neither of us was saying, yet I was convinced word would get out.

After Tunis, the windfalls from Tommy increased. Not immediately or in frequency but in size. After Tunis, too, I stopped seeing Tommy as regularly as I had. I resented him for having asked me to do the job as much as I disliked myself for having done it. A sneaky resentment, based on collusion. Understanding the company he kept put the other deals in context. But I needed the money.

THE sky was darkening steadily and by the time I reached Chalk Farm station the rain was bucketing down again. My studio is the first floor of a decrepit building in Soho which is bound to be torn down in the next burst of urban renewal. The front room is spacious and well proportioned, with a high ceiling and long windows. Once upon a time it was a pretty Victorian drawing-room, now it is jammed with my gear: aluminium boxes full of cameras and lenses, arc lights, transformers, coils of cable, movable panels, rolls of paper and coloured materials, a big table heaped with odds and ends that also doubles as my desk. Across the landing is a smaller room I use as a dark room. Once upon a time I had a secretary, a witty and depressed woman with a fine line in gallows humour, but she got replaced by a word processor. A black joke she appreciated. These days I have an assistant when I'm working but between jobs I make do with an answering machine. The loneliness of the late 20th century: machines may cost less but they're not very companionable.

There were two messages waiting for me on the answering machine: one from my agent, the other from Inspector Rogers of Scotland Yard.

Inspector Rogers was very polite. We understand you were a friend of the deceased. No doubt you've heard there were certain irregularities, a suspected break-in. Perhaps we could ask you a few questions. Of course, it must be very upsetting for you. A matter of routine, you understand. Explore every avenue. No, it would be easier, I think, if we came to you. As you say, Mr Constantine, no time like the present.

I wandered round the studio clearing away the bits and pieces that seem to accumulate on my chairs and sofa without any apparent help from me. Then I thought, Fuck it, and phoned Helen Donovan.

An American voice, young-sounding but tired. Not one I recognised but the telephone does funny things. I explained I was an old friend of Tommy. I told her about the letter.

'He asked me to keep an eye on you.'

'An eye. That's rich.'

Tommy and his troublesome women. He worked on his erotic life like he worked on his business deals, each one a battle, a new challenge, a potential source of glory. No wonder his heart gave out.

'Are you all right? Do you need anything?'

'I feel lousy, if you want to know. How else am I supposed to feel? I also feel pissed-off. Like he's left me in the lurch.'

There was reggae music in the background, syncopated percussion, a girl's voice singing, 'Tonight, tonight is the night of all nights.'

'It's rotten for all of us. He was my oldest friend.'

The music ended. A cheerful voice said, 'The next request is from Edith Valentine of Bexley Heath.'

'Don't get me wrong,' Helen said. 'It's just that I don't know what I'm going to do without him.'

She sounded young enough to be my daughter. Tommy should have stuck to women nearer his own age. I don't need this, I thought.

'I'm terribly sorry. Maybe I can help in some way.'

'Help? Is that what you do when someone dies?'

'At least I could buy you a drink.'

'Why not? Tommy talked about you. A drink to our mutual friend. It'd be nice to see a sympathetic face.'

We arranged to meet at the Museum Tavern at 5.45.

'I'm tallish, middle-aged, not much hair. I'll be wearing a leather coat,' I said. 'I don't look like a refugee from the British Museum Reading Room.'

'Neither do I.'

The voice behind her said, 'That one was produced by the Mad Professor.'

INSPECTOR Rogers surveyed the studio and seemed not to approve of what he saw. He had a stern face, pale hair, flickering eyes that seemed to take in everything. He had brought a constable with him, a burly eager young man in a grey herring-bone jacket one size too small for him. The constable hitched up his grey flannel trousers to protect the creases, perched himself on the edge of the sofa and took notes.

I told them what little I knew. Yes, Tommy and I were old friends. Yes, he cut me in on business deals from time to time, but purely out of friendship, not because he ever needed my money. No, I hadn't seen him for weeks, but that was nothing unusual. It happens in middle age, right? No, I didn't know what he was currently involved in. All I knew was that the deals seemed to be getting bigger and Tommy now appeared to be very comfortably off.

Rogers took the pad from his assistant and read through the notes. There was a long silence, as though he were waiting for me to say something. He leaned forward. 'I believe there was a letter, sir. To you, if I understand correctly. Sealed. From the deceased.' When he spoke his jaw muscles flexed as though with the effort to contain his irritation.

'A personal letter.' I looked him righteously in the eye.

'What we have here, sir, is an on-going investigation.' The jaw muscles seemed to have a vigorous life of their own, separate from his stony face. 'We'd appreciate your co-operation.'

I fished around in my jacket pocket and handed him the letter.

'Ah,' he said. He read it through, then handed it to his assistant. 'Mind if we keep this?'

He had been one step ahead of me, waiting for me to make a mistake, prove I was unreliable. Louise, of course, had told him everything. Louise couldn't resist telling anyone everything. Maybe she had steamed the letter open and wanted revenge.

'One thing,' I said. 'Do you have to tell Miss Schapiro about this other girl? She's upset enough as it is.'

'We'll do our best.' He grinned, one man to another. 'Bit of a lady's man, was he, your friend?'

'That sort of thing.'

'Well, I don't see why it need come up.' Now he was ahead of the game he was all smiles. When he thanked me for my help I realised that all he had come for was the letter. As he was leaving, he turned at the door and said, 'This Helen Donovan, have you contacted her?'

'It seemed the least I could do.'

'What did she say?'

'Nothing much. She sounded young and upset.'

'Well, she would be, wouldn't she?' said Inspector Rogers. He paused, then added, 'I hope you won't take that any further, sir.

Just leave it to us.' His voice was serious, avuncular, full of authority.

'Of course,' I said.

I PREFERRED Helen with her clothes on. The clean-cut American look, blonde hair cut short, fresh and efficient and wholesome despite the strain lines around her dark eyes, around her soft slow mouth. Another creature entirely from the girl I'd seen in Tunis, with her head full of drugs, her body slippery with sweat, her high cheekbones that were so tricky to light.

My ankle began to ache. Seeing her again made me feel old and uneasy. We had this secret in common, a favour we'd done for Tommy, now we had another secret, another favour for our friend. She looked at me critically but with no sign of recognition. In Tunis I had been a floating face among the other faces, figures in a Quaalude landscape. I wondered how she'd managed the simple logistics, the plane, customs, a place to stay. Maybe Tommy had been there all along, waiting in the hotel, chewing a cigar, afraid to show his face yet not wanting her to come to harm. He must have known she'd been out of her skull or he'd never have asked me to call her.

Trustworthy Joe. Knows how to keep a secret.

She asked for Bacardi and ice. I watched her while I waited for the drinks. She looked carefully round the bar, checking the other customers. There were not many of them at this early hour: a couple of postmen drinking Guinness; a group of tourists wearing new Burberries and expensive cameras; a fugitive from the British Museum Reading Room staring wearily into his glass of beer, a large briefcase on the bench beside him. She studied them methodically, one by one, then kept her eyes on the door.

I had ordered doubles, which was as well since she drank half hers down straight off.

'I reckon I owe you an apology,' she said. 'Tears on the telephone, that's not my scene. I guess I was just all over the place.'

'What else were you supposed to be?'

'It's like all your worst imaginings come true. Him of all people. Tommy the unsinkable.'

She jiggled her glass, making the ice cubes clink, then touched its cold edge to her cheek, experimentally, like she'd put the beer can between her breasts.

I asked her when she had heard.

She shrugged. 'Does it matter? Last night, this morning. I heard. We saw each other all the time, anyway.'

'You know how he died?'

'Badly, I guess. At the wrong moment. Like everyone else.'

'I mean the details?'

'Only that he was in his office. He had a heart attack. What's there to know?'

She studied the rum in her glass, sipped it slowly, lovingly, as though she meant it, extending her upper lip to absorb the full flavour. A serious drinker.

'A rotten thing,' I said. 'Rotten for him, rotten for us all.'

'I can't get my mind around it. But it makes sense in a gruesome way. You ever meet a guy who ran like he did?'

'It was part of his charm. All that energy, all that optimism. I don't know about you, but I loved him for it.'

'I loved him for all sorts of things. But he pushed his luck. He mixed with some terrible people.'

'Thanks for the recommendation. Should I feel offended?'

'I mean people he did business with. Hustlers, heavies. People like his friend Fernandez, for instance.'

'Anyone I know?'

'Fernandez and Company. Import and export. Entertainment and leisure. Other things, too. Other levels of activity. Investments, property, companies within companies. If you're a friend of Tommy you know the scene.'

'How do you know they're so terrible?'

'I work for them.'

You worked for me, too, I thought. 'Is that how you met him?' I said.

She nodded. 'Girl Friday. PR, receptionist, a bit of typing. A pretty face to be nice to the customers. You get the picture.' She drank more rum. 'The boss is Sun Belt American, so he claims, but they're Spanish mostly and I guess Spain got kinda left behind by the rest of the world. They don't belong to the twentieth century, those people. Shiny teeth, slick hair, no foreheads. All machismo and phoney dignity. Creeps. But there wasn't any nonsense about work permits and they pay me partly in cash.'

'No wonder you liked Tommy.'

'He was kind and he made me laugh. He treated me like a human being.'

'You can't be short of volunteers.'

'I came over here to get away from the volunteers.'

'Where from?'

'Where the sun always shines and the fruit always grows. Southern California. I'm one of the mindless golden young they talk about. I spent my childhood at the beach when I should have been at school learning about things. One morning I woke up and realised I was pig ignorant and if I didn't do something about it I was going to stay that way. So I split to sophisticated old Europe.'

'Tommy wasn't exactly Henry James.'

'He wasn't exactly a beach boy either.'

'What did your parents say?'

'Pa is four marriages on, Mom two. They send me cheques when they remember.'

She sat there with her youthful glowing skin and felt sorry for herself. I studied the pink ear under her blonde hair, the subtle curve of her mouth, as if I hadn't seen them before. I wondered how they would taste. Wholesome, outdoors, small-town Californian, the perfect specimen you see in the movies and never meet.

'Perhaps it's time to go home,' I said. 'Back to Lotos Land.'

'I am home. This is where I live now.'

'What about Fernandez & Co? Are they home, too?'

'I wish I knew.'

Sorrowful eyes, wistful voice. One moment street-wise, the next little girl lost. I had watched her with the skinny youth and the tough little oriental, exploring each other in slow motion, entwined, 'the red rose and the briar', like Barbry Allen. Yet I couldn't imagine her aboard hairy old Tommy. Tommy with his weight problems, his smoking problems, his business problems, his alimony problems, his Yiddish oaths. She could have been the daughter he'd never had, neither of us had ever had.

I told her the letter from Tommy had said he might have to go away for a bit. I asked if she knew what he was up to.

'I couldn't keep up. You know what Tommy was like. Every deal was going to be the big one that changed his life. Every girl too, I suppose. That's why I liked him.'

'It's as good a reason as any.'

'The best,' she said. 'Believe me.'

I went back for more drinks. The bar was filling up now as the offices emptied. The postmen and the man from the Reading Room had gone, their places taken by young people jostling to be served. Half of them wore office suits and dresses, the others had interchangeable clothes: draped suits with shoulders like an NFL linebacker's, sheepskins over T-shirts, leather jackets, jeans. A babble of accents from county to cockney with all the shadings in between. Bikers, casuals, young fogies, Sloane Rangers. I was older by about twenty years than anybody there.

A tweed-suited youth standing next to me at the bar said, 'A nice glass of whisky, old boy. That's what's needed to keep the gastric ulcers at bay.'

'Good thinking,' said his tweed-suited friend. 'Pre-emptive strike, what?'

Neither of them was a day over twenty-five but they had the mannerisms, the ripe voices, of two old buffers at the Athenaeum.

Helen was still watching the door, checking each new arrival. I gave her her drink and said, 'Who're you looking for?'

'Just looking, I guess. Watching the passing show.'

'You don't need to be so nervous.'

'With Tommy gone what else am I supposed to be?'

A young couple in office clothes sat down at our table. They talked in low voices, heads together, his hand on her thigh.

'He looked after me,' Helen said.

'He looked after us all.'

Another group of cameras and new Burberries trooped in. It was a mistake to have picked the Museum Tavern. It was more like the English-Speaking Union than a pub.

'You weren't actually living together,' I said.

'A technicality.'

'Louise'll be glad to hear that.'

'Who's Louise?'

'His lady in residence.'

'Louise was living on borrowed time.'

'Everybody was, it seems now.'

That silenced her. She stared at the door for a while, then said thoughtfully, 'You know what I miss?'

'About Tommy?'

'About Lotos Land. The big skies, the feeling of space. Everything is so cramped over here.'

'The way things are going, it's getting more cramped by the minute.'

She smiled for the first time and said, 'Now who's nervous?'

I wanted to touch her young face. It looked new-minted, fresh from the mould, with the shine still on it. Her neck was smooth and there was a faint down on her cheeks, like the skin of a peach. I wanted to forget where I'd seen her before. I reached across the table and took her hand. 'I've known Tommy nearly twenty years,' I said. 'All my adult life.'

She kept her hand in mine and looked at me soberly. Dark eyes, blonde hair, soft mouth. Lucky old Tommy. 'I've only known him for eighteen months,' she said. 'But it feels the same: all my adult life.'

I tore a sheet out of my diary and wrote down my telephone numbers – the studio and home. In case you need help, I said. In case anything goes wrong.

She shrugged. 'It's already gone wrong.'

As we got up to leave, I said, 'Someone from your firm paid me a visit last night. A man called Riley.'

'That asshole. What was he after?'

'Something about missing merchandise. Where does he fit into the scheme of things?'

'He's the gofer, the jack-of-all-trades. He drives the boss, runs errands, fixes the plumbing. He has a permanently dripping nose. I don't think he's your kinda guy.'

'But he had my name and address.'

'You were a friend of Tommy's. It stands to reason. This is a large and efficient outfit. They have computers, they keep tabs, check things out.'

'Why should I be on their computer?'

'Maybe you were on Tommy's.'

We elbowed our way through the crowd. Dense voices, canned music, the ping of the fruit machine. I had to lean close to her to catch what she was saying. All I heard was, 'They're bad news.'

Outside the pub we paused a moment, face to face. It was the moment to kiss her and say everything would be all right. She seemed to be expecting it. But first I'd have to apologise, tell her I preferred her with her clothes on.

'Take care,' I said.

'Don't even think about it.'

She turned and walked briskly away in the direction of New Oxford Street. It was still raining.

WHEN I told Judy about the meeting she looked at me quizzically and said, 'You've got a funny look on your face. Was she that attractive?'

'She was that young.'

'Same thing at our age.'

I woke up in the night thinking I heard noises downstairs. A creak, a door closing, footsteps. I lay in the darkness, listening, intent as a gun dog. But noises did not come again and all I could hear was the heavy thud of my heart. The rain had ceased, the wind had dropped, the air was very cold. Maybe it would freeze at last. Maybe we would have a real winter.

I turned and looked at Judy. In the bluish light her profile was delicate, her skin purified of wrinkles, as though she had shed years in sleep. The expression on her face was attentive, but not as if she had heard the noises I had imagined. Instead, she seemed to be listening to something soothing and far off. I had the curious feeling that I was looking at her for the first time. How beautiful she is, I thought. And went back to sleep.

But the next morning she woke me, terribly upset. She had dreamed she was in America and the President – she didn't know which – had pushed the button. Oh well, she thought, they'll get round it somehow; they always do. Then she was half walking, half crawling to an underground shelter. The bomb had been dropped and it was all over. At the mouth of the shelter three old men were dancing hand in hand. Inside were rows of mutilated and dying. Someone was saying, 'There's not a mark on me but I have these dreadful pains inside. Am I all right?' And someone else replied, 'That's how it always starts.' Sitting up in bed, Judy hugged herself. 'Where do I get such terrible dreams?'

'Maybe it's to do with Tommy,' I answered lamely.

I SPENT most of the morning with an advertising agent and his client, discussing a campaign for a new brand of cat food. The client was a carefully made-up woman wearing a yellow suit and a great deal of gold jewellery. She had hair like a magic carpet, curled up front and back as if ready to fly, and seemingly too big for her head.

'Pet food,' said the agent. 'Basically, we're talking love here.' He was young and dark and wolfish. He fluttered his hands when he spoke. 'We're talking about a very special relationship.'

The client ignored him. 'I've seen those jeans ads of yours, Mr Constantine.'

'You want mouth-watering,' said the agent. 'The way Joe shot them, those girls had backsides on them you wouldn't believe.'

The client glanced at him irritably. 'All that fifties nostalgia. I found it quite admirable.' Her voice was drawling and upper class and she spoke carefully, almost pedantically, as though to blot out some earlier and still unreconstructed accent.

I gave her my charming smile and murmured, 'I'm so glad.'

The agent said, 'Joe's one of the best we have. No question of it.'

'I don't doubt that.' The woman brushed him aside impatiently.

'But what we have here is a rather different problem.' She fixed me with her sharp, carefully made-up eyes. 'How do you feel about pussycats, Mr Constantine?'

I turned the smile up a couple of notches. 'Mostly they're smarter than models,' I replied. 'But you can't tell them what to do. It's a question of patience.'

'I'm not talking about technicalities, Mr Constantine. I wouldn't presume. I'm talking about empathy. The question was, How do you *feel* about them?'

'Beautiful creatures,' I lied. 'I like their independence.'

'"I am the cat that walks by himself and all places are alike to me,"' she intoned. 'Kipling had their number. We try for that and we'll have a great shoot.'

'It's all a question of concept,' said the agent.

'That's what I'm paying you for,' she answered.

After she left, the agent stayed to gather up his papers. 'How do you like that bitch?' He waved his hands, as though shaking water from them. 'It's the accent that gets me.' He pursed his mouth and enunciated with great care, pausing for effect, ' "And how do you feel about pussycats, Mr Constantine?" You know where she started out? From a stall in Queen's Crescent is where, selling cut-price dog biscuit and minced horsemeat.'

'What's this *we* she was talking about, this *great shoot* stuff? Is she planning to sit in on the sessions?'

'You know how it is.' He sighed deeply. 'They want a little fun for their money. They like to feel part of the creative process. What can I do, old man?'

'Just keep her off my back.'

'Back?' he echoed. 'You should be so lucky.'

At lunch time I walked over to Tommy's office. A policeman was standing at the main entrance to the building. I walked past slowly, trying to think of an excuse for going in. I pictured Inspector Rogers ploughing solemnly through Tommy's scattered files, checking out the improbable deals, examining, God help me, the dubious photographs. He was a man without tolerance, without a sense of humour. I wanted to say, Forget the sleaze factor, admire the chutzpah and imagination, the enjoyment of wheeling and dealing, the curious creative energy Tommy invested in his business affairs. I didn't know what Rogers was looking for, but all he was going to find was the sort of evidence that would make the tax man's hair stand on end. This case needed an auditor not a policeman.

When I got back to the studio I found, once again, that I was missing my secretary. There were no messages on the answering machine and only junk mail in the post. I threw the junk mail away unopened but that was only a short-term satisfaction. I needed my secretary's companionable gloom, her black jokes, her dire reports on the six mangy strays who shared her life, but the only presence in the room was the computer. The blank grey face waiting to come alive at the press of a button. 'Let me help you be alone with your own thoughts,' it seemed to be saying. 'Let me bring order to your chaos.' I switched it on, called up the directory that contained my correspondence and looked at the letters I had written Tommy. Notes accompanying cheques I had sent him when he cut me in on deals: down jackets from Taiwan, electronic insect repellers from Hong Kong, and three lots of goods from Hungary – pullovers (again), bottled cherries, kitchen ware. The Hungarian connection was obviously thriving since each of the deals had made a tidy profit. Maybe Tommy had cousins there who managed to juggle the system to their advantage.

Years ago, before I got into fashion photography, I spent a week in Hungary. It was in the days when I fancied myself as a photo-journalist, and I had gone east for a German travel magazine to photograph the Prague spring. It seemed logical, while I was at it, to go on to Warsaw and Budapest to see what winter looked like. Warsaw was much as I had expected: pinched and deprived, like London during the war, with dreadful food and shabby clothes and lively passionate talk. In Budapest nobody said anything that might remotely be held against them but the shops were crammed with consumer goods and the restaurants were marvellous. I photographed the handsome leather-faced old men preening and sunning themselves in the public baths, and I heard a nightingale singing its heart out in the garden of a spacious villa in Buda, while two elderly journalists complained bitterly about the bad old days before 1956 when Rakosi's police brought you in for questioning if you ordered a second bottle of wine with your meal. I came away with the impression that it was a country where anything could be arranged, Marxism notwithstanding, and there would never have been an uprising if the cooking had been better. If an operator like Tommy was going to do business with the Eastern bloc, Hungary was the natural choice.

A light tap on the door.

'Come in,' I called.

Nothing.

I tried again. 'It's not locked.'

Still nothing.

I got up irritably and opened the studio door. A well-groomed young man was waiting patiently on the landing. Neat moustache, clean-cut features, olive complexion. He wore a pale shirt open at the neck and a leather jacket, wide at the shoulders, tight at the waist. He smiled pleasantly. 'Mr Constantine? Could you spare me a moment?' His voice was light, soothing, heavily accented. *Constan-teen.*

I led the way into the studio and went back to my seat behind the word processor, while he settled languidly in the chair I had cleared for Inspector Rogers. 'Gutierrez,' he said. 'Hector Gutierrez. I work for Fernandez and Company.' He smiled pleasantly again. His eyes were small and stony.

I waited.

'Your friend Mr Apple – the late Mr Apple – had dealings with us.'

'He had dealings with a lot of companies. I never tried to keep up.'

'But you did business together.' *Beezness.*

'Occasionally. He was a friend, not a partner. Not that it's any concern of yours.'

'Sure, sure. No problem.' Hector looked me up and down with care, slowly, as though trying to memorise the details.

So much attention made me uneasy. 'This is the second visit I've had from you people. First a man called Riley, now you. I want to know where you got my name, where all these details come from. My deals, Tommy's deals. That's private information, none of your damn business.'

'We make a point of knowing when our money's involved.'

'Money?' I gestured at the chaotic room. 'That's a laugh. You want details, I'll give you the name of my bank manager. See what he has to say.'

The man called Hector looked pained. 'The subject is Tommy Apple.' He stared at me with his flat eyes. 'I guess you just don't understand. We're talking beeg money.'

'The estate will pay. It's in the hands of the lawyers now.'

'Lawyers don't understand this kind of debt. Debts without paperwork.' He flashed his charming smile. 'Misappropriated property.'

He stood up and began to wander vaguely round the room. He picked up one of my Nikons and examined it carefully, turning it over and over in his hands, as if he had never seen a camera before.

'Tommy was a successful business man,' I said. 'He didn't steal things. He wouldn't have known where to start.'

'Tommy was in over his head. Believe me.'

He opened a filing cabinet and flicked idly through the folders of photographs. 'Preety girls.' Another charming smile.

'One of the perks of the trade.'

Above the filing cabinet was a blow-up of Judy, Judy when young, Judy when we first met.

'Someone special?'

'My wife.'

'You have a preety wife also. Very preety.'

'I'll tell her you said so. She'll be flattered.'

He came behind the table and stood over me, so close that I could smell him – aftershave and garlic.

'Tommy's affairs aren't my concern,' I said.

He stretched out his hand and took hold of my shoulder with fingers like steel pincers. He bent slowly down until his bleak eyes were close to mine. The smell of garlic was very strong. 'You were a friend, Mr Constanteen. A close friend. You the best we got.' He turned his head and glanced at the computer screen with a letter to Tommy displayed on it. He smiled at me coldly and said, 'See what I mean?'

'I was checking up. There's nothing there. Just bits and pieces.'

He slid his hand up to the base of my neck and tightened his grip. I gasped, twisting around, trying to pull free. His other hand went to my neck, pinning me to my chair.

'Why should I believe you?' he asked. 'Writing things down on paper don't mean a thing.'

'Why should I lie? It's got nothing to do with me.'

He turned my head slightly in his grip and looked at me in a disinterested way, as though I were a specimen waiting for him to experiment on.

My neck ached. 'Please,' I said.

'Pleeze,' he repeated. He looked at me with distaste and let go of my neck. 'Don't give me trouble, friend. You wouldn't enjoy it.'

'Someone's fucked up.' I was standing now, facing him, rubbing my neck. 'You got the wrong guy.'

He stood with his hip cocked, his hands hanging loose, smiling and pleased with himself. 'I could make your life seriously miserable,' he said. 'Think about it.'

He turned at the door, still grinning. 'We'll be in touch.'

'WHY pick on me?' I asked. 'Riley, Hector, Helen. Two creeps and a girl. It sounds like an MGM musical.'

The moment I mentioned Helen I realised that I had made a tactical error. Even devoted wives with devoted husbands prefer not to hear about potential opposition.

'You can't blame the girl,' said Judy primly. 'You phoned her, remember?' She sipped her drink and stared determinedly at the gas flames flickering in our imitation coal fire.

'You're missing the point. The point is, why me?'

'Maybe what the Spaniard told you is true. Maybe you're all they've got.' She did not sound sympathetic.

'That doesn't make sense. Tommy had dozens of friends. He was doing business all over town. Tommy was a very popular man. I was just another member of his fan club.'

'Be that as it may,' said Judy.

I got up, took her glass and mine, poured fresh whisky into them, then went and stood in front of the phoney fire and listened to the rain pattering against the windows.

'It's like my Dan Air marriage all over again,' I said. 'Everybody knows I'm being made a fool of. Everybody except me. I want to be let in on the secret.'

Mention of my erratic ex-wife did the trick. Judy smiled at me fondly and said, 'Paranoia can seriously damage your health.'

'I'm not paranoid, I'm merely being persecuted. People are coming at me from all over.'

'And they all know something you don't. Well, that's one way of looking at it.'

'You'd better believe it.'

'You could always tell the police.'

'I get the impression they wouldn't believe me either.'

'Who does that leave?'

'You,' I said.

Outside, the wind had dropped and the sound of the rain against the windows was small and secretive.

'Oh, I believe you,' said Judy. 'For what that's worth.'

That night I lay awake a long time, listening to the rain. The tree outside our window was lit by a street lamp and the shadows of its branches moved restlessly on the ceiling. I thought of Hector, his olive good looks and dead eyes. I couldn't imagine what he was doing in my life, or what he had been doing in Tommy's. Tommy lived in a world of hustlers, all calculation and false bonhomie, with a little shady give and take on the side. He ate too much, laughed too loudly at his own jokes, married the wrong women, then bobbed up again, clamouring for more. Hector was pure psychopath, a clammy mirthless presence.

'No fun and games for you with the tax man?'

'To each his speciality.'

Stonehouse waved the papers vaguely in my direction. 'This all there is?'

I nodded.

'Of course,' he went on meditatively, 'if the deals were strictly cash, there's no reason why you should have kept records of them all.'

'They weren't. I wrote cheques.'

Stonehouse showed his yellow teeth in what was supposed to be a diffident smile. 'What if we have evidence to the contrary?'

'It would be crap.'

Rogers said, 'Put it another way: when did you and Tommy Apple last see each other?'

'If you want the date, it's probably in my diary.'

'I thought you were close friends.'

I shrugged. 'Time goes by. Like the song says.'

Stonehouse leaned forward on the sofa and showed his teeth again. 'Then why do you figure so prominently in Apple's diary? Your name is circled. It has arrows attached to it pointing in all directions. You figure, Mr Constantine. You were part of his plan of attack.'

'It's a plan he didn't get round to telling me about. All he did was write me a letter and you've got that. It's not a letter that says he and I were in the middle of something.'

The two men looked at each other.

'Ask my wife.'

'Are you a man who tells things to his wife?' said Rogers.

'Who else can I tell?'

'Why tell anyone?' said Stonehouse and went back to winding his arms around each other.

Rogers stared at me stone-faced. 'What did Hector Gutierrez want?' He sounded bored.

I felt bone-tired, as if the previous night's vigil had suddenly caught up on me. 'How do you know about him?'

'Mind your own bloody business.'

'Are you watching my house as well?'

'We wouldn't want you to come to any harm, would we?'

So at least I hadn't dreamed the presence in the parked car outside.

'About our mutual friend Hector,' said Stonehouse. He took a pipe from his pocket, blew through it noisily, then pulled out a tobacco pouch and began to fill the pipe.

'He wanted to put the frighteners on me, I suppose.'

Stonehouse lit a match and began to puff. He glanced at me through a cloud of blue smoke and said, 'Did he succeed?'

'You bet.'

Stonehouse nodded. 'It's one of the things he's good at.'

'What did he say?' asked Rogers.

'The same sort of thing that you're saying. That Tommy and I were in on something together. Something to do with Fernandez and Company. He talked about misappropriated property.'

'What did you tell him?'

'I said I didn't know anything about it. I said Tommy wasn't a crook.'

'Did he believe it?' Stonehouse asked from behind his cloud of smoke.

'He said he'd be back.'

'Did *you* believe it?'

Stonehouse's pipe had gone out. He lit a match and sucked patiently. The pipe made a low gurgling sound.

'I don't like your chances,' said Rogers. He stared at me with distaste. 'Hector and his friends think you and Tommy were deep into a scam. We think so, too.' He paused. 'Tell me.' His distaste intensified. 'Do you make a habit of handling stolen goods for your friends?'

'I never handled anything. I put up the money and left it to Tommy.'

'That's your story.' Rogers leaned forward, blunt hands clasped tightly, as though holding himself back. 'We have information from Interpol that leads us to believe that those Hungarian goods of yours – the pullovers, bottled fruit and kitchen utensils about which you corresponded so openly with your friend – were nicked, all nicked.' He glared at me like a hanging judge. 'You've been dealing in stolen property, Mr Constantine. Fact.'

Stonehouse seemed to be enjoying himself. He scratched the back of his head and twinkled benevolently from behind his smoke screen.

'Tommy wasn't like that,' I said.

'Oh yes he was. And we have documents to prove it,' said Rogers.

Stonehouse took his pipe out of his mouth and smiled. A lifetime of pipe smoking had left an arch-like dent in his yellow teeth and his smile was ragged. 'Of course, the matter doesn't necessarily have to go to court.'

'We'd like you to be on our side, you see,' Rogers said.

'And if I'm not, you'll have me for stolen goods? Thanks.'

Rogers laughed. 'You should be so lucky. Do you have any idea what goes on out there? Your friend Tommy Apple died of a heart attack. Very sudden, very sad. So you sit down and have a good cry. He was overweight, you say. He smoked forty a day. He was excitable. It stands to reason, you say. A bad insurance risk. Right?'

He was leaning forward. Broad shoulders, ramrod back, eyes gleaming with pleasure.

'Let me tell you about excitable, Mr Constantine. According to the post mortem, there were marks on the wrists indicating that Apple had been tied up, probably to his executive chair. There were also marks on his body suggesting that someone had worked him over with a sharp instrument. These are serious people, Mr Constantine, professionals. They enjoy their work.'

I sat still to attend to this. What he had said sounded so removed from my own measured life he might as well have been speaking a foreign language I understood only remotely.

'But you can protect me?' I mumbled.

'At this moment,' Stonehouse gestured with a long arm, as though he were paying me an elaborate compliment, 'that is our sole aim in life.'

'What do I have to do in return?'

'Be helpful. Be nice. Be friendly.'

'To you?'

'To Fernandez and Company. Co-operate with them. Tell them what you know.'

'But I don't know anything.'

'We'll help you out,' said Stonehouse expansively. 'Trust us.'

I got up and walked over to the window. The rain had stopped for the moment and the wind had dropped. But the heavy clouds were low over the roof tops and the air itself seemed grey and sodden. I went back to the table, facing the two strangers, and opened a metal case. My camera lenses were ranged in it, each in its separate velvet-lined slot. Reminders of an orderly and precise world.

Stonehouse was lounging back on the sofa, puffing his pipe. He had a hand between his thighs and his legs were crossed. When I looked at him he smiled encouragingly.

'How did I get into this?' I asked.

He pulled an ear-lobe with his free hand. He seemed unable to leave himself alone. 'Maybe your friend Tommy wasn't such a friend,' he said. 'Maybe he was looking for what our American friends would call a fall guy.'

'The poor sod is dead. He can't defend himself.'
'He couldn't when he was alive, either. Not when it mattered, could he?'
Rogers watched me stonily, his face a rictus of disapproval. He said, 'You and the deceased were very close. He did you a lot of favours. Do him any favours in return, did you? Anything you're prepared to talk about?'
'What kind of favours?'
'I mean something in your professional line of work. I can see a man like Tommy Apple might need a smudger from time to time.'
'Tommy didn't use advertising. That's not how he functioned.'
'Advertising isn't what I had in mind.'
'The answer is no.'
'You're quite sure about that?'
'Unless you want to hold family snaps against me.'
'You're getting upset.' Stonehouse held up a warning hand. 'That's not the way.'
I went back to my chair. Rogers was smiling, a scrubbed self-satisfied smile.
'What shall I tell my wife?' I asked.
'Nothing they would want to know,' said Stonehouse.
There were soup stains on his MCC tie. His suit looked as if it had been slept in. But his smugness, his sense of superiority were impermeable. In the end, it was more than I could take. 'Home Office, what's Home Office?' I asked. 'Who the hell are you?'
Stonehouse ducked his head and showed his yellow teeth. 'I'm official,' he said. 'The rest is none of your fucking business.'

TOMMY, who believed in nothing, got a slap-up Orthodox funeral. His ancient mother wept in the front row, next to the four grim ex-wives. Louise wept forlornly at the end of the row.
The little chapel was packed to overflowing with men like Tommy, middle-aged business men and their overdressed women. The place smelled of wet mink and Crombie overcoats. Closed umbrellas made little pools of water on the stone floor. At the back of the chapel was a crowd of seedier figures – solemn funeral faces but black ties askew, grubby shirts, collars mostly unbuttoned. Tommy had always been a keen poker player, but his enthusiasm was greater than his skill and his steadfast optimism – his unassailable belief in a next card that would redeem an unplayable hand – had made him a popular figure with the rocks at the Beachcomber. Now

all the rocks had come to pay their final respects: Gentleman Dan, Greek George, Pete the Pump, Fat Jack, Persian Ali, Omar the Turk and Hungarian Mike. As the rabbi rattled through the prayers, I leaned close to Judy and whispered in her ear, 'It's not a funeral, it's a poker hustlers' convention.' 'Shush,' she hissed and stared gravely at the rabbi.

Helen was standing at the back near the delegation from the Beachcomber. She was wearing a camelhair overcoat, a scarf over her blonde hair, like a 50s college girl. I thought of pointing her out to Judy, then changed my mind.

When the rabbi finished at last we followed the coffin out into the rain. It was balanced on an old-fashioned wooden cart, the kind rag-and-bone men used to push. The wheels crunched on the gravel. We trudged after it to the far side of the cemetery where the earth was raw and the headstones were all new. I had Judy on my left, Hungarian Mike on my right, all of us trying to shelter under the one umbrella. Hungarian Mike leaned his shoulder against mine and said, quite loud, 'Poor old Tommy. He's gone all in at last.' Judy let out a snort of laughter, turned it into a cough and squeezed my hand.

Hungarian Mike seemed not to have heard her. 'You believe in life after death, Joe?' he asked.

I shook my head. 'There's nothing much I'd fancy for eternity. But I suppose a celestial poker game would be all right.'

'Just as long as the cards ran better for me than they're running now. Imagine eight-three off-suit for time everlasting.'

At the graveside, the rabbi said Kaddish while the rain came down, then the coffin was lowered unsteadily and Tommy went to his last resting-place head first, settling with a subdued bump. Hungarian Mike nudged me again. He nodded towards the other poker players, with their paunches, their grey stubbly faces. 'I don't know why any of us bother to go home. Get the cards and the chips, we might just as well stay here.'

I filed forwards in my turn and shovelled a little mud on to the coffin. It looked cold and wet and lonely down there, worse than up here, but at least Tommy was out of all that. I hooked my arm through Judy's and we walked back to the car, huddled together under the umbrella. There was no sign of Helen among the mourners at the grave.

Hector was waiting at the cemetery gates. He wore a Burberry, tightly belted, and an Irish tweed hat with a neat brim. Mr Riley stood behind him in his shabby blue mac. He held an umbrella in one hand, a handkerchief in the other and his cold seemed worse than before. His red nose twitched, his watery eyes behind their glasses were fuddled.

I squeezed Judy's arm, looked straight ahead and prepared to walk past them. But Hector stepped forwards, smiling his film star's smile. 'I need a word with you,' he said.

With his dark features and county gent's clothes he looked like a bookie's tout, faintly absurd in the rain-sodden cemetery. He turned the smile on Judy. 'A pleasure to meet you, Mrs Constanteen.'

'This isn't the time,' I said.

'It'll have to do.'

'A friend has just been buried.'

Hector looked stonily at the sombre couples moving past and said, 'Everybody's friend.'

The cold I felt had nothing to do with the dark sky and the rain. Hector brought with him intimations of the day of judgment. In his presence I seemed to remember all my sins.

He turned to Judy and switched on his smile again. 'You can spare him for five minutes.' It was a statement, not a question.

Judy looked nervously from him to me and nodded.

'Wait for me in the car,' I said. When I tried to smile my lips felt stiff and unusable, like they'd been injected with Novocaine.

Judy smiled politely, as if all this were normal. My stand-up wife. She paused as she walked away and called over her shoulder, 'Don't be too long.'

I followed Hector to a black Jaguar parked on the opposite side of the road. Mr Riley trotted behind, miserable as a toy poodle in the pouring rain. Hector held the Jaguar's rear door open for me, then he and Riley climbed into the front. Helen was sitting in the corner of the back seat next to a plump smooth man who, despite the weather, wore dark glasses. His charcoal grey suit was immaculately tailored and the cuffs of his white shirt protruded enough to show diamond cuff links. He wore a slim watch with a blue face, diamonds to mark the hours and a delicate band of platinum links.

When I squeezed into the seat beside him he offered me a hairy manicured hand and said, 'Ray Fernandez. I'm glad you could come,' as if he were the host of a smart dinner party. The accent was lazy American, deep and assured.

'I didn't have much alternative.'

'Ah, Hector.' He smiled indulgently at the back of Gutierrez's head. 'I hope he wasn't too forceful.'

'He made his point.'

'Ah well.' Fernandez made a hostly gesture with his hands. 'I guess you've already met Helen Donovan.'

I looked at her, prepared to fake whatever was appropriate, but Helen kept her eyes fixed on the front seat, as if none of this had anything to do with her.

'I haven't got long,' I said. 'My wife's waiting.'

Fernandez glanced at his watch, then ran a finger caressingly around its expensive face. 'I won't keep you. You were a close friend of Tommy's. I think you can help us.'

'I'm an ignoramus, an innocent abroad. Talk to Tommy's lawyer. Like I told your boy here, he's the man in charge now. If you need it, I can get his name for you, no problem.'

'Most kind. But lawyers tend to be kinda rigid in their outlook. I'm looking for someone with a more flexible response. A friend.'

'We'd drifted apart.'

'Please.' Fernandez held up a warning hand. 'The problem is quite simple. We were doing business with your friend and a shipment has gone missing. A shipment from Hungary.'

'What kind of shipment?'

'Toys,' he said. 'Hand-made wooden toys. Very high quality goods.'

'That sounds like Tommy. Always full of surprises. How about Hungarian pullovers? We did them a couple of times and doubled our investment.'

The surly mouth beneath the dark glasses tightened. 'I am asking you politely, Mr Constantine. Do me the courtesy of answering seriously.'

'I'm sorry but wooden toys don't strike me as the kind of investment Chase Manhattan is going to lose sleep over. And you seem like a very wealthy man, Mr Fernandez.'

A nod of recognition, a small satisfied smile. 'To me, it's important. Trust me.'

I looked at Hector behind the steering wheel, eyes front, pretending not to listen. 'I don't know a thing. It's weeks since I spoke to Tommy. But I'll do what I can.'

Fernandez's smile widened. His teeth were white and even. American teeth, a triumph of orthodontistry.

'Now you're being smart. You won't regret it.' He patted Helen's knee in a proprietorial way. 'Isn't that right, hon?'

The girl blinked, looked down for a moment at his hand, then went back to her study of the back of Hector's head. She did not answer.

'What do you want me to do?' I asked.

'You were his pal. You knew his little ways. Trace the shipment for us.'

I tried unsuccessfully to see the eyes behind the dark glasses. Fernandez was so sleek and expensive that he filled me with dismay. 'What if I can't?' I said.

'Sure you can, Mr Constantine. Look on the bright side.'

The windows of the Jaguar were beginning to mist up. Across the road, a forlorn group stood under umbrellas. Tommy's mother, Louise and the rabbi. The rabbi had his arm consolingly around the old woman's shoulders. He was a short man but stout, and she seemed tiny in comparison, as though diminished by grief.

'Where do you think I should start?'

'If I knew, I wouldn't be asking. The shipment has simply disappeared.' Fernandez gestured elegantly. 'Pouf. Gone with the wind. Vanished.'

'Are you certain it arrived?'

For a moment, Fernandez's elegance deserted him. His jaw tightened and he leaned his face so close to mine that I could smell his sharp breath and see the angry dark eyes behind the dark glasses. 'Of course it fucking arrived. Why do you think I've got you here? Why should I waste my time?' The rage evaporated as swiftly as it had arrived. He leaned back comfortably against the leather upholstery. 'Or yours either.'

I felt as lost as Tommy's mother. But at least she had the rabbi to console her. 'I'll make a few phone calls, talk to some friends. Maybe somebody out there has an idea,' I said.

'You'll think of something, no question.'

'And if I draw a blank?'

'I'd hate to think you were holding out on us. That's not the way to go.'

'I've got nothing to hold out. Please get that clear.'

'That's what you tell us. For your sake, I hope it's true.'

'Mr Fernandez, I'm a photographer. I know about lighting and composition. Tommy's deals were always beyond me, even when I was in on them.'

He glanced at his beautiful watch, then sighed resignedly. 'Get me my goods, Mr Constantine,' he said. 'Hector will keep an eye on you.'

'Is that part of the deal?'

He smiled benignly. 'I guess so. But don't worry. You keep your side of the bargain, you'll find he's all smiles. Isn't that right, Hector?'

Gutierrez tilted his profile towards us and showed his teeth.

When I got out of the Jaguar Helen glanced at me quickly but made no sign. As I crossed the road, hunched into my overcoat against the rain, it occurred to me that she had not said a word the whole time I was in the car. As if we had never met. I had pictured a scenario in which she wept on my fatherly shoulder, mourned our mutual friend, intimate in shared grief. She's got the boss now, and maybe she had him while she and Tommy were planning a romantic future together. Then I remembered the expression on her face, peaked and strained, eyes a little too wide, head too still. That's not distance, I thought. That's fear.

'TELL me what's happening,' Judy said as we drove away.

'I'm like the leprechaun in the old joke. The police have one of my balls in their hands, Fernandez has the other. Between them they have my undivided attention.'

'Leave your balls out of it. Just this once. Tell me what's happening.'

'I wish I knew.' The wipers thumped monotonously, the tyres hissed, the endless rain swept down. 'Tommy was doing one of his import deals with Fernandez and somewhere along the line the goods disappeared. Fernandez is upset about it. He seems to think Tommy's double-crossed him. And the police think the same. What beats me is why they all take it so seriously. These are toys we're talking about, wooden junk from Hungary, just in time for the Christmas rush, the kind of half-assed deal Tommy used to cut me in on. Two grand up front and double your money in a year. Fernandez looks like he'd have twice that sort of change in his back pocket. He dresses like a merchant banker: hand-built suit, diamond cuff links, a pair of matching bodyguards. He was wearing a Piaget watch that must have cost more than all the toys in Hungary. Yet there he is, breathing fire and destruction. It's a mad world, my masters.'

'That's all very well,' said Judy. 'But what's it got to do with you?'

'If I knew that I'd sleep better. The police say Tommy left my name around, scribbled all over his diary. The implication is, he and I were in this together.'

'He'd have told you.'

'Maybe he was intending to and hadn't got round to it.'

'Then why didn't he mention it in that letter he never sent?'

I stared out at the sodden suburban streets and the cars probing slowly along with their headlights on. 'Maybe he had something to hide. Maybe he had a fiddle going and was using my name as a cover.'

'Why would a friend do that?'

'Perhaps he thought I owed him one for favours past.'

'What kind of a hustler was he, after all?' She shook her head wearily. 'This was the guy who married us off, darling.'

'I suppose things just got out of control.'

'I'm glad you're being so philosophical about it.'

'What else can I be? The poor bastard is dead.'

'And he's left you in charge of the sinking ship. Remember what that black comic used to say? "Never speak nuttin' but good of the dead. He's dead. Good." '

We drove in silence. Although it was only four o'clock, the light was going fast. I turned into the side street where Tommy's mother lived and began to look for a place to park. We were late for the wake and the kerb was already lined with expensive company cars.

'What worries me is how Fernandez knows your name was all over Tommy's diary,' said Judy.

'Perhaps he doesn't. Perhaps Tommy simply mentioned my name to him.'

'Or perhaps they were in his office when he died.'

'I was afraid you were going to say that.'

I finally found a slot a hundred yards down the road from Mrs Apple's house. I backed in and switched off the motor. We sat for a minute listening to the creaking settling noises of the car's engine and the rain drumming on its roof. When I turned to Judy I saw she was watching me intently, as though trying to remind herself what I looked like.

'In a previous incarnation,' I said, 'before I married you, I sometimes used to wonder what it would be like to fuck up on a grand scale.'

'Welcome to the big time,' Judy said.

THE next morning my ankle ached so badly that it hurt to get out of bed. The face in the bathroom mirror seemed to belong to someone I didn't recognise, someone much older than myself, with a lined forehead and pouches below his blurred eyes and not much hair. I kept my eyes fixed on the spot I was shaving and tried not to take in the whole, then stood for a long time under the shower hoping that the hot water would soothe away some of the ache.

I told myself nothing had happened, it was all a misunderstanding. For twenty-odd years Tommy had acted the fairy godfather. If the deals had been bent, he'd made sure I didn't know. I didn't even know for certain there were any deals. He could have put the money on a horse or a poker game and it wouldn't have mattered. He always made sure I got back more than I put in. It was his way of helping out, of being a pal. And when he finally asked a small favour in return I'd complied willingly without a second thought. What are a few dirty photos among friends? Not my style of work but I was glad to oblige, no questions asked. If he had wanted another favour, he had only to ask. Yet all the letter had said was, Keep an eye on Louise, call Helen. No mention of any shipments, Budapest to Heathrow via Malev, no hint that he was setting me up.

He must have doodled my name in his diary while thinking of something else entirely and the police had latched on to me because they had no other leads. Likewise Fernandez. They were all thrashing around in the dark and they had happened to blunder into me. In due course, they would realise their mistake and blunder off again. When I had phoned Rogers the previous evening to tell him about Fernandez, he'd said, 'Keep up the good work,' like some mindless blimp in an old war movie. How was I supposed to take that seriously? There was always Hector, with his handsome smile and bad breath. But even Hector had limited his threats to an iron grip on my shoulder. It was all about nothing.

Judy stuck her head round the bathroom door and said, 'I'm off early, darling. I've got to make up for yesterday afternoon.' She looked bright and fresh and at least twenty years younger than me.

'How come you're so full of fun?'

'I live right,' she said. 'And for once it's not raining.'

A cold wind had dried the streets and the sun shone palely, as though through a gauze curtain. A burly man was sitting in a car a few yards up the street. He was unshaven and puffy-eyed and there was a paper coffee cup on the seat beside him. I smiled at him as I passed, walking as briskly to the tube as my ankle would allow, but he pretended not to see me. It was nice to know Rogers was taking me seriously but somehow I was not reassured. I glanced round when I reached the top of the road. The burly man had got out of the car and was walking slowly after me.

Because I was late the rush hour was over, the tube almost empty. I walked to the far end of the platform and waited for the burly man to appear. A pale stricken youth was walking up and down, muttering to himself. He wore a long overcoat, sneakers and no socks, and he glared at me each time he passed. 'Capitalist bastards,' I heard him say. 'They think they can get away with it, don't they? Think nobody's watching, nobody's keeping count.' He wandered off down the platform, turned and wandered back again, muttering as he went. When he was level with me again he swung suddenly around and said in a high thin voice, 'The signs are all around us. Open your eyes.'

I smiled at him for the benefit of the people down the platform. Then I turned my back on them. 'Fuck off,' I said.

His pale face became paler, his mouth trembled. His eyes glared, but glared past me. 'Dirty Jews,' he muttered. 'Jews everywhere. Contaminating the proletariat. Go back where you came from.'

I turned away briskly and walked down the platform to where the other passengers were waiting. The burly man was among them and I was even relieved to see him. The pale youth followed me. 'Send them back where they came from,' he was saying. 'Filth, scum.'

The people on the platform moved uneasily away from the rails and looked at me sympathetically.

The young man drew himself up and addressed them. 'And the Lord said unto Satan, Whence comest thou? Then Satan answered the Lord, and said, From going to and fro in the earth, and from walking up and down in it.' He gazed fiercely around the embarrassed faces, as though expecting an argument.

Two teenagers with rucksacks giggled and an elderly woman clucked her tongue disapprovingly. I opened my newspaper and pretended to read. The pale young man stared at me with wide crazy eyes. But the fire had gone out of him and he no longer seemed convinced. Maybe I hadn't spoken to him after all; maybe he had imagined it. He seemed to be struggling with his inner voices, no longer certain which was them and which was me. I smiled ruefully at the elderly lady and she smiled back. The young man stalked off down the platform, muttering, gesturing, watched by the rest of us.

The burly man came with me to Tottenham Court Road, travelling discreetly in the next carriage, but left me at the corner of my street. I wondered if he would go back to collect his car or leave it in place for the next man on night shift. I felt vaguely disappointed to see him go. It was like having a bodyguard; it made me feel important, a person of consequence, like Fernandez. There were two men digging a hole in the pavement in front of my studio. It crossed my mind that they, too, might be working for Rogers. But maybe that was just another illusion of grandeur.

The door of my studio was open and Stonehouse was sitting at my table-desk in front of the computer. I had the impression that he had had it on and had switched it off when he heard me trudging upstairs.

'Sorry to barge in unannounced,' he said. 'Thought you'd be here by now. The cleaning lady let me in.'

I studied him without pleasure. The expensive shabby suit, the yellow teeth and diffident smile. 'Be my guest,' I said. 'This is all part of co-operating with you, right?' Stonehouse shrugged and looked sheepish. 'So put it on the record that I'm being co-operative.'

'Don't take it that way, old boy. No percentage in getting miffed.' His long face sagged, he seemed genuinely upset. 'When it comes down to it we're all on the same side.'

'Glad to hear it. Now I can sleep safely at nights.'

Stonehouse got up from my chair and went over to the sofa. He slumped down dejectedly and began twisting his arms together.

'I met a madman on the tube,' I told him. 'A paranoid schizophrenic who thought the Elders of Zion were out to get him. How come other Jews walk all over London and nobody accuses them of crucifying Christ? One look at me and they know I did it single-handed.'

'Maybe you're too sympathetic. They see it in your face.'

'I wasn't even brought up as a Jew. My parents didn't believe in that stuff. At my C of E school we had prayers every morning and chapel twice a day on Sundays. I know the New Testament better than my Presbyterian wife does. I got a distinction in Divinity in School Certificate, for Christ's sake.'

'It doesn't seem to make much difference in the end, does it?' Stonehouse said sympathetically.

'Even my nose is a fake. I broke it playing rugger.'

'I understand.'

'So why is it that when anyone accuses me of anything I always see the force of their argument?'

'Because you're a nice man, self-effacing.'

'Guilt,' I answered. 'Jewish fucking guilt.'

'What's there to be guilty about?'

'Nothing. That's the whole point. It's self-generating, self-fulfilling and self-defeating. Heads you win, tails I lose.'

Stonehouse looked embarrassed. The conversation languished. Finally, he said, 'Tell me about Fernandez.'

'I already told your friend Rogers.'

'It always sounds better from the horse's mouth.' He pulled out his pipe, cleaned it, filled it, lit it, then leaned back against the sofa, one hand tucked between his legs, smoking peacefully, while I told him about the meeting.

'I wonder where that shipment went,' he said when I finished. 'Clever man, your friend Apple. I can see why Fernandez is irritated.'

'Am I supposed to believe you don't know more than he does?'

'Less, probably. At that point, we weren't looking. All we know is the shipment cleared customs on the twelfth of last month and was driven away in a van.'

'Who by?'

'Not Apple. He was minding the shop. Having lunch with his bank manager, to be precise. You can't get a better alibi than that.'

'You've been through his papers. There must be warehouses he used for all the stuff he had through his hands.'

'Of course there are. Regular little magpie he was. We've found goodies you wouldn't believe. But there's no sign of Hungarian toys.'

Stonehouse slouched on the old sofa, pipe in his mouth and one hand clamped between his thighs. With his other hand he scratched tentatively at the side of his nose. I had never met anyone who found his own body so fascinating.

'You have no idea how weary all this makes me,' I said. 'There's you, with your Whitehall manners, coming on like we're dealing in state secrets, and there's Fernandez who looks as if he has enough money to start World War III all by himself, and what are we talking about? Wooden puffer trains. I feel left out.'

Stonehouse looked at me coldly. 'I see you're a man who likes all the "i"s dotted and "t"s crossed. I suppose I'd rated you higher than that.'

'Sorry to disappoint you. Go ahead, dot an "i" or two. I'm not proud.'

'You should concentrate,' Stonehouse said in a schoolmasterly tone. 'A man of your intelligence. Why do you think I'm involved in a routine police investigation? Because I've got nothing better to do with my time? We're talking about drugs, Mr Constantine. Cocaine, to be precise. I would have thought it was glaringly obvious.'

'Bullshit,' I said. 'Tommy was a nice Jewish boy. At heart.'

'I fail to see what religion has to do with it.'

'Jews don't drink. And all in all, they don't take drugs. Hippy poets apart, and at least not in England. Our vices are domestic, not social. We suffocate our children and vote for liberal values.'

'What a sentimentalist you are, to be sure.' Stonehouse wagged his pipe at me, more schoolmasterly than ever. 'When I said involved I didn't mean hooked. I meant drugs was just another line of goods he was importing. Like those Hungarian pullovers but with far larger profit margins. The sky's the limit with coke. Get it pure, double it up with a little borax and you make a fortune. And you don't have to worry about the tax man. The drawback is the company you keep.'

'Like Fernandez and friends?'

Stonehouse nodded. 'A difficult man. Not someone to cross.'

I remembered the tête-à-tête in the Jaguar. This is what my old pal has landed me in. First porn, now cocaine.

'What's all that got to do with Hungary? I thought drugs was the only problem the Eastern bloc didn't have.'

'There's the mystery. You wonder about the Jews, I wonder about the Hungarians.'

'I wonder about me,' I said. 'What am I supposed to be doing in all this?'

'Whatever Fernandez asks you to do. Show willing. Wag your tail when he whistles.'

'What he wants is information. He wants his goods. If I'm to feed him, you'll have to feed me.'

'That's not impossible. After all, you're an old friend, an occasional partner in crime. You might know where some of the skeletons are buried. The unit on the Mahatma Gandhi Trading Estate in Camberwell, the lock-up in Kilburn.' He picked up his battered briefcase, fumbled around in it, and brought out two keys, each of them tagged. 'Here you go,' he said jovially. 'Now you're lord of the manor.'

'He's probably checked them out already.'

'You're not to know. This way at least you'll be showing your heart's in the right place.'

'I aim to keep it there. Hector notwithstanding.'

Stonehouse gave me his lopsided smile and said, 'Faint heart never won fair lady.'

'All very well for you. You're not on the sharp end.'

'Where's your sense of adventure, Mr Constantine?'

'I lost it when my second decree absolute came through. I'm middle-aged. I devote a good deal of energy to avoiding trouble.'

'That's defeatist talk. For a man with an open mind, life is full of surprises.'

'That's what I'm afraid of.'

Stonehouse gave a little snort of pleasure. He seemed possessed by a kind of bony jocularity that depressed me deeply.

'I wouldn't want you to get into trouble,' he said pleasantly. 'You see, I feel a kind of fondness for you, a sympathy with your work. Photography's an art I've always admired. Done a bit myself – in a strictly amateur way, you understand, nothing I'd want a professional like yourself to see. Only the other day I was saying to the wife, Hester, when I retire maybe I'll go back to the lens.'

He watched me carefully, massaging the inside of his thigh. Here we go again, I thought.

'We found some rather interesting photographs in the deceased's files. What we call the gilt-edged type. You know, art work. Imaginative stuff. Mark you, all that's been overtaken by video these days. Amazing what you can rent for a couple of quid. But I suppose it's nothing to what'll be available when satellite television really gets going. In the States, I'm told, there are whole channels specialising in that kind of stuff.'

My ankle was aching again. I stared at him poker-faced and waited.

'I suppose you've never taken that kind of picture?' Stonehouse said casually. 'You know, model work. This is off the record of course, strictly between you and me. Surprising the people who will involve themselves. But I suppose the money's not to be sniffed at.'

He watched me with his bluff blue eyes. A cricketer's eyes, blood-shot but unblinking. I looked away and rubbed my ankle.

'Silly question.' He snorted again, enjoying a private joke. 'A propos of sniffing, let me ask you another silly question: You ever handle coke for your old friend, did you?'

My armpits and back were running with sweat but I felt ice-cold. 'I don't even know what it looks like,' I said.

'A cross between table salt and flour. Very unimpressive, considering the price.'

'I don't have to answer this sort of question.'

Stonehouse's stare hardened, the corners of his mouth turned down. 'We're talking about drugs, Mr Constantine. Drugs and pornography. Serious charges. I can ask you any damn question I please.'

'I'm not charged with anything. I don't have to answer.'

Stonehouse lowered his head and when he looked up again he was smiling. He took his hand from between his thighs and patted the air between us. 'Don't get upset, old boy. All we want is a little co-operation. Stick with us and you'll come to no harm.' His voice was reassuring, carefully modulated, the kind of voice you use to a frightened child. One minute the Wicked Witch of the West, the next minute Nanny. He was giving me his whole repertoire and it was hard to keep up.

'Why do they call them gilt-edged?' I asked.

'Damned if I know. It's a phrase I picked up from my colleagues in the Met. I suppose they picked it up from their customers.'

'A dirty picture by any other name.'

'That's the ticket. Look on the bright side. "Nothing is good or bad but thinking makes it so." Or that's what they say.' Stonehouse took out a leather jotting pad with gold reinforced edges and wrote on it briefly. 'You just pass these addresses on to Fernandez and see how grateful he will be.'

I glanced at the piece of paper: the Mahatma Gandhi Trading Estate and the Kilburn lock-up.

'I assume there are others.'

'All in good time. We've got to play him a little, give him some line.' He rubbed the side of his face, then ran his hand beneath his nostrils as though to smell his own scents. 'You mustn't think badly of your friend,' he said. 'When I was in Germany after the war everyone was on the fiddle. It was how you survived if you were smart.'

'I should have known you were a spook.'

'Just a spooklet, nothing grand. I speak the lingo, you know. I did interrogations, none of your cloak and dagger stuff.'

'I bet that's what you say to all the boys.'

'It's all long past. I missed it at first, but not any more. Now I'm just another functionary, a peaceable fellow like yourself.'

'I'd like to stay that way,' I said.

Stonehouse uncoiled himself from the sofa. He was a tall man with a big frame and I could see that at one time he might have been an athlete. But his shoulders drooped, the skin at his neck was loose and there was a boozer's network of broken veins in his cheeks. I couldn't imagine him now wielding any weapon more threatening than an umbrella.

'One question,' I said. 'How do you hide cocaine in toys?'

He smiled at me sadly. 'You're what they call a literalist of the imagination. First we find the shipment, then we worry about how the stuff is hidden.'

He moved towards the door, then paused. 'I don't suppose,' he said hesitantly, 'you have a bottle anywhere on the premises?'

Before I could answer, he sighed deeply and shook his head. 'I forgot. Jews don't drink.'

I got up and walked across to my old steel filing cabinet. 'You don't listen,' I said. 'I'm a public school lad, I went to university, I've had all the advantages.' I pulled open the bottom drawer and took out a bottle. 'Maybe I'll join you.'

JUDY

I think they are watching me. When I walk down the hill to my studio in the morning I feel I'm being followed. I dawdle, look in the shop windows, see a smeared image of myself in my black military raincoat, umbrella shouldered like a rifle, rain hat pulled down around my ears. Yet when I glance casually back there is never anyone to be seen. The problem is there aren't many shops on Haverstock Hill and it's difficult to stroll convincingly in this foul weather. Even so, I'm sure that I'm seen to my door each morning by an invisible escort. Ours or theirs? And who, precisely, is ours, who theirs?

My studio has been searched. I haven't told Joe this; there seems no point in adding to his troubles. But I'm certain of it. Not that they left a mess. If anything, the place was too neat, but in a shadowy unreal way. I'm a naturally tidy person and I know where all my things are. Nothing was out of place, yet nothing was where it should have been. It was as if all my bits and pieces had been picked up and put down again just a fraction of an inch out. I felt I was looking at a *trompe l'oeil* picture and if I stared hard enough the studio would transform itself into another place entirely, somewhere I'd never seen before, a looking-glass world.

I hope, for their sake, that they found what they were looking for, though I can't think what there was to find.

They must have had a hard time of it. The studio is crammed with papers – folders of them, boxes, files, folios – with books and paints and bottles of ink and all my instruments. Cupboards full of stuff, shelf after shelf of it, a lifetime's detritus. All of it has been checked, every last item, and scrupulously replaced. It feels odd to be the object of such attention. Like being in the lens of a devoted scientist. Am I worthy of all this effort?

Now when I sit at my drawing board I have the spooky sensation of not being alone. I feel I'm being watched, even with the door closed and all the lights on. I imagine a huge spider crouched just out of sight, its evil little eyes fixed on my back, waiting to make its move.

Maybe it's all my imagination. Maybe nobody follows me,

nobody searched the studio, nobody cares. Maybe I've dreamed it all up because of what happened to Tommy and we'll all live happily ever after, despite everything. Maybe it's just a generalised anxiety because, at heart, I can't believe my luck in finding a man who turns me on and keeps me interested, then actually marrying him. I was brought up to believe marriage is a duty, a question of making the best of a bad job. The idea of happiness goes against my Presbyterian conscience. It fills me with foreboding, like holding a valuable crystal glass in my hands and waiting for it to break.

So I sit at my drawing board, balancing the invisible glass that I know is going to shatter. I listen to the rain and what do I think of? I think, of all things, of the sea: of hot beaches and small waves, the prickle of salt water drying on my body, and the smell of Ambre Solaire, the smell of being young, unmarried, restless, unhappy. I think of the sea, its tang, its soothing sound, while the central heating thumps away, the strip lights buzz and the rain pelts down outside.

We hardly ever get to the beach any more. Joe says he hates the whole scene – the bodies frying in rows or parading themselves to each other. He says the feel of sand between his toes sets his teeth on edge. More likely he's self-conscious about his belly and thickened waist. As I should be, I suppose. Forty is a serious age for a woman. But I do my Jane Fonda and work at the stretching exercises and keep dread at bay for the time being. Joe has shots he took of me when we first met pinned to the walls of his studio, then tells people, 'She's got to stick with me because I'm the only guy around who remembers what she used to look like.' Everybody laughs, me included. As I get older, laughter seems the nicest form of tenderness, and the rarest.

Years ago, when I first came down to London, I spent a weekend on a boat with a friend from college and her husband. He was a teacher there, forty and counting, a patriarch from where we stood. She was half his age, his brand-new second wife. At night the boat rocked with their love-making. They sent ripples clear across to the opposite bank and I listened with awe. But in the morning, when I listened again, I could hear them lying in their bunk giggling like children. No one had ever told me that laughing and fucking went together. After all the cant and histrionics I'd absorbed from Lawrence and Henry Miller, it was a revelation. I decided then that that was the kind of marriage I wanted. The miracle is, I got it.

Joe and I seemed to have known each other before we even met. After the first hour we were finishing each other's sentences, as though we were speaking a private language. We seemed singled out, attracted in ways profounder than sex. Not just looks and excitement but something chemical, a question of smell and taste and texture. A perfect match, the million-to-one shot that comes off. What Yeats called 'the yolk and white of the one shell'. We kept breaking up, uneasy with the idea that this was it, there were no more choices. But even apart we stayed eerily in touch. The first time I went to bed with someone else, Joe and I hadn't seen or spoken to each other for two months, though I knew, from Tommy, he had another girl. But he arrived on my doorstep at seven in the morning, holding a bunch of bedraggled roses he'd stolen from a garden in Fellows Road. 'I couldn't sleep,' he said. 'I was thinking about you all night.' I told him to give me an hour, bundled the other man out of my life, and met Joe for breakfast at a coffee bar in Swiss Cottage. Destiny. Three months later we split up again but each separation felt more wilful, more aimless than the last and finally there seemed no point in pretending. When we married it was like coming home.

Now I don't know where he's got to. He is furtive and apprehensive, looking over his shoulder all the time. It makes sense of course, considering what he's got on his back: the police, a Whitehall mandarin, an American businessman who comes on like he was second cousin to the Godfather. It would be laughable if Joe weren't so haunted by it, so zipper-mouthed. Something is going on that he won't talk about. Something to do with Tommy and his deals. Our dear friend the crook, now deceased. Or maybe it's the American girl. Whatever the reason, a veil is down and I don't trust him. He treats me as though I were one of them, to be buttered up and kowtowed to. He buys me flowers, treads softly, lays on the charm. He'd pull back my chair if I gave him the chance. He scurries off to the studio when there's no work to do and placates me when there is nothing to placate. I'm not a shrew, I'm not his conscience, I'm his wife. For better or for worse. And I don't know what's on his mind any more.

Whatever it is, he brings it to bed. No more giggling, no more fooling around. Our love-making has become ferocious, anonymous, full of grief. He burrows down between my breasts as if he were trying to hide. As if it were our first time or our last. Full of doom, full of fear. As if some immense event had taken possession of him. The more we make love, the more I think I've lost him.

I turn the central heating a notch higher and go back to my drawing board. It's peaceful here with my inks, stencils, curves and set-squares. The rain patters against the window and the traffic sounds a long way off. But I can't concentrate. The great sheet of white paper is waiting for me to fill it. I brush my hand over its blank moon surface tenderly. There is nothing more pleasing than Indian ink on thick white paper, each sign in its right place and each balancing the others. But today it won't come right. I take a sketch book and try to rough out what I'm after in pencil but nothing seems to work. All I can think of is Tommy's death and the grief it's brought us. After all those years of friendship and good will, it seems a kind of insult.

I get up and pour myself a cup of coffee. It's ten o'clock but the morning outside the window is dark, as though we were up near the Arctic Circle – Bergen, not London – where the sun scarcely lifts above the horizon and the light is squeezed out like miser's gold. When the telephone rings it sounds like an explosion.

'You sound terrible,' says Louise. Her voice is whiny and intimate at the same time. The kind of voice that encourages confession, then never lets go.

'Bloody weather,' I say. 'It's enough to get anybody down.'

'I know.' She sounds suddenly on the edge of tears. I should have known better than to say anything that would encourage her. Even the weather is off limits. She goes on, the tears coming steadily closer to the surface. 'I've been sitting here thinking of Tommy.'

'Funny you should mention it.'

'I still can't believe what's happened.' She sobs, sniffs loudly, sobs again.

'I'm *so* sorry,' I say. The sobbing continues. 'It's just awful,' I murmur. 'Awful.' And in a way, my heart goes out to her. But she has been calling me every morning since it happened, weeping monotonously into the telephone, and my patience is wearing thin. While her sobs rise and fall over the telephone line, I wonder how many other people are on her calling list. I also wonder how genuine it all is. If Tommy was really preparing to leave her for the American girl, she must have known something was wrong. Now the poor bastard is dead and gone, her grief is a way of reclaiming status as the woman in residence.

She subsides slowly, very slowly, like a summer storm moving off into the next valley. Finally, she blows her nose and swallows noisily. The main purpose of the telephone call has been accomplished: she's had a good cry.

'Darling,' I say, 'do you have any idea of what he was really up to?' I mean Joe, not Tommy, but why tell her?

'What do I know?' she asks rhetorically. ' "We're going to get rich", he'd say. And when I said "We're rich already", he'd shake his head and say "This is comfortable. I mean seriously rich". As though it mattered. It was just a game really. It wasn't about money, it was about winning.'

I imagine her sitting in her over-furnished living-room, with her big comfortable breasts, her hair like a fright wig. I look tenderly at the clean uncluttered paper on my drawing board. It is everything that she isn't.

'What do the police say?' I ask.

Louise snorts indignantly. 'They don't *say* anything. I've had six of them in here, picking over our belongings, emptying the drawers, shuffling through the papers. I don't know whether they're investigating the break-in or Tommy.'

'They must have said something.'

'They say Tommy's death was suspicious. What's suspicious about a heart attack I want to know? He just did himself too well. If they'd seen him lashing into the smoked salmon they'd know all about the cause of death.'

'Talk to your lawyer.'

'Why make trouble? Anyway, how can I with them around all the time? I haven't even had my hair done. I look awful and no wonder, but I don't like to leave the flat. There's even two sitting outside in a car. Every hour on the hour I take them cups of tea. The neighbours are at their windows. Like this was Golders Green, not Reddington Road.'

'They're probably listening in to your telephone calls.'

'I hope they're enjoying themselves. Maybe we should talk dirty and give them something to listen to.'

Poor Louise. She hasn't got much in her life to talk dirty about now.

'Those were the days,' I say, and suddenly she is crying again, long measured sobs, Atlantic breakers rolling in. 'Oh Judy, Judy darling, I'm not going to get over this.' By the time she has calmed down, I am exhausted.

I hope the listeners have enjoyed themselves.

After that, there is no point in even trying to work. I put on my coat and hat and walk quickly to Chalk Farm tube station. The rain has let up for the moment and the clouds have lifted. The white façades of the comfortable Victorian houses in Provost Road soak up the wan light, the trunks of the bare trees glisten dully. I look back a couple of times but see no one loitering with intent behind me. But then, if they knew what they were doing, I wouldn't, would I?

By the time I come out of the tube at Oxford Circus a watery sun has broken through and the world seems unnaturally bright. Crowds saunter along Oxford Street admiring the Christmas tat in the windows. Street decorations blow in the breeze. The shop windows make me depressed. Women's fashion this season is a cross between Rita Hayworth and Superman. Outlandish shoulders and tiny waists. I'd need to be six foot tall and thin as a stick to carry them off. I hurry past, feeling old and overweight.

John Lewis is crowded with Christmas shoppers and the air is like some man-made substitute, hot and smelling of perfume. I push my way through the crowd to the escalator. As I ascend slowly above the seething heads, I watch the street door I came in by but all I can see are harassed women like myself.

I need to buy hand towels but the choice is overwhelming and it is a long time before I can catch the attention of one of the surly assistants. She takes pleasure in telling me what they haven't got but finally, despite her, I find more or less what I want. As I am waiting for the girl at the cash desk to check my bank card, I glance over my shoulder. The one they call Hector is standing near the arch that separates the towel department from curtains. I look away quickly, not wanting to catch his eye. His Burberry is open and he is carrying his hound's tooth tweed hat in his hand. He looks very much at his ease, a compliant husband waiting for his wife to make her purchases.

My ears buzz and I feel cold, although beads of sweat are standing out on my forehead. When the girl at the cash desk asks me to write my address on the back of my cheque the words don't get through and she has to repeat herself – with a great show of irritation. My hand shakes when I write. Yet what I feel is anger: anger with my body for being so out of my control, anger with Hector for making this happen, above all anger with Joe. What right has he? What right has anyone?

The girl at the cash desk expresses her disapproval by wasting time; she rings for a supervisor to OK the cheque. I stare at her stony-faced and refuse to respond. While we are waiting, I turn towards where Hector was standing, ready now to take him on. But Hector has gone.

I pick up the green and white bag of towels and stroll, as nonchalantly as I can, towards the curtain department. No sign of him. I saunter on, pausing to finger the racks of materials, glancing around each time I finish. I can feel the sweat under my armpits and between my breasts. I take out a tissue and wipe my forehead. When I get to the escalators I look around again, then go up to the next floor. I look back as I rise. He has broken cover and is walking quickly towards the moving stairs. I cross to the down staircase, force myself to count ten so that he is committed, then hurry back down. Directly the up stairs come into view I can see him, sandwiched between two hefty women. He flashes me his seducer's smile, as though we had known each other for years, and tries to barge his way up. But the women are broad-beamed and truculent; they have bags spread across the steps and they have no intention of giving way. I hear him say, 'Fuck you, lady,' then outraged noises from the women as they rise out of sight.

I shove my way down, saying, 'Sorry', 'Excuse me', 'Sorry'. On the ground floor they are playing 'Jingle Bells' and the smell of scent is very strong. I push my way through the shoppers and make for the Oxford Street exit, wondering if the ferret-faced man is waiting for me outside. I dart across the street against the lights. A bus-driver stares at me, appalled. A taxi brakes violently and the driver shouts at me. I cut down into Hanover Square, then over to Regent Street, wanting to run but making myself walk. I go in the front door of Dickens & Jones – more perfume, more 'Jingle Bells' – and out at the back into Argyll Street, past the music shops and television companies in Marlborough Street, and into Soho.

By the time I reach Joe's studio my clothes are wet with sweat but not until he has locked the door behind me do I let the tears come. Joe stands awkwardly over me, patting my sweaty head and murmuring, 'It's all right, darling, it's all right.'

'Oh no it isn't,' I reply.

JOE

I was astonished at how long she wept. Usually, Judy cries only under extreme provocation, and when she does it is over quickly. Her grim Scottish parents brought her up never to indulge in self-pity and she looks down on women like Louise who use tears as a weapon. Now she sat on my untidy sofa and wept her heart out. Her face streamed with tears, her hair and neck were wet with sweat. She did not look like someone who was grieving, she simply looked bedraggled, as if she'd been out in the rain without a coat or an umbrella. It was only when the tears went on and on that I realised that they had nothing much to do with either grief or fear. She was crying because she was truly pissed off. With herself, above all, for having let Hector Gutierrez make her run.

'He caught me off my guard,' she said when the tears finally began to subside.

'There's no need to apologise.'

'Even Louise would have behaved better.'

'Louise would have had hysterics right there in the towel department. He has a gift, has Hector, for putting the fear of God into people.'

'Why should I fall for it? In the middle of John Lewis, for Christ's sake, with hundreds of people around?'

'Join the club. Intimidation is how he makes his living.'

'What kind of consolation is that? He's probably outside now.'

'I thought you lost him.'

'He'd know where I was heading.'

I went over to the window. The hole in the pavement outside was bigger today and the workmen had erected a little striped red and white awning, like a beach hut, to protect themselves from the weather. I hoped Rogers had put them there to keep an eye on us. I surveyed the street carefully but there was no sign of Hector. That did not necessarily mean much. He could have been lurking in a doorway out of sight. More likely someone was standing in for him. Waiting was not Hector's style.

'All clear.'

'Rot him, anyway,' said Judy. Wet tissues were scattered around her on the sofa and her face was flushed from weeping.

'You're a very attractive woman,' I said.

'Not to myself, not at this moment. I feel like the girl who let the hockey team down. What Katie didn't do.'

I walked back to the sofa and bent to kiss her. 'You were taken off guard. It can happen to anyone.'

She stood up abruptly. 'I need a wash.' She unlocked the door and went out to the little toilet on the landing. I waited by the open door of the studio and watched the stairs. When she came out five minutes later her hair was combed, her face made up and her eyes had a glint in them.

'Well,' she said, when the studio door was locked behind us again, 'what are we going to do about it?'

'I don't see that we've got a lot of choice.'

'That's because they know what they want and we don't.'

'Oh, I know what they want, all right. Or what Stonehouse says they want.'

'The omniscient Stonehouse. Our Delphic oracle. So what's the word from on high?'

'You won't believe it, anyway.'

'Try me.' She probed her cheek with her tongue. Something she does when she's angry. Always a bad sign. 'You know me. Open-minded to a fault.'

'The word is drugs. Cocaine. Probably in that shipment they've all gone bat-shit about.'

'You're crazy, both of you. Out of your tiny minds.'

'It's nothing to do with me.'

'That's what you tell me. Give me one good reason why I should believe you.'

'Why should I lie? We're in this together.'

'You're in this. You and your late friend. Leave me out of your shabby little deals.'

'It's too late.'

'Don't you believe it, buster. I could wash my hands just like that.'

'It's the wrong moment. If you won't believe me, who will?'

'Good old Judy. Always there when she's needed.'

'That's not what I mean.'

'Softening of the brain.' She leaned forward, her face sharp with anger. 'Male menopause. It goes with the American girl. Poor Tommy wanted to join the young. Maybe he thought it was going to be like the sixties all over again. Flowers in the hair and give peace a chance. A man of his age ought to have known better.'

'Maybe he thought it was just another business deal, with bigger risks and bigger profits.'

'For a man who came on as a high-rolling gambler he got the odds seriously wrong.' Her tongue probed her cheek again. 'What I don't get is where you fit into the plot. Is this the kind of deal you've been doing with your pal all these years?'

'You know better than that.'

'I know nothing, except that I don't trust you.'

'I think the only reason Tommy used my name is *because* our deals were so trivial. That way, this number would look like just another shipment of Hungarian pullovers.'

'He stuck you with it, your bosom friend. He really landed you in the shit.'

'How could he have known what would happen?'

'He read the papers, didn't he? Every day another drugs crime. He knew he wasn't playing games with the Girl Guides.'

'He's not playing games with anyone now, poor bastard.'

'But where does that leave you?'

I shrugged. 'As messenger boy between Oliver Stonehouse and Ramon Fernandez. For the time being, that is. Until I can find a way out.'

'Who are you trying to please now, for Christ's sake?' Her cheeks were red, her eyes shone with righteous fury. 'You suck up to me, you suck up to them. What's on your conscience that makes you so submissive, Joe? We've got coke, a heart attack that isn't a heart attack, a relationship between Tommy and you that's a total mystery to me, and now you say you're going to run like a poodle between these terrible people.' She sat very straight on the sofa and gathered up the pieces of tissue she had scattered while she wept, as though to remove all evidence of weakness. 'We had a good life before this happened, a real marriage. Now you're willing to sit still while these buggers trample all over us. What the hell's got into you, Joe?'

'My, but you're sexy when you're cross.'

'Don't patronise me.' She got up abruptly. 'I thought you had balls.'

'They got caught between the hammer and the anvil,' I said. 'Between Stonehouse and Fernandez.'

'I'm not fooling.' She walked over to the filing cabinet where I keep my prints, pulled open one of the drawers and began to flick through the photographs. She took out one of the fashion shots I'd done on location in Tunisia: a model in profile against a glittering sea, sand on her young breasts, nipples erect, wet jeans plastered to her spectacular backside.

'You used to be serious,' she said. 'Look at you now.'

'If you knew the amount of time it took to set up that shot you'd know how serious I am.'

'Remember Prague? What happened to the man with an eye for truth?'

'You design letter-heads. I don't ask you what happened to the Sistine Chapel.'

'I never had any ambition to do anything else.'

'And I had the ambition but it ran out. It happens with age. Besides, we both like the good life and somebody has to keep this circus on the road. You pay for your own studio and buy your own clothes, and somehow you think that entitles you to take the moral high ground.'

'Don't start in about morality.' She held the picture to the light, brooding over it. 'I remember her. That was in Djerba, wasn't it? The shoot that took six days instead of three. Miss Perky Tits. Miss Twenty-one-inch Waist. No wonder you took your time.'

I affected weariness. 'I told you a dozen times: the clients came with us and wouldn't leave me alone. To top it off, we had a sandstorm.'

'Excuses, excuses.' She shrugged. Slowly, grudgingly, her anger was deserting her. One of the redeeming features of my life with Judy is that our flare-ups never last long. 'What the hell,' she said. 'It gave me a scare. It was after that I decided to do the Jane Fonda exercises. Since I couldn't join it, I might as well beat it. I suppose I owe the girl something.'

She slipped the print back into its file, closed the drawer and crossed to where I sat in front of the blank computer. She stood over me, looking down. The angry flush had gone from her face and the expression in her blue-grey eyes was sad, disappointed.

'You know what's wrong with us?' she said. 'We're complacent. Because we have good sex and don't fight much, we think we're special. Favourites of the gods or something.'

'What would you prefer? Squabbles and affairs? I've tried that twice and, believe me, there's no percentage in it.'

She reached out and touched the side of my face. 'I'm as bad as you are,' she said. 'I feel superstitious about us. I think it can't last, we're going to have to pay for it. But now I'm beginning to wonder if the whole thing isn't some kind of mutual delusion.

Skin deep. Nothing to do with reality. I mean, what does it take to break through this complacency of ours?'

When I started to speak she spread her fingers, as though in warning, across my mouth. 'I'll tell you what it takes. The death of the man without whom none of it would have been possible.'

I took hold of her hand and held it against my face, wanting to comfort her.

'That's pretty strong medicine,' she said.

'You know what I think?' I replied. 'I think Louise has been getting to you, making you feel guilty you have a live husband. And one who isn't about to ditch you for some Californian beach girl.'

Judy smiled at last. 'How do I know?'

'Because the beach girl hasn't asked me yet.'

She bent down and kissed me on the mouth. 'You sure know how to make a lady feel loved, Mr Constantine.'

I put my arms around her but she straightened up and moved away. 'Tell me,' she said, suddenly business-like, 'does Stonehouse really know how they brought the drugs in?'

'Along with those wooden toys from Hungary, he thinks. But God knows how.'

'I see.' She took a piece of paper from my desk and scribbled on it: 'Do you think this room is bugged?'

I thought of the men digging a hole in the pavement outside and their red and white British Telecom awning. I nodded.

She slid down on to my lap and kissed me seriously on the mouth. 'It's been a rotten day,' she said, louder than was necessary since her mouth was by my ear. 'I need you.'

'Are you propositioning me, lady?'

'Could be, mister.'

I slid my hand under her sweater and caressed her smooth back. When my fingers reached the fastenings of her bra she wriggled free.

'What's wrong with the here and now?' I asked.

'I don't like your casting couch. I never know who's been there before me.' She stood, took my hand and pulled me up after her. 'Let's go home,' she said. 'Come on. You won't regret it.'

'Have I ever?'

We walked hand in hand to Tottenham Court Road and, because the clouds had lifted and the rain was holding off for the moment, we found a taxi almost immediately. Judy glanced around before we got into it and began kissing me as soon as the door was closed. But her heart clearly wasn't in it and when I opened my eyes I saw she was watching the traffic out of the rear window. I straightened up indignantly and said, 'What gives?'

'Stay close,' she whispered. 'Just in case we're being followed.'

She lay back with her head turned towards me and I did the same. Seen from behind, we would have been two profiles, touching and not touching.

'I've got news for you,' she murmured, mouth to mouth. I waited. 'You know someone called Geary?'

I shook my head, inhaling the smell of her breath, and her scent. I touched her breast beneath her coat.

'Tommy's solicitor. Plummy voice, big hollow laugh. Well, he phoned me. Said he had a letter for me from Tommy. To be delivered personally in the event of his death. Would I care to pick it up or should he send it round by messenger? He sent it.'

I moved away a little, offended that she and Tommy should have had secrets, even posthumously. 'Why didn't you tell me?'

She put her face to mine. Her hair brushed my forehead. She was smiling and pleased with herself. 'Don't get worked up, sweetheart.'

'You haven't answered.'

She took my hand and put it back on her breast. 'I didn't want to upset you. I thought you had enough on your plate.'

'Why should I be upset?'

She lay still, her head against the taxi seat. We had stopped at the Euston Road traffic lights. A bus was drawn up behind us. The driver had a black beard, a turban, the face of a warrior king. He was watching us impassively.

'It was a kind of love letter,' said Judy. 'A muddled love letter.'

'Dear old Tommy. Now he tells you, poor bastard.'

The taxi moved forward, picking up speed towards Camden Town.

'He told me something else, too.'

'Go on.'

'I don't know for sure but I think he was saying where to look for that stuff you're all after.'

I took her face in my hands and held it away from me. 'Darling, you're a star.'

'That's what I've been trying to tell you, in so many words.'

We kissed again and held it all the way through the traffic jam in Camden Town. 'I didn't know being followed could be such fun,' I said eventually.

'What are the chances the house is bugged, too,' Judy asked.

'Even money.'

'Then for God's sake, let's be careful.'

When I paid off the taxi-driver he winked at me and said, 'Have a nice afternoon, mate.' We went in quickly without pausing to see if any other car had turned into Glenilla Road after us. I bolted the front door.

Judy took off her black raincoat, with its epaulets and buckles, and hung it up. 'Come on,' she said. 'I'll show you.'

'Uhn, uhn.' I shook my head. 'We've got to keep up our cover. First we make love, then you show me.'

She smiled sweetly. 'Anything you say, boss.'

A SINGLE light glowed in the corner of the room. The radio by the bed played Mozart, the Divertimento in E-flat, three instruments talking together in lively serious voices, subtle as running water. My favourite Mozart. I even knew the date, 1788, Mozart's bleakest year, when he had never written better or been more desperate for money. I wondered how he managed it, hustling for commissions, cadging loans, writing music that sounds like God, in a tender mood, musing on the creation.

When I need money – nearly always these days – I shoot adverts for cat food or sit by the telephone hoping that Tommy will call with one of his cryptic messages. 'You want to do yourself a favour, Joe? Thursday morning you phone your broker and tell him to buy Natty Suitings. Not Tuesday, mind. Not Wednesday. But Thursday first thing. And sell by the following Wednesday. No later. Mortgage the house if you have to. You won't be sorry, believe me.'

Dear Tommy, I always believed you and I was never sorry. What am I going to do without you?

Judy had fallen asleep with one arm flung out wide, a generous gesture, full of welcome. The sheet was twisted across her, from one leg to the opposite shoulder. I stroked the sweet curve of her hip softly, so as not to wake her. She kids herself about the Jane Fonda exercises but I'd hate her skinny.

The music ended and there was a burst of applause. Judy stirred and opened her eyes. 'What's the time?' she said. 'I feel I've been asleep for hours.'

'Not hours but long enough. It's coming up to eight o'clock.'

She sat up in bed and rubbed her neck lazily. 'There's nothing like sex in the afternoon. It even makes marriage feel illegal.'

'Well now, I just thought we were having fun.'

She got up and walked into the bathroom, saying, 'Darling,

anything that much fun can't be legal.'

I heard her turn on the shower. She was singing: 'Isn't this a lovely day to be caught in the rain.'

'Leave the shower on for me,' I called.

So Tommy's bequeathed her a love letter. The world is always stranger than you think. Oddly enough, I felt no jealousy at all.

We sat side by side on the freshly made bed. The radio was turned up loud on the evening concert for the benefit of the listening mikes. Judy rummaged in her handbag and pulled out an envelope: 'For Mrs Judy Constantine, 226A Steele's Road, NW3. To be delivered only in the event of my disappearance or death.' The writing was Tommy's, large and extravagant:

> Dear Girl,
>
> You know I love you and have always loved you. If things had gone different maybe you and I should have been married, though with my track record, how long would that have lasted? Anyway, if you ever get to read this letter it will mean it's too late for all that.
>
> As it worked out, it was Joe who saw what you're worth, and you saw him. That'll do fine for me. Because I love him too. I love you both. You're the best couple I know and I'm proud that I helped bring you together. I may not be that much older but I think of you as the kids I never had and I want things to go well for you. It worries me that Joe is always so skint. It's no way for a nice Jewish boy from a good family to live. No way for either of you to live.
>
> So I want to do something about it and I've made arrangements. In the mean time, go to Bournemouth and see my Aunt Rosie Graham. She's at the Green Lodge – where else? – along with all the other old Jews. She's got something for you.
>
> Maybe I should be writing to Joe but all in all I think you've got a better head on your shoulders. Don't tell him that. I'd hate to hurt his feelings.
>
> So be lucky, both of you, luckier than I suppose I'll have been by now.
>
> Love you,
>
> Tommy.

The radio was blaring away. 'I hate Tchaikovsky,' I announced.

Judy sat very still and said nothing.

'So you've got a better head on your shoulders than I have. Well, screw him.'

Judy said gently, 'Don't talk like that. I told you it was a love letter. A pass from the grave, poor bastard.'

'He always had a rotten sense of timing.'

'You know it's not like that. You loved him as much as I did. More, probably. It's just terribly sad.'

'Then why did you keep it to yourself?'

'Because at first I couldn't bear to open it. I thought I knew what it would say. He was always sending me letters: "I've been wanting to get into your pants for fifteen years." In so many words. I just threw them away. It was like a nervous tic. He couldn't help himself.'

'You must have encouraged him.'

'That was years ago, before we were married. But it didn't work out, did it?'

'I'd be the last person to know.'

'It's ancient history. Don't take it to heart.' She sat close to me on the bed, holding my hand. Her voice was low and unhappy, as though she were telling a mournful bedtime story. 'It was during one of our off periods. Tommy asked me and asked me to go away with him. Finally I said, OK, why not? You were God knows where, with one of your Sloaney blondes. I didn't want him, Joe. I wanted to get at you through him.'

'Should I be flattered or sorry for you?'

'It didn't work out. We went to Torquay. To the Imperial, of course. And when it came to the crunch I just couldn't handle it. We finished up in separate rooms and drove back to London the next morning. It was sad, not sexy. I wanted to apologise to everybody: him, you, the whole bloody world. I loathed myself for behaving like a spoiled bitch.'

'He liked spoiled bitches. Look at Louise.'

'It's all over. Dead and gone, like Tommy.'

'So now I know.'

'There's nothing to know. That's what's so stupid. I still feel bad about it. I wish I could have told him I was sorry.'

I walked over to the window, pulled back the curtain and looked out. Nothing moved on the street but I assumed the watchers were out there with their flasks of coffee, their cigarettes and their two-way radios. I glanced at my watch: ten past eight. Fifty minutes to go before they changed guard. I'd seen them do it two nights in a row, one car pulling out, the other waiting, lights flashing, to take up the treasured parking place.

I turned back to Judy and said softly, 'I suppose we'd better do something about it.'

I took her by the elbow, led her to the booming radio, put my mouth to her ear and whispered, 'Put our toothbrushes and stuff in your handbag. We're going to Bournemouth.'

I switched off the radio and said, loud and clear for the benefit of the listening mikes, 'I'm starving. Let's go eat a Chinaman.'

Judy picked up her handbag and went into the bathroom, saying, 'I'll just put on some lipstick.'

I called after her, 'How about the one in Wardour Street, the Chu Chin Chow or whatever it's called?'

'Chuen Cheng Ku,' she answered cheerfully. 'The number's in my address book by the bed.'

I called the restaurant, repeating its name carefully when they answered. I booked a table for nine o'clock and spelled out my name to an uninterested receptionist.

'No plobrem,' she said.

Then I called the local taxi firm. They asked for my destination and said they'd have a car round in ten minutes.

I thought of the watcher outside, looking at his wristwatch, anxious to get home to his wife and a hot meal. I assumed that whoever was bugging our phone was speaking to him now.

Downstairs, I poured whisky for us both. Judy's eyes were shining and when I handed her a glass I could feel her hand trembling faintly with excitement.

'You're full of sparkle this evening,' I said.

'Love in the afternoon. Love and confession. What do you expect?'

The taxi arrived before we had finished drinking. 'Better leave the lights on,' I said, hamming it up for the listeners. 'This is Hampstead, darling. Thieves' paradise.'

We went out and double-locked the front door. As we drove away, I glanced back and saw a car pull out behind us. I nudged Judy and said, 'Here we go.'

'They don't even care if we see them,' she said indignantly.

'They're bored. It's too easy for them. Now's the time to mix them up a bit.'

The car stayed with us all the way to Wardour Street, stopped when we stopped and waited while I paid off the taxi. When we walked into the restaurant it drove off.

'What do you bet they think we're safe for an hour?' I said. 'Attending to our post-coital appetites.'

'They might be waiting inside.'

'They wouldn't waste the money. Not now they think they've got our number.'

The receptionist greeted us with a smirk that registered disapproval rather than welcome. As she led us to our table, I muttered to Judy, 'Just stick with me.'

The restaurant had once been two establishments, one in Wardour Street, the other in Rupert Street. But they had knocked down the walls between, leaving a noisy dog-legged room with high ceilings, bright lights, red dragons on the wall. The receptionist placed two menus on an empty table and waited for us to sit down. The menus were stoutly bound and seemed to have as many pages as a collection of contemporary verse. The place was famous for its exotic range of dishes – pigs' maws and duck webs, chicken gizzards and jellyfish.

I looked embarrassed and muttered, 'Toilet, please.'

The woman's disapproval became outright contempt. She nodded towards the back of the room. I stood back politely for Judy to lead the way. When we reached the dog's leg I said, 'Keep going.' We walked out the back entrance into Rupert Street. Opposite was an arcade of shoddy boutiques. We bustled through it but no one seemed interested in us. When we came out on to Coventry Street a taxi was at the kerb, setting down a sombrely dressed city gent. I shoved Judy in and said 'Waterloo' before he had finished paying. He stared venomously and said, 'I say,' in a shocked voice.

'Goin' to miss the last train, are you?' the taxi-driver asked.

'We've got quarter of an hour,' I said since that was what he wanted.

'Easy,' said the driver.

I watched the back window all the way to Waterloo but no one followed us.

THE station was filled with seasonal muzak: 'God Rest You Merry Gentlemen', 'In Dulce Jubilo', 'Tidings of Comfort and Joy'. Swooping strings and harmonious brass. When the 9.30 to Bournemouth pulled out Big Ben showed its illuminated face briefly between the brightly lit office blocks. We moved towards the suburbs past Christie's warehouse, Rapid Results Tutorial College, Wimbledon Squash and Badminton Club. Then the city slowly faded into a scattering of yellow lights and the reflection of the carriage rode steadily against the darkness. Sliding smoothly through the night, a faint pressure on the ears from the train's speed. At Southampton there were cranes behind the Royal Mail parcels depot and a sense of the sea close by. At Brockenhurst a solitary woman in a bright pink ski-suit stood under a platform lamp.

It felt strange to be going back to Bournemouth, a strangeness that had nothing to do with Tommy's Aunt Rosie or his letter. It was the place we went for summer holidays when I was a little child, summer after summer after summer. When I was tiny we stayed at the Metropole, a vast Victorian palace of red brick, marble pillars at the entrance, a cupola, chimneys built like Corinthian columns. I remembered the dining-room with stiff linen on the tables and a glass conservatory wall opening on to a garden.

My father stayed in London with his business and his girlfriends and appeared reluctantly at weekends. Mother spent her days drinking tall glasses of lemon tea with her cousins (never friends, in my recollection, always relatives), women with big diamond rings, colourful clothes and a limitless flair for gossip. One of them had spectacular red hair and was a great beauty; she spent the last twenty years of her life in a wheelchair, tended by her handsome husband.

I went to the beach every day with Nanny and my sisters. The changing huts smelled of wood and salt water and woollen bathing costumes that never seemed to dry properly and made me shiver when I put them on in the morning.

I remembered a small town, always in sunshine, a place where it never rained. Donkey rides. Cones of soft ice-cream from a kiosk called Nottiano's.

Bournemouth station was as old and draughty as ever, but there was a shiny new glass building opposite it with yellow double-decker buses drawn up in front. Instead of arcades of little shops and streets lined with pine trees, there were pedestrian precincts, chain stores, endless roundabouts, urban sprawl. The taxi driver had never heard of the Metropole, so he took us to the Royal Bath, an ornate building, long and low and white, facing out to sea like a fortress. Inside it was pink and spacious, with subdued piped music and porters in blue uniforms. We made love again in a canopied bed, lazily, taking our time. Out in the bay were vertical strings of lights in the blackness. I fell asleep wondering what they could be. Next morning when I looked out of the window, I saw a gas rig about a mile offshore, a derrick and two tall towers of girders. Three support vessels moved slowly round it. The sea was flat and grey, like stone.

I phoned Tommy's Aunt Rosie and explained who I was. She said she had been expecting me. Then she said angrily, 'What sort of a way is that to die, dropping dead in the prime of life, a nice boy like him?'

'It's a terrible thing. Everyone's in shock.'

'I wanted to come to the funeral, show my respect, sit shiva with Dora. God knows what she must be going through. But my doctor, the schmuck, said no.'

'He had a great turn-out. Everyone was there.'

'What do you expect? A popular boy like him. Everybody loved him.'

'Let me buy you lunch. Tommy's favourite aunt. I've heard all about you.'

'I've heard about you, too.'

I said I'd collect her at 12.30.

'Come for a stroll down memory lane,' I said to Judy. 'It's been nearly forty years. They ordered things differently in those days.'

It had rained during the night but the clouds were lifting and the day was grey and raw. We walked down the slope, past a car park, to the sea. The buildings on the promenade were shut and padlocked. The Westover & Bournemouth Rowing Club, founded 1865. A fish-and-chip shop, two ice-cream kiosks, a grandiose Victorian public toilet. Someone was mending deck-chairs in the storeroom of Happyland Amusements and Bingo.

'Blank,' I said. 'All I can remember is Nottiano's ice-cream and they've gone.'

'Don't let it get you down,' Judy said. 'Most people have a hole where their childhood used to be.'

'It seems such a waste, all that time gone for nothing.'

An elderly couple came towards us, arm in arm, bundled up against the cold, their old dog plodding beside them. We passed a row of bathing chalets with pointed roofs, the eaves painted red and yellow and blue, faded curtains in their windowed fronts.

Nothing.

'Maybe I just imagined it all.'

Beyond the chalets were smaller cabins, windowless with pitched tarpaper roofs. Each of them had a little wooden platform outside, hinged back and up, padlocked against the door. 'These have got to be the ones we rented every summer. Funny that I can remember how they smelt but not how they looked.'

'You shouldn't take it so personally.'

'What else do you do with your past?'

We walked back along the promenade in the cold still air. The ticket office at the entrance to the pier was closed but the gate was open. We passed a locked amusement arcade, our steps echoing on the wooden planks. From the end of the pier, the gas rig looked quite close, a huge structure of intricately meshed steel, lights still burning in its accommodation modules. A solitary fisherman stood on a lower platform at the end of the pier, patiently casting into the yellow-grey water, reeling in and casting again. Off towards the shore, a man in a wet-suit paddled busily out to sea on a surfboard, then rode in again on the slow small breakers. The cliffs above the promenade were littered with high-rise buildings.

'I think I'm missing the point,' I said.

'What point?'

'That I'm old enough to know better.'

'It was a gamble,' said Judy. 'Who knows what you might have found?'

We walked back down the pier. The little wooded park opposite was hung with peacocks and butterflies made of coloured lights. I recognised the park from a photograph my mother kept of me and my nanny, smiling warily into camera, trees in the background. But I did not remember the place. The traffic was heavy between the pier and the park.

'It's not like I had a happy childhood,' I said. 'I don't want the time back. I just wonder where all the money went.'

'The last of the romantics,' said Judy.

We climbed the hill past the Royal Bath Hotel, past a roundabout blocked with midday traffic, towards the centre of town. The avenue of pines was still there, but at the end of it was another congested roundabout, and in place of the old Metropole was a wedge of concrete and glass with a fast food joint at its base, a shoddy new pub, a kebab take-away, a used-car dealer's.

Judy squeezed my hand and said, 'They build over everyone's past. Always have.'

'Thank God that's not why we're here.'

Rosie Graham was living in a residential hotel not far from the sea front. There were potted plants in the entrance hall and a large number of armchairs, all of them occupied. Old men with newspapers and walking sticks, old ladies placidly knitting, their walking-frames parked beside them. Aunt Rosie was waiting in a chair opposite the door, a wiry old woman with a nose like a tomahawk and a head of thin curls, carefully permed. She had a gold-topped malacca cane at the ready and she got up the moment we came through the door. As we went out again, she hissed, 'Take a look at the old bird in the corner.'

The woman in the corner had rolls of comfortable fat and iron-grey hair drawn up in a tight bun. She filled her armchair so completely that it was hard to tell where the chair ended and she began.

'A newcomer,' said Aunt Rosie scornfully. 'Dumped here by her children two days ago.' She walked briskly between us, flourishing her cane like a weapon. 'So I introduced myself, wanting to be nice, make her feel at home. And what did she say? She said, "Graham? What sort of a name is that for a Jew?" You know what she's called? Jones. Married a goy and never looked back. The chutzpah of some people never ceases to amaze me.'

We were out under the pine trees again. The clouds had lowered but the rain held off. When I asked her where we should have lunch she said, 'You want we should eat with the rich Jews, the place to go is the New Ambassadors, just round the corner.'

The New Ambassadors was gloomy and deserted. 'Lunch is at one sharp,' said the surly receptionist. 'Through the bar on the left.' The bar was empty except for two elderly couples, neither of them drinking. Both the men wore knitted shirts. They stared at us resentfully, then looked at their watches, waiting for the starting signal.

'Not a lot of action here,' I said to Aunt Rosie. 'Let's go to the Royal Bath. Live it up a bit.'

She giggled conspiratorially. 'As long as you're paying.'

We walked back down the hill, hunched into our coats, waiting for the rain. 'Florida it isn't,' she said. 'Even so, you'd think they'd make us welcome. It's not like they don't need the business.'

It was midweek, so only half a dozen tables were occupied in the vast pink dining-room of the Royal Bath. We sat by the window with a view of the garden and the new sports complex. The waiters made a fuss of the old lady, guiding her through the elaborate menu, telling her what was good. She settled on warm salad with asparagus and smoked game, followed by sole with truffles and lobster.

'Lobster,' she said. 'Poor Sammy, God rest his soul, would turn in his grave if he knew.'

I thought of my grandfathers, upright successful men who ate in the best restaurants and had no compunction about ordering forbidden food. Tommy's relatives would think of them as traitors, hiding out in the middle of their enemies, their beautifully tailored clothes their protective colouring. In America, the Jews stay as they are and become Americans; in England, they remain outsiders until the distinguishing marks have disappeared.

Rosie sipped her wine and pretended to admire the room but she kept eyeing Judy sidelong. Quick sharp glances, sizing her up, woman to woman. Finally, she coughed and said, 'Excuse me for asking, but you're not Jewish, are you?'

Judy smiled. 'Afraid not.'

'In most ways, she's more Jewish than I am,' I said.

Rosie gave me a beady look. 'Don't tell me that means much.'

'I have this fear I'm going to come home one Friday evening and find the candles lit.'

'There are worse things could happen to you.'

'I'm Presbyterian,' said Judy. 'Or rather, I started out that way. From a long line of bigots. When I told my mother I was going out with a Jew she thought about it for a while, then said, "Well, at least he's not a Catholic."'

'It's not easy being a mother,' Rosie said philosophically.

'It was her way of cheering herself up.'

'As long as you're both happy.'

The waiter brought the food. The old lady ate appreciatively, taking her time. 'A nice place, this,' she said. 'Reminds me of London.'

'You miss London?'

'All the time. When we came here we had a bungalow in Westcliff but after Sammy died I moved into town. To the home, you understand. When you're in a house of your own, maybe the neighbours talk to you, maybe they don't, this being England. And if they don't, you might as well be dead. So I moved for the company and because it's nearer the shops.'

'What's it like, the home?'

'An elephants' graveyard. All we do is wait. Wait for meals, wait for visits. What we're really doing is waiting to die. But they don't like to mention that.'

The waiter cleared the plates away and brought the sole. It was garnished with large pieces of lobster and Rosie glanced quickly round the room before she tasted one. 'Something this delicious,' she said. 'What else could they do but forbid it?'

The food put her in a good mood. She began to talk about the old days, about relatives long dead and Whitechapel streets where Bengalis live now. She had reached that point of her life where eighty years ago was like yesterday and yesterday itself was blank. The Applebaum boys, her brothers, Nate, Abe, Barney and Lou. Nate, Tommy's father, went into the schmatte business and got bought out by C&A. Abe, the bookie, had a stroke one night at the tables at Crockford's and spent the last six years of his life in a wheelchair, unable to speak. Barney was the ne'er-do-well, the one who gave them headaches until they clubbed together and bought him a passage to Jo'burg, where he got into diamonds, then came home, opened up in Hatton Garden and ended up richer than all of them. Large men with large appetites, now deceased.

Judy was listening wide-eyed. She has a passion for the Jews, God knows why, and secretly feels cheated that she married such a watered-down specimen. 'What about Lou?' she asked.

'Lou.' Rosie's face softened. 'He was the quiet one, the nebbisch. Built like a bull but soft, you understand, soft up here.' She tapped her forehead. 'He finished up in a mental home. But not altogether meshuggah. When they took him there he looked at the clock over the entrance and said, "Is it right?" They told him of course it was. "Then what's it doing here?" he said. A sweet man. Harmless.'

The waiter brought hot apple dumplings with vanilla sauce. Rosie leaned forward over the plate and sniffed appreciatively.

'It's all a long time ago. Dora and me, we're the only ones left. The two little sisters.'

When the coffee came I asked her why she had said she was expecting us.

'Tommy told me. He sent something for me to look after for him, and a note with it, saying he'd collect it soon and if he didn't a friend would. Meaning you. Not that you're altogether a stranger to me. He used to come and see me, did Tommy. Schlepped all the way from London every month or two. He was fond of his old aunt. And he talked about you. About you both. As a couple. He said you were the only happily married people he knew. I told him, "Thanks a lot, what about me and Sammy?" "That's different," he said. "In your day, people weren't so dissatisfied." '

'What was it he sent?'

'A packing case. It's in the storeroom at the home. I didn't want it cluttering up my room, which is small enough as it is.'

I looked at Judy but she was watching the old lady. Her expression was tender, abstracted, as though she wasn't taking in the words. She's an only child and she needs a family, I thought. Not just me. We should have had kids, relatives, someone to see at Christmas. It had never occurred to me before that she might be lonely.

We walked back to Green Court, Judy and Rosie arm in arm, gossiping like old friends.

The packing case was in the storeroom, along with cabin trunks and garden furniture and old washing machines. It was quite small – about four feet square – but when I lifted one side it felt heavy.

'Young Bernie brought it,' said Rosie. 'Tommy paid him fifty quid to pick it up at Heathrow and bring it on down here. Fifty quid plus his petrol. It was one way to make the little momser pay a visit to his great aunt. That's the sort of thing Tommy would have thought about.'

I took a taxi to the Avis office, leaving Rosie to introduce Judy to the old people in the reception hall. Both women seemed delighted to be rid of me. When I got back an hour later, Judy was flirting with an old boy in a pearl grey suit and a rose in his button-hole. 'They say youth is wasted on the young,' he was saying. 'But believe me, darling, wisdom is wasted on the old. Look at us.'

The hotel porter was a surly young man with a bright boozer's face. He helped me heave the crate into the back of the rented station wagon but looked at the tip I gave him contemptuously.

Rosie hugged Judy, then said, 'Wait a minute. I got something else I almost forgot.' She stalked to the lift, tapped her stick impatiently until the doors opened, waved it at us when they closed. Five minutes later she was back with a pink plastic bag marked 'Jennifer's Lingerie'.

'A memento,' she said. 'He wanted you should have it.'

A framed photograph. Tommy and me with our arms round each other's shoulders, laughing into the camera. I'd taken it myself using the self-timer when he had come to my studio to tell me about a deal. I think it was down jackets from Taiwan.

'He sent it with the packing case,' Rosie said. 'Happy days. Something to remember him by. Something to remember us both.'

She came out into the drive to see us off. It was dark now and beginning to rain. 'God knows what you've got in the case,' she said. 'But be very careful. He was a lovely boy, Tommy, but straight he wasn't.' She waved to us as we drove away, standing in the brightly lit doorway, a small woman, erect as a drill sergeant, with an animated face and thin hair.

On the way out of town, I stopped at an ironmonger's and bought a hammer and chisel. We stopped again on the Southampton road, on a stretch of heathland studded with gorse bushes. I climbed into the back of the car and prised open the lid of the crate. Long distance lorries thundered past, trailing plumes of spray.

The crate was full of long boxes, glossy and brightly coloured, the kind you hope to find under the Christmas tree when you're very young. The words said Toytown Express and the picture was of a train speeding through a landscape of cows, bushy-topped trees and thatched cottages, a church spire on the horizon, a bright blue sky. I took one of the boxes out of the crate, nailed the top down again and climbed back into the car. I handed Judy the box.

'Father fucking Christmas,' I said. 'Ho, ho, ho.'

She opened the lid and pulled out a wooden train. 'Who'd have believed it,' she said. 'What you see is what you get.'

'Not with Tommy and his friends, it isn't.'

She turned to me. Her face was clouded, full of trouble. 'Let's go home, Joe. I can't stand the thought of that old woman on her own like that. All those old people. I don't want to end up like them.'

'They're the lucky ones. Think what that place charges.'

'That's what I love about you. You always know how to cheer a girl up.'

'Do you think Tommy was paying her rent?'

'I don't want to talk about it.' She switched on the radio and the car filled with canned laughter. A man with a Yorkshire accent said, 'Yes, I've been married twice. Both me wives died. The first died from eating poisoned mushrooms, the second died from a fractured skull.' He paused. The audience snickered in anticipation. 'She wouldn't eat her mushrooms.' The laughter boomed out again. Judy twisted the dial, looking for music. 'We must look after each other,' she said. 'Take me home.'

She slept all the way to London, cradling the box in her arms like the baby she had never had.

I PULLED off at the service station before the Hammersmith flyover. I got out the *A–Z*, and examined the labels on the keys Stonehouse had given me. The Kilburn lock-up was on the way home, more or less, down a steep hill off West End Lane, at the end of a row of dingy houses. The garage was clean and dry and half full of boxes marked Sony Trinitron. Maybe Inspector Rogers had been right about stolen property but I couldn't see why Tommy had bothered.

I backed the station wagon up to the garage entrance and together Judy and I heaved out the crate and shoved it against one wall. Then we drove to the Avis office at Marble Arch, returned the car and took a cab home.

The moment we got out of the taxi, the watcher in the car parked opposite our house picked up a telephone and began to talk into it urgently. When I waved at him he glared back and went on talking. His face was dark with stubble and his eyes were red and puffy.

I closed the door behind us and pushed the bolt home.

The toy engine was pale varnished wood, solid and beautifully made. Its funnel and wheels were painted red. The carriage windows, too, were red, their outlines delicately chiselled. When I hefted one of the carriages in my hand it felt disproportionately heavy. I carried the toys down to the cellar where I have a rudimentary workshop left over from the days when I fooled around with cars and liked tinkering under the bonnet. I put one of the carriages in a vice, placed a chisel against its smooth surface and tapped it hard with a hammer. The blow left a discreet dent but no visible entry wound.

'This is a very expensive number,' I said. 'It must be made of some exotic hardwood.'

'Trust Tommy,' said Judy. 'Nothing but the best.'

I tightened the vice and hit the toy again as hard as I could. A faint hairline crack opened under the chisel. Then I remembered that the house was bugged. 'What we need here,' I said, 'is a little music while we work.'

'Come on,' she said impatiently. 'One thing at a time.'

I touched a finger to my lips. 'Just in case.'

She went upstairs and came back with the portable radio turned up high. I tapped the blade of the chisel into the hairline crack and hit it again. The crack deepened a little and spread. I unfastened the vice and put the toy on the floor. Judy knelt beside me and held it steady while I banged away at the chisel. The crack widened slowly. I twisted the chisel, first one way, then the other. Inside was a roll of a hard white substance, neatly wrapped in plastic. I probed it with my finger.

'It's been compressed,' I murmured under the music. 'More weight, less volume.'

Judy stared at it with wide eyes and said nothing.

'Beats me what Tommy was up to.' I ran my hand over the smooth wood, then probed the crack again. 'I'd have given good odds, any money, that Stonehouse had got it wrong.' The plastic-wrapped package nestled in the centre of the toy like a nut in its shell. 'Better keep it like this,' I whispered. 'Just to prove we're straight.'

'Who's going to ask?'

Back upstairs, we lit the fake fire and settled into our armchairs, the toy train on the carpet between us.

'Darby and Joan,' I said softly. 'The folks on the hill.'

'Haverstock Hill.'

'What are we going to do now? Tell Stonehouse?'

'That's one alternative.' Her eyes were still wide and deep. She seemed overawed by the seriousness of the occasion.

'Better than telling Fernandez.'

'Well,' she said slowly, 'there's always private enterprise.'

I looked at her in astonishment. My Presbyterian wife.

'We wouldn't know where to begin.'

'The way things are working out, we seem to have begun already.'

'What did you say about Tommy? He should have known better. These are serious people. And at least Tommy was an operator. We don't know which end is up.'

'Wouldn't you like to get your own back on those bastards?'

'Sure I would. The bastards who hurt Tommy, above all.'

She got up and came and sat between my knees, staring at the fire. On the radio, someone was playing a Schubert sonata. 'It's so sad,' Judy said.

'What is?'

'Everything. The music, Tommy, Aunt Rosie, this happy marriage of ours. Even those packets there are pretty damn pathetic.'

'Maybe I should phone Stonehouse and get it over with.'

'He'd probably throw us to the wolves, just to see what happens.'

'So let's cut out the middle man and go straight to the wolves.'

Judy looked at me with her large troubled eyes. 'We're not ready for them.'

'That's the question, isn't it? What are we ready for? What do we want out of this mess?'

'We're a couple of yoyos,' she said. 'Whatever that stuff means,' – she nodded at the toy on the floor beside her – 'we don't deserve it.'

We sat, watching the fire, while the music ran on. Finally, Judy said, 'I'm exhausted. Let's sleep on it.' She rubbed her cheek against my thigh. 'What do I have to do to cheer you up?' she asked.

I put my hands gently on her head and answered, 'I'll show you.'

I WOKE slowly and reluctantly, feeling as if I had aged years in my sleep. Someone once said that, after seventy, if you wake up without any pains, it means you're dead. By that standard, I was well and truly alive. Every bone in my body ached, beginning at my bad ankle and spreading up through my legs and shoulders to my neck. I lay for a while with my eyes closed, not yet ready to face the morning, then turned heavily, put my hand on Judy's warm side and inhaled her smell. She smelt of sleep and sex, a soothing combination. At that moment, the tea-maker started hissing and its alarm went off. Judy rolled over and switched it off, still three parts asleep. I opened my eyes and sat up slowly. The bedroom window was full of winter light. On a chair beneath the window was a Waitrose shopping bag containing the box o

'The way I feel,' I whispered, 'I could use a little sn

Judy smiled at me sleepily. 'Snort,' she said. 'What know about coke? Do you sniff it, mainline it, or use it to the dishes? Have a cup of tea instead.'

'I need my youth back.'

She sat up, her hair round her face, her breasts half out of her nightdress. She is a woman who makes up carefully and wears neat well-cut clothes to work, brisk and business-like. The disorder and the skin like silk are secrets she reserves for me. 'Do your exercises,' she said. 'You'll feel better when there's some blood flowing in your veins.'

'Blood, lady? I run on anti-freeze.'

While Judy showered, I did my push-ups and pull-ups and sit-ups, twisted my trunk from side to side and swung my arms. By the time I had showered and shaved and brushed my teeth, my aches had more or less gone and I had made up my mind. I carried the Waitrose bag downstairs and dumped it on the kitchen table next to the coffee pot. When I switched on the radio the room filled with the cheerful sound of Handel. Judy watched me over the morning paper and said nothing.

'Let's not get cute,' I told her. 'We give it to Stonehouse. Unless you think that'll turn me into a bloody poodle again.'

'I'm sorry I said that. You're a good man.' She looked at me sadly. 'Too good, probably.'

'Forget good. I don't give a shit about the drugs, the police, the rights and wrongs of it. What I care about is friendship. I want to find out what really happened to Tommy. I want to nail the bastards who hurt him.'

We took the tube down to Tottenham Court Road and walked to my studio without once looking back to see if we were being followed. Somehow it didn't seem to matter any more.

I locked the studio door behind us and called Stonehouse.

'I've got something to show you,' I said. 'It's important.'

There was a muffled sound as Stonehouse put his hand over the receiver and spoke to someone else. Then he said, 'Sit tight, dear boy. I'll be over straight away.'

He arrived within half an hour, clattering in with his overcoat flapping and his brolly at the ready. He obviously had not expected to see Judy and gave her a beady look. But he took her hand and inclined over it in a courtly fashion, as though he were about to kiss it. 'Such a pleasure to meet you at last,' he murmured. Judy seemed amused. She settled herself into the chair in front of my computer, her knees pressed demurely together, and Stonehouse flopped, as usual, on the sofa.

'You shouldn't have done it,' he said sadly. 'You cannot imagine the trouble you've caused.'

'You shouldn't have harassed us,' I replied. 'What's needed in this situation is a little mutual trust.'

Stonehouse shifted around on the sofa. He seemed all bones and awkward joints, held together by an old worsted suit. 'We have our duty to do. Enjoying it isn't necessarily part of the job.'

'I'm sorry you've had a hard time.'

'Rogers was beside himself. He wanted to get a warrant for your arrest.'

I walked over to the window. The hole in the pavement was still there. A man huddled miserably under the red and white shelter, blowing on his finger nails. His breath steamed briefly in the freezing air.

'All's well that ends well,' I said. 'We've brought you a present.'

I took the boxed train out of the Waitrose bag and handed it to him. He turned the carriage over and over, caressed it, ran a finger delicately along the split and probed the plastic package inside. Then he placed the thing carefully beside him on the sofa, clasped both hands between his thighs and leaned back, as though trying to uncork a difficult bottle. 'My!' he said, and 'Oh yes!' and 'I say!'

Judy watched him contentedly.

He looked at her with respect and asked, in a hushed voice, 'Where did you get it?'

I answered, 'That's for us to know and you to find out. What matters is, we've got the lot.'

'The whole shipment?'

I nodded.

Stonehouse sighed. 'Dear boy,' he said. 'My dear, dear lady.' He picked up one of the carriages, held it up to the light and peered along it, turning it slowly. 'Beautiful workmanship. Not a trace of a join.'

'I thought you'd be pleased.'

'Pleased!' Stonehouse made an expansive gesture. 'Pleased is hardly the word.'

Now's the time, I thought. This is where they open the cage and let us go. The secret of modern surveillance is ignorance. You understand it so little that you put yourself out of action. Once you believe your every move is followed and every word bugged, your paranoia becomes self-fulfilling; you reduce yourself to impotence without any help from your persecutors. For all I knew, nobody read the reports of the men who followed us and the voice-activated tape machines switched themselves on and off without anyone bothering to play them back. But that didn't prevent us talking in whispers and glancing back every time we turned a corner.

'Mr Stonehouse,' I said.

'Oliver.' He bared his long yellow teeth in what was supposed to be a friendly grin.

'Oliver,' I repeated. 'We're doing our bit, aren't we?'

'Understatement, dear boy.'

'Good and faithful servants, and all that stuff?'

'No question of it.'

'Then can I ask you a favour?'

'Name it and it's yours,' he answered recklessly.

'Call off your watch dogs. Switch off the tape recorders.'

Stonehouse cocked his head and looked at me in silence but the grin stayed in place. 'They're for your own good, old chap. We're only looking after you.'

'I cannot tell you how demoralising they are.'

'I know, I know. But we worry about your safety.'

'Worry about our sanity. We wouldn't try and cheat you. You must know that now, even if you didn't before.'

'Of course, of course.' His face was still flushed with pleasure and his eyes twinkled. 'But what about your friend Hector?'

'I've thought about that,' I said. 'Maybe I should take the train to Fernandez. Show willing. Get him on our side.'

Stonehouse ran his fingers lovingly along the unbroken side of the toy. 'It's an idea,' he said, without much enthusiasm. 'I'd have to talk to my superiors. There could be legal problems. And Inspector Rogers may have objections. He's a great one for playing everything by the book.'

'I have the impression he'll play it any way you tell him to.'

'Dear boy.' He patted the air in front of him, feigning modesty. 'You mustn't overestimate my powers. I'm just a small cog in the machine.'

'What does that make us?'

'You're our key players. Our stars.'

'Then give us room to shine. We're doing our best but you keep crowding us.' I looked him in the eye. 'We can't even fuck without someone listening in.'

Stonehouse blushed and looked away.

'Don't mind him,' said Judy. 'But see it from our point of

view. We're ordinary people. Civilians. We're not used to this sort of thing. It's like being invaded.'

Stonehouse kept his head down and his eyes fixed on the floor. 'It's all very distasteful,' he mumbled. 'But we have a job to do.'

'Don't think we don't appreciate it,' said Judy. 'But there are degrees, after all. We have to get on with our lives.'

He raised his head slowly. He was still blushing. 'I can only apologise. If I'd known how you felt . . .' He twisted the wooden toy in his bony hands. 'It's a great embarrassment.'

'Don't take it personally,' said Judy. 'We're not blaming you. We're just asking you to help.'

Stonehouse uncoiled himself from the sofa. He stood awkwardly, like a chastened schoolboy, not looking at either of us. I couldn't tell if he was in shock from the idea that Judy and I occasionally made love or that we had caught him listening in.

'Dear lady,' he said. 'I'll do what I can. You mustn't be inconvenienced.'

He put the toys into his battered briefcase and struggled into his overcoat. When he reached the door he paused and said, 'I think you have a point about Fernandez.' As if we had been arguing about it.

THE cafe on Old Compton Street had the usual tea urn and coffee machine, wilted pastry under glass domes, the usual smell of old frying oil. The little woman behind the counter was round and muscular, like a basketball, and her upper lip was shadowed with down. Three stocky men in leather jackets stood opposite her, leaning against a shelf where their coffee cups were perched, and chatting with her in Spanish. A twittering cadenced sound like bird song.

There were half a dozen booths at the back of the cafe. Helen was sitting in the furthest corner next to a young man in a flak jacket and tinted granny glasses. Another young man in dark glasses sat opposite her. His hair was cut short and he wore a bulky leather jacket with shoulders stretching from elbow to elbow.

Helen nodded at the youth with granny glasses. 'This is Karl,' she said. 'And that's Danny.'

'Joe,' I said. They looked at me without interest and didn't answer. Their blankness was studied, an effect they were working hard for. It went with the languid slouch and sullen mouths.

Helen ignored them. 'I'm glad you phoned,' she said.

'I'm glad you're glad. I didn't expect it, not after your performance in the car. I thought we were going to have to be introduced all over again.'

The corners of her mouth lifted in a smile. 'Life is full of surprises.'

'So I'm learning.'

Karl yawned ostentatiously. His lank blond hair curled over the collar of his jacket. He had a sharp nose and his eyes, behind the prim glasses, were blue and staring. I shifted a little to get a better look at Danny: meaty Irish nose, long upper lip, dimpled chin, a complexion pitted like no man's land.

'I need to speak to Fernandez,' I said. 'Urgently.'

'Mr Fernandez is a very busy man.'

'Is that why he sent you?'

'I guess so.'

'And young Karl here, and Danny?'

Karl glanced at me with his empty eyes. 'We are friends of Mr Fernandez.' His voice was precise and colourless, his accent faintly German.

'Friends and associates,' said Danny. 'That's the kind of company it is. One big happy family. We do him favours and he does favours for us. A mutually beneficial arrangement.' The soft brogue, the Irishman's love of the rolling phrase. His smile was intimate but calculated.

'It's OK,' said Helen. 'We're all friends here.'

'That's nice,' I said. 'But with all due respect, it's Fernandez I need to see, not his little helpers.'

Helen smiled again. 'Gee, Mr Constantine, and there was I thinking it was me.'

'That, too. But Fernandez is the one I've got business with.'

Karl studied my ski jacket and polo neck sweater. 'Funny,' he said, 'you don't look like a business man.'

'I'm a photographer. Haven't they filled you in?'

Karl cocked his head and looked at me with something like interest. 'A photographer, yes? What kind of photographer?'

'Fashion mostly. Advertising. That kind of thing.'

Karl's interest waned.

'Organising a little promotion for Mr Fernandez, are we?' said the Irishman. 'Just what he always wanted and was afraid to ask for.'

'Are these your minders,' I asked Helen, 'or did you actually invite them along?'

She looked away, suddenly bored. 'Take it easy.'

It seemed important to get her attention back. At my age the problem is not that girls like her don't respond any more; they don't even *see* me.

'Here's how it is,' I said. 'I have business to do with the boss, business I'm sure he'll be interested in, and suddenly I can't get hold of him. Up till now it's been all I can do to get away from the guy or his messengers. Now, when I want him, he plays hard to get. It doesn't make a lot of sense.'

She was looking at me again with her dark slanted eyes. She seemed amused, almost fond. This one really does see me, I thought. More to the point, I'd seen her. Naked, spotlit, drifting, in a tangle of slippery bodies. We had a pact, a secret in common. I wondered if she remembered, however vaguely.

'I may have something he wants.'

'I'll pass on the message. No problem.'

'Sooner rather than later.'

'I hear you, Joe. Don't be so uptight.'

Bored and impatient. She studied her fingernails, then raised her hand to her mouth and thoughtfully nibbled a piece of skin that bothered her. The bird voices at the front of the cafe rose and fell. Children, I thought. I am wasting my time with children. One has a lovely face, a taut and elegant body, and she thinks this gives her privileges. The others are playing roles they've picked up at the movies: tough guys, laconic, self-possessed, ready for anything. Kids' stuff. I wondered if they had been there when Tommy had his heart attack. I wondered if they were the ones I was looking for.

The Irishman twisted in his seat and tried to catch the eye of the tubby woman behind the counter. But the tubby woman was pouring coffee for a couple of teenagers and pretended not to see him.

The teenagers brought their cups to a booth and settled themselves in. The girl had long blonde hair, hanging loose, and was wearing three sweaters over a collarless shirt. The boy huddled, as though freezing, in a dirty sheepskin coat.

'Three quid an hour,' the girl was saying. 'And for that the sod thinks he can order me around like dirt.'

'Tell him to stuff his job,' said the boy.

'It's convenient. Think what I save on fares.'

'There's gotta be a better excuse for taking shit.'

'I don't need you to tell me, thanks all the same.'

I turned away from them. Karl was studying me with his pale staring eyes. 'Fashion photographers are very well paid,' he announced.

'Some of them. It depends.'

'And you, Mr Constantine? Are you one of the high flyers?'

I shook my head. 'Strictly small time.'

'Such lack of ambition in a man of your years.'

I shrugged. 'What about you?' I asked. 'What do you do for a living?'

Karl's stare hardened. 'I am a poet.'

'Now there's a turn up for the book.' I was careful not to smile. 'And Fernandez is your patron?'

'Mr Fernandez is a man of many interests.'

'A published poet,' said Danny, seeming impressed. 'In the little magazines, to be sure. But that's where the real action is.'

'You know about these things, too?'

'Ah well, I'm just a reader, you understand. I don't have the gift myself.'

'What kind of poems do you write?' I asked.

'Come on now, Mr Constantine,' said Danny. 'What sort of a question is that? He'll think you're stupid.'

'Is that what you think, Karl?'

'Stupid. Bourgeois. The terms are interchangeable.'

'I get it,' I said. 'A poet of the revolution.'

Karl did not blink. 'In Thatcher's England what else should the young be?'

Helen got up abruptly. 'OK, fellas, enough literary chat. Time to go.'

'Just when we were getting to know each other,' I said but she took no notice.

We followed her out into the noisy street, watched sullenly by the girl with long blonde hair. At the intersection of Old Compton Street and Wardour Street the traffic was solid in both directions. As we walked past the fuming cars towards Charing Cross Road, I muttered, 'Who are these creeps? Baader-Meinhof and the IRA?'

'Don't provoke them.' But it was her well-being she was worried about, not mine.

I needed cigarettes, so I left them at the newsagent near Dean Street. When I came out the three of them were at the corner of Charing Cross Road, Helen walking between the two men like a prisoner under escort. The youth in a dirty sheepskin coat and the girl in three sweaters were sauntering along hand in hand, a block behind them. I should have felt irritated that Stonehouse hadn't kept his word but all I felt was relieved. Someone had to be looking after Helen.

JUDY

I know he has seen her before he says a word. The shifty look, the hearty talk about the Kraut and the Paddy. 'We were like an old-style dirty joke,' he says. 'A German, an Irishman and a Jew.'

'What about an American girl?' I ask.

And he answers, sheepishly, 'Bingo!'

'Odd how reluctant you are to mention her.'

'Odd how up-tight you are on the subject.'

'It's not you I distrust, it's the expression on your face.'

'She's young enough to be my daughter, for Christ's sake. I feel protective towards her, working for those monsters.'

'She was young enough to be Tommy's daughter and what difference did that make?'

'Tommy was a business man. He had the tycoon syndrome. He thought if you get to a certain age and make a fortune, you trade your old lady in on a newer model. If it hadn't been Helen, it'd've been a Ferrari. Something sporty to make him feel young again.'

'That's the sort of talk that makes me want to join Women's Lib.'

'Darling, it's Tommy I'm talking about, not me. Twelve years on and you don't know any better? Listen, we talk, we make love, we even like each other. What more do you want?'

I lean over and kiss him on his balding head, almost fondly. 'I still don't trust you,' I say.

'I love you, too,' he replies.

Dinner is over, the washing-up is done, we are sitting in front of the fire. A picture of domestic bliss, except for the toy train in an airline bag in the bedroom.

Stonehouse returned the train two days ago, a new carriage in the same pale and polished wood in place of the damaged one. Along with the train came his official sidelong blessing: 'See what you can do, dear boy.' Since then we have been waiting. Two days isn't long. Less than two days. Thirty-six hours. But they seem endless. It is like waiting for a death, a new element in our settled life, random and dismaying. I think of my father, lying stiff and remote in the upstairs bedroom of the unheated granite house, while the undertaker's men measure him for his coffin and cut the signet ring from his finger. I am wearing the ring now. I have small hands and even on my middle finger it feels clumsy. I twist it round and round and stare into the fire. 'We should never have got into this,' I say.

'We didn't have an alternative,' Joe answers. 'We were press-ganged, remember? We might as well make the best of it.'

His calmness irritates me. Better calm than placating, but either way I don't trust him. I run my finger lightly over the surface of the signet ring, tracing my father's initials: J.S.M. John Stewart Macdonald. He's with O'Leary in the grave. Or rather, with Harriet Flora, 'beloved wife and mother'. Now there's no one between me and the ticket-office and no one to follow me.

'We should have had children,' I say.

Joe looks at me oddly and doesn't reply.

When the telephone rings we both jump.

Joe hurries across the room and picks up the receiver. 'Hello,' he says. 'I've been expecting you . . .' He straightens up and stands at attention, a subaltern taking orders from his senior officer. 'Right . . . Right . . . My wife is here . . . No, I think she should come . . . OK . . . OK . . . See you.' He puts down the phone and smiles at me with genuine pleasure.

'Fernandez,' he says, then bursts into song, 'Grab your coat and get your hat, leave your troubles on the doorstep.'

Riley must have been waiting outside at the end of the car phone because he rings the bell moments later. He is wearing a shiny navy suit, like a chauffeur's, but no cap, and the effect is spoiled by a grey V-neck pullover.

I smile at him and say, 'That was quick.'

Joe says, 'How's the cold?'

Riley sniffs but does not answer.

The Jaguar is double-parked, its engine running. Inside is warm and silent and smells richly of leather. Riley drives faster than I would have expected and more aggressively. Whenever another car slows him down, he sniffs irritably. Around the edge of Primrose Hill, behind Camden Town, down Gower Street, into Covent Garden. Joe and I sit close together in the back. I hold his hand, needing reassurance, but he takes no notice of me. Although the car's rear seats are like club armchairs, he sits upright, alert and watching, holding the airline bag on his lap with his free hand. I can feel the tension in his body, an electric charge waiting to spark. He hums softly to himself, 'Just direct your feet to the sunny side of the street.' Every time I look up, Riley is watching us in the rear-view mirror.

We stop outside a new office block at the end of Long Acre. Riley hops out smartly and opens the car door for us, then leads the way into a glitzy reception hall where a security guard is sitting behind a semi-circular desk. We sign his visitors' book and take the lift to the top floor.

There is a closed-circuit camera watching us in the lift and another facing the doors when we get out. There are more cameras in the brightly lit corridor and another over a door marked Ramon Fernandez and Co., Importers. The office is functional and elegant, black leather and stainless steel. On the receptionist's desk is a computer, a small switchboard and a television screen with a view of the empty corridor. A couple of smudged paintings of what might be Spanish landscapes hang on the walls. Riley ushers us across the room and knocks discreetly on a door. With his shiny suit and his pullover, he looks out of place in these smooth surroundings. He opens the door for us but does not follow us in.

Fernandez's office is big and shadowy, lit only by the Tizio lamp on his desk and a shaded standard lamp behind a sofa. A deep armchair faces the sofa, more black leather and steel. I try to see what pictures he has on his walls – an old art college tic – but all I can make out is the thick impasto. The huge window behind his desk is filled with the lights of the city.

Fernandez is short and plump and beautifully dressed. His teeth, when he smiles, are as white as his shirt. He has a sheen to him, like a man whose barber visits him daily with hot towels and cologne, clipping and shaving. He exudes wealth and bed, a mindless confidence, like one of Goya's royal portraits. When he takes my hand, bowing over it slightly and murmuring, 'Such a pleasure,' he holds it too long in his manicured fingers. I smile back and say nothing. He looks like a man who expects women to have big bosoms and wasp waists and no conversation, so why disappoint him?

'A drink?' he asks. 'A little brandy, perhaps?'

'Fine,' says Joe.

Fernandez opens a cupboard that lights up automatically to reveal bottles, glasses, a decanter. We settle ourselves on the sofa. Fernandez takes the armchair.

'I've been getting messages,' he says.

'You're a hard man to reach,' says Joe. 'I've been trying for days. Finally, I got Helen. In desperation. Even then I wasn't sure.'

'You know Helen?' Fernandez asks me. 'Lovely girl but Californian. How do the kids say it these days? Flaky. God knows what controlled substances she's ingested in her time. She's got holes in her head like Swiss cheese. You can never be sure the synapses are going to work.'

We smile at each other as though we were discussing one of Joe's lovable weaknesses. Fernandez has bleak eyes and his smile is like a titbit thrown to a dog, a gesture with nothing behind it. It's ten o'clock at night yet he's in no hurry to know why we're here. As if we were somehow below the level of his attention. He makes conversation but has more important things on his mind. It's a way of showing his power.

But Joe wants to be taken seriously. He sits forward on the sofa, body tense, eyes bright with excitement. 'If I didn't know better, I'd say you'd been avoiding contact,' he says.

Fernandez spreads his hands in a gesture of peace. 'I'm a businessman. I travel a lot. I have the executive's occupational disease, jet lag. Did you know,' speaking to me now, the object of his small talk, 'in Sweden young businessmen are refusing promotion? They want to stay home with their families, preserve their marriages. They don't want to live out of suitcases in expensive hotels.'

'You have a family?' I ask, since it seems required of me.

'Three children, almost grown.'

'Here in London?'

'In Arizona. Where the sun shines.'

Living in London makes him homesick for the sun. I wonder if he has closed-circuit television and security guards back there in his house in Arizona. A spotlight on the perfect pool, guard dogs roaming loose after dark.

'I've news for you,' says Joe. 'Don't you want it?'

Fernandez swills the brandy round his glass, sips it, smiles patiently. 'You're going to tell me anyway.'

'I wouldn't want to bore you.' Joe is sulking. He has a surprise to spring and the atmosphere is wrong. He wants attention, a little buzz of expectation, a hush for his big moment, not this small-talk about jet lag and children and a home in Arizona. He is a man bearing gifts and he feels entitled to respect.

Fernandez spreads his hands, smiling. 'Mr Constantine, why do you think I'm here at this time of night? We're both serious men, realists. Tell me what you have for me.'

Joe unzips the flight bag and takes out the Toytown Express in its bright cardboard box. He leans forward and hands it to Fernandez across the carpet solemnly, like a sacrificial offering. Fernandez, in turn, leans forward in his low-slung chair and takes it in both hands. There is a moment of silence. I hear a siren wailing faintly in the glittering city far below and the soft hum of the central heating.

'Well,' says Fernandez. He examines the gaudy box, turning it this way, then that. He opens it, takes out the train, fondles it, holds it up to the light. 'Real craftsmanship,' he murmurs. 'Like toys when I was a kid.'

Odd to think this barbered manicured man, in his expensive clothes, has ever been a child.

Joe says, 'It's what you were looking for?'

Fernandez nods. He puts the train on the carpet and pushes it gently, a child with a Christmas present.

'I have the whole case,' says Joe. 'It's yours when you want it.'

Slowly, as though unwillingly, Fernandez looks up from the train and fixes his bleak eyes on Joe. 'I'm in your debt. I owe you.'

'What's yours is yours. You owe me nothing.'

Fernandez cocks his head, the beginnings of a smile on his heavy mouth, a different style of attention – wary, amused. 'You're full of surprises,' he says.

Joe leans back on the soft leather sofa. 'Tommy was my dear friend. I had nothing but kindness from him. I don't want to think there are these loose ends, these accusations. He treated me honourably and that's how I want him remembered. I don't believe he was trying anything cute with you. I think there was a misunderstanding. So now I have traced the goods, it's only right you should have them.'

'And?'

'And nothing. The stuff is yours. There was a misunderstanding and now I've put it right. I want to clear my friend's name.'

Fernandez's smile broadens. 'A man of principle.' He, too, is leaning back in his chair now, enjoying the show. 'But do you really think your friend would have cared? He was a good businessman. For him, sticking to the letter of the law was a form of stupidity, a sucker-play. The first thing he looked for was space to manoeuvre in.'

'And that's what brought you together.'

Fernandez shrugs. 'He was very well connected. He knew people all over and everybody liked him. Also, he was discreet, he didn't ask unnecessary questions.'

'Is that important to you?'

'There! You see!' Another smile. He is enjoying himself. 'That is precisely the kind of question Tommy would never have asked.'

I wish this conversation were over. We have come here to clear up the mess, to set ourselves free. But all that's happening is we are getting in deeper. An intimacy is developing between my husband, with his intelligent eyes and broken nose, and this smooth fleshy potentate. It's a question of male pride. A macho game. They're egging each other on.

'I'm nobody,' says Joe. 'You can tell me.'

'It was a minor deal. Tommy claimed to have connections in Budapest, people who produced quality goods. We wanted to see how reliable they were, what their workmanship was like. The shipment itself was beside the point. Your friend misunderstood this. We had a difference of opinion. I don't even understand what he thought he was doing. Double-cross? On a nothing deal like this? It's not even feasible. Maybe he thought he could put pressure on us. On *us*? A clever man like him. It hardly seems credible.'

'Why do you say us, not me?'

'Don't be taken in. My name is on the door but my company is just part of a much larger organisation. A wholly owned subsidiary. I'm answerable to all sorts of people. Bankers, accountants, a board of directors, a chairman. A modern business is like the army; it has an intricate chain of command.'

'That wasn't how Tommy operated.'

'Tommy was a free spirit. Which is why I liked him. Mostly he operated in mid-air.'

He gets to his feet, goes across to the bar for the decanter and pours more brandy into our glasses. Despite his weight, he moves precisely, with a certain grace. A plane traverses the window, lights winking, sloping down towards Heathrow. He sets the decanter on the carpet in front of him. The cut glass sparkles in the lamplight, glints of yellow and blue.

He swirls the brandy round the balloon and sips. 'The first time I saw Tommy he caught my eye as someone special. It was at the Beachcomber, the poker room.'

Joe nods serenely. I want to kick him, tell him not to be taken in, but he's gone, remembering the good old days before he started losing.

'They were playing seven-card low-ball, a very big game. Pot limit, twenty-five-pound rolling antes. Seven players, high card brings it in for twenty-five means the opening raise is two hundred.'

'Big medicine.' Joe goes on nodding like an idiot. 'Since my time.'

'It's my game. I learned it in Vegas from the crazy Texans. Anyway, Tommy is playing and going very well. That's why I noticed him, and because he was dressed in this odd way: a Conway shirt but no tie and a snazzy leather jacket. I suppose he kept the jacket in his car and put it on when he left the office. So the game breaks up early and one of the hustlers says to Tommy,

"Come on, why don't we play heads-up, you and me, twenty grand each, freeze-out." I guess he's half-joking, pushing his luck. Tommy just shrugs and says, "Sure, why not?" He fumbles in his side pockets and pulls out fistfuls of £1,000 chips. Dumps them on the table, doesn't even bother to count them. Then he reaches into his inside pocket and takes out a handful of big green plaques, £10,000 each. He must have had a hundred grand on him. You could see the hustler change colour. Greed, fear. He didn't know whether it was Christmas or Armageddon. When he goes to the bathroom to wash up someone says to Tommy, "You really want to play that guy?" And he just shrugs and says, "What can happen? So I lose twenty grand." A man after my own heart, I thought. A gambler with a sense of proportion.'

'He must have come a long way since I last played with him.'

'I had the impression he was in control, a regular winner.'

'Finish the story.'

'That's it. The hustler changed his mind, of course. It was a bluff and Tommy called it.'

'In the old days they used to hang out the flags when Tommy walked into the club.'

'People change, they harden with age, some of them. I read somewhere, self-pity is the world's favourite indoor sport. But comes a point when losing is no longer attractive.' He is still smiling but he watches Joe steadily, sizing him up. 'Which side are you on, Mr Constantine?'

I look quickly at Joe, wanting to say, Don't take the bait. But he's there before me. He shrugs it off. 'I've given it up. I don't gamble any more.'

'You're missing out on the good things in life. When I got talking to Tommy that evening he said, "Gambling-money is the best money in the world. It costs you nothing, so you spend it with a free conscience." That's when I knew he was the man for me.'

To change the subject I say, 'When did all this happen?'

'A year or two ago.'

'So you've done other deals with him.'

'Madam, Tommy and I were tight, like that.' Fernandez holds up two fingers crossed. 'I relied on him. This thing that happened' – his eyes hold mine, giving nothing away – 'it came as a terrible shock.'

Joe says, 'So we're here to finish the business.' He fishes in his pocket and takes out a key. 'The packing case is in a lock-up in Kilburn, safe and dry.' He tosses the key to Fernandez. 'But there's other stuff there. I'll need the key back quickly.'

'I'll get it copied. You'll have it back tomorrow morning.'

'The address is on the tag.'

Fernandez raises his glass in salute. 'A pleasure to do business with you.'

'We're not doing business. We're closing the account. Here's to that.' He sips the brandy. 'One thing I should tell you. The police have been following me. The chances are they're keeping an eye on the lock-up. It's something you should know when you collect.'

'I appreciate your thoughtfulness.'

'Not that I'd try to teach you your business.'

'Like I said, I'm in your debt.'

'Don't even think about it.'

We get up and he walks us to the door. Riley is at the reception desk, feet up, reading the sports pages. On the television monitor the bright empty corridor is waiting for us.

Joe pauses at the doorway and says, 'What really happened to Tommy?'

'What sort of a question is that? You know what happened. He had a heart attack. A terrible tragedy for us all.'

'There'd been a break-in. He got worked up, over-excited. Then his heart gave out.'

'These are tough times, pal. We spend a fortune on security.'

'That's not the point. I mean why should there have been a break-in?'

A long slow smile, full of sympathy and understanding. 'I wish I knew the answer. He was my friend, too. But who am I to know what happened? So there was a break-in and something got out of hand. He was a man with a short fuse. All his life he trod a fine line.'

They face each other. Fernandez extends a hand and Joe takes it.

'As I see it, it was a question of confusion, of crossed lines.' Fernandez's voice is earnest, conciliatory. 'Your friend, I mean, he must have been confused, outraged, when he should have stayed cool, and it was the wrong moment to lose control.' He keeps hold of Joe's hand, as though to emphasise his sincerity. 'I'm guessing, of course. I don't know the facts. But as I see it, what we are dealing with here is a mistake, a tragic stupid mistake.'

Joe relinquishes his hand. Riley is on his feet now, waiting at the door, the newspaper folded and stuck in his jacket pocket.

'It's for my peace of mind, you understand.'

'I empathise, Mr Constantine. Don't think I don't. But a man like you, a man of principle, it's not a problem you have to worry about.'

'As long as we understand each other,' says Joe.

At the outer door Fernandez presses my hand, all warmth and sincerity. His flat eyes flicker from mouth to breasts to hips to mouth. He smiles as though we had a secret understanding. I know the look; it automatically undresses you and finds no surprises. I smile back, feeling no resentment. I don't even feel singled out. This is habit, the seducer's tic.

'I'm very glad we had this meeting,' he murmurs.

I hold the smile in place and say, 'We all are.'

It's over, I think, as we follow Riley down the silent corridor. Over, as the lift doors slide together behind us. Fernandez, I suppose, is watching us on the flickering monitor but that no longer matters. No more Fernandez, no more Hector, and no more Riley, once the ride home is over. The questions are still not answered but they are void.

So why this feeling of community, of complicity, of something beginning?

The pubs are emptying and the streets are still full – of young people mostly, hand in hand, heads down against the biting wind. The northbound traffic is heavy and aggressive, everyone impatient to be home out of the cold. Riley muscles the Jaguar up Tottenham Court Road, past the cut-price hi-fi stores, not giving an inch. The rage of this ineffectual little man astonishes me. Joe and I sit silently in the back, cocooned in soft leather, watching the lights swish past. On Primrose Hill bare branches are moving against an orange sodium-lit sky. There is a brief sense of space and night, the encompassing winter darkness. Then we are back among the lamplight and parked cars of familiar streets.

We shut our front door behind us and shoot the bolt into place. I go upstairs, leaving Joe to check the answering machine and switch out the lights, make sure the oven is off and the windows shut, the homely rituals. I drop my coat softly on the bed and begin to undress. I have my slip over my head, halfway off, when Joe comes into the bedroom. He closes the door behind him and stands there watching me.

'You have lovely breasts.'

It never fails and his response never fails to give me pleasure.

'You're such a sucker, darling. Still. After all these years.'

'Fernandez seemed to like what he saw.'

'Fernandez looked at me like I was so much meat. He's not the kind of man a nice girl like me would want to go to bed with, not in a million years.'

'He hasn't asked you yet.'

'Not in so many words. But a man like him, he doesn't ask, he assumes.'

'I saw the look. I thought you'd be flattered.'

'Flattered? You fancy me as a whore, Joe? That turn you on?'

He crosses the room, touches my face gently, then brushes his lips over the sensitive space between my breasts. 'So, Señora Constanteen, we make beautiful museek together, yes?'

'Eef you weesh eet, señor.'

He sits heavily on the bed and begins to unlace his shoes. His bony face is lined and tired. He is coming down from his high. 'Even so, this time round I quite liked the guy. All that threat he exudes, that's just his way of doing business.'

'Who does business by menace? That's not what the game's about. He's a creep, sweetheart. Don't let that buddy-buddy, Gamblers Unanimous stuff fool you.'

'What do we know about business, you and I? There's a whole world out there. Data bases, spread sheets, telexes, fax machines. Corporate men in grey suits talking about petro-dollars. Bankers, risk-analysts, hopping jets as though they were buses. London, Zurich, Bahrain, Tokyo, New York. Full of energy and strategies. I used to play squash with them back in the old days. I'd assume they were jet-lagged but they were hard to beat. Jet-lag was their natural condition. They lived off adrenalin.'

'You're such a romantic. You even think the corporate life is sexy.'

'Why not? All that know-how about third world budgets, about which political party is tight with which terrorist faction. At least they're living in the real world.'

'What makes it any realer than ours?'

He undoes his shirt slowly, as though each button were an effort. 'We have us. You, me, our half-arsed work.'

He struggles out of his shirt and trousers, then collapses back on the bed, feet dangling over the side, hands behind his head.

'I like Americans,' he says. 'I like their energy and their openness. I like the imperialist state of mind. Taking power for granted, doing business wherever there's business to be done. All the confidence we had a hundred years ago.'

'Fernandez didn't start out American, neither did Tommy. Tommy was a hustler, a freelancer like us. He lived out of his back pocket.'

'Same but different. And what do we know about him? Maybe he'd graduated to bigger things.'

'Like smuggling coke?'

'Our old friend. What kind of sense does that make?'

'Maybe he caught the imperialist fever, wanted to build himself an empire right here in NW3.' I sit beside him on the bed and stroke his damp forehead. 'Brush your teeth, come to bed. You look beat.'

Wearily, he pulls on his pyjamas and goes into the bathroom. The rain has started again. I hear it pattering against the windowpanes, the trees creaking in the wind. Joe comes back in, pulls open the curtains, lowers the window a couple of inches, then stands there, peering out.

'I wish it would snow,' he says. 'I wish, just once, we could have a real winter.'

He climbs into bed and puts his arms round me. 'I love your smell,' he says. Then he is asleep.

JOE

A couple of years ago, when my mother died, we inherited the house I was brought up in. We live in it now. A square and solid Edwardian mansion, gone slightly to seed. Red brick, cornices, stained-glass windows in the hall, carmine and purple and emerald, sculptured banisters, everything built to last, no expense spared. It's far too large for us, too full of the echoes of my family, all of them dead, and of the swarms that once filled the place: Nanny, Minnie the cook who ruled the roost, the parlourmaids, Peggy and Lizzie, and Violet who came on Fridays to polish the silver. Sometimes I think I can hear them in the empty upper rooms. Bustling feuding presences, vanished now.

Perhaps it was a mistake to move back. It's too big, too expensive to run. A family house and we have no family, only each other. I feel like a dubious Balkan monarch – Zog of Albania, Peter of Yugoslavia – returning unexpectedly from exile, without a following, without resources, knowing his moment has passed. By rights, we should sell our separate studios, break our old links, and transform the vacant upstairs spaces into offices, his and hers. But it is hard to give up old habits and we are both fond of our shabby studios. Anyway, the property market is dead for the time being. A couple of years ago, while we were dithering, there was crazy money to be made. But directly we put the studios on the market, the mortgage rates went up and the buyers disappeared. We grit our teeth, phone the estate agents every week and ignore the bank manager's starchy letters.

It's time someone stopped the downward slide. Two generations ago the family was wealthy. My grandfathers had chauffeur-driven Rolls-Royces, huge flats overlooking Regent's Park and small armies of servants to go with them. One grandfather was a JP, a club man, a pillar of the Anglo-Jewish establishment. The other was a dandy, a lady-killer who spent most of his time in the members' enclosure at Ascot, Goodwood, Kempton Park. Edwardian figures with fob watches and sapphire tie-pins, masters of the grand style.

Gradually, all the money seeped away. My father hated business, a one-man financial disaster zone, although in those days it cost less to keep up the appearances of middle-class life. But crumbling, uneasy, my mother forever nagging him because the rest of the family were richer than we were, a perpetual sub-text of money worries. My father was a diffident man, not inclined to lay down the law. The only piece of advice he ever gave me was, 'Whatever else you do, don't go into the family business.' I listened to him and look where it's got me. By the time he died, the business was bankrupt. The executors paid eight pence in the pound. My mother kept the house – it was in her name, a wedding present from her father – but her last years were hard. Now I am back. We cleared out her cumbersome furniture, repainted the rooms, put in a modern kitchen. But I still hear voices from my childhood, the money worries and recriminations. Maybe we were foolish to imagine they would fade and we could start out afresh. And there are no children to reverse the slide.

My father was a romantic, a martyr to powerful but confused feelings. He loved classical music and women – in that order. Not any women, indiscriminately, but women who were kind to him and thought him marvellous, something that my mother, one of life's realists, never quite managed. Music and sentimental affairs were his way of filling his life, and he preferred music. When I was home from school or university I used to sit with him every evening, listening to records. We rarely talked and sometimes he slept, but that listening together was his most eloquent form of communication. My sentimental education. I can't remember him dressed informally. He wore three-piece suits and never loosened his stiff white collar. He smoked continually and sometimes, when he dozed off, ash would drop on to his hand-stitched lapels. But mostly he listened intently, head cocked, gently beating time with his foot or hand, filling himself with everything he did not get elsewhere: feeling and order, sweetness and clarity. Or that's what I thought then. Perhaps he was thinking about money, fretting about his overdraft, his bank manager, his expenses. Shortage of money was the continuum he moved in.

He died of a heart attack in his sleep. At 2am, after an evening of Haydn quartets. I like to think Haydn was a sign that, just for once, he wasn't brooding about finances and he went to bed feeling cheerful, his head buzzing with healthy witty music. I was shooting hair-spray advertisements at the time and the four models – blonde, brunette, red-haired and black, none of them older than nineteen – were particularly mindless. We were behind schedule and the agency was on my back. So I never had time to mourn him properly or come to terms with his abrupt departure. I still think he'll reappear and we'll be able to say goodbye. I see him sunk in his armchair in front of the booming gramophone. I fill the house with music in his honour.

When my mother realised that the man lying next to her was dead she didn't phone me immediately. She knew I was working, she said, she knew I needed my sleep. So she got out of bed, wrapped herself in the eiderdown and spent the rest of the night on the floor in front of the electric fire. I got a phone call at 7.30. Her first words were, 'I hope I didn't wake you.' How do you explain that, except by a lifetime of believing that everything she did was wrong?

Yet after my father's death she began to change. Her own father, the martinet, the race-goer, had died a few years before and finally she was free. She walked her dog, cooked lavish meals, acquired friends who were not related to her, and rattled unperturbed around the shadowy crumbling house until arthritis stopped her short. She used to say, 'I want to die with my boots on.' Instead, she spent her last years dragging herself around on a walking-frame and died of cancer of the liver, aged eighty-four, having outlived her daughters.

The iller she became, the more her natural cynicism flourished. She carried on a running battle with Mrs Pickard, who came to look after her when her legs gave out. Mrs Pickard was a doctor's wife, a lady who had come down in the world. She was even older than my mother, bent like a question mark, and she moved around the house in shrewdly calculated bursts, from one piece of furniture to the next, pausing to rest and catch her breath at each stop. But she perked up disgracefully when my mother finally took to her bed.

'I don't know how long I can stand this,' my mother whispered to me, making certain that Mrs Pickard could overhear her. 'As I get iller, she gets more cheerful.'

Mrs Pickard tottered out of the room, tunelessly humming a snatch of Cole Porter to show she hadn't heard.

My mother seemed liberated by the prospect of death. She had always avoided doctors, preferring to patch herself up when she had an accident and swallow aspirin if she felt ill. So when the doctor started visiting her daily she was not deceived. 'Every time he bustles in he seems astonished,' she said. 'He can't believe I'm still here. I think he's secretly disappointed.'

'What did he say?'

She raised her eyes to the ceiling. 'What do you think he said? "You're on your last legs." '

Long, hot days. Her bed had been moved downstairs into the old drawing-room with its Chinese silk carpet that used to be forbidden territory when my sisters and I were children. Outside the French windows, the garden was going to seed.

'At least we don't have to pay a gardener this year,' my mother said.

But mostly she chose to ignore the obvious, preferring to talk about Judy or me or Mrs Pickard's dreadful cooking.

'What do the goyim know about food, anyway?'

In the three months it took her to die, she only made one direct reference to the future, and she waited until she was on her death-bed for that. 'All that stuff about the after-life,' she said. 'It's just fairy stories, isn't it?'

The cancer was everywhere by then and the doctor told me she had only a few days to go. I wanted to say something encouraging but when I saw how she was watching me, beady-eyed and amused, I shrugged and said, 'I think so.'

'Thank God,' she replied.

Two days later she was in a coma.

My mother loved the house and was terrified of hospitals, a fear I understand. It seemed the least I could do to make sure she died at home. For the last weeks of her life, I hired agency night nurses, so that Mrs Pickard could get some sleep. The nurses were mostly from New Zealand, plump efficient young women, habituated to death. For them, this was just another job and they discouraged shows of emotion. They washed her emaciated body with strong deft hands, cheerfully cleaned up her wastes, injected her briskly with Brompton Cocktail which subdued the pain and brought hallucinations: a huge hand that opened and closed in front of her eyes, disembodied voices gossiping about unfulfilled promises and unpaid bills. Threat and malice and money worries. Even when she became used to the drug and the hallucinations passed, she fretted about the expense. 'How are we going to pay for this,' she would ask. And when I replied, 'It's only money. Don't bother about it,' she'd shake her head and say, 'You're just like your father.' But fondly, without a trace of recrimination, as though finally even she could see there was no point in worrying any more.

The confusions were vanishing, layer by layer. As her body wasted away, the bone structure of her face became clearer and I could see her as she must have been when she was young, before I was born. Dark eyes, almost black, oval face, long delicate mouth, a beauty in her time. Then she was gone. After three days in a coma, her body trying to die, her heart refusing to give up. There were long moments when she seemed not to be breathing, then she would sigh deeply, pant, sigh again, mouth loose, tongue lolling. The nurse wiped her lips with a damp pad, felt her pulse, smoothed the pillows. She groaned, panted, sighed, sighed again, arm braced, fist clenched. But still her heart would not give up. Later, there were convulsions. I had no idea it could be so hard to die.

Two deaths. One a magician's trick with no visible strings or trapdoors, no rustling curtains, no farewells. The other a slow dissolve, day by day, inch by inch, lasting months. But in their different ways they both died well: my father with his head full of Haydn, my mother with all jokes blazing, until she lost consciousness and the terrible sighing began.

It is a long time since my parents made an appearance in my dreams – vague friendly presences, always disappointed – but I often wake up in the big first-floor bedroom, their bedroom, thinking about my inheritance, worrying about money. The bedroom has a wall of built-in cupboards with doors heavy enough to keep out the weather. At their centre, above what was once a fireplace, are two glass doors with ogive panels opening on to another cupboard where my parents once kept their mysterious medicines: cardboard boxes of pills and silver-wrapped suppositories, dark brown bottles.

Grey winter light.

The street outside is a short cut to nowhere so the traffic is light. The milkman's electric cart, early morning learner-drivers grinding gears, mothers on the school run with car-loads of children. The street vendors of my childhood have all gone – the rag-and-bone men, the lavender woman with her lingering musical call, 'Won't you buy my swee-eet lavendaar . . .' We live in a richer, more corporate society where nobody bothers about small change or sells bunches of lavender, the stems bound with silver paper.

My inheritance. The burden of being short of money seems to have been in place since I was a child. Not broke, not poor, just chronically short. I carry the weight of my father's fecklessness, my mother's unwavering preoccupation. A difficult combination. I worry about money; then, when I have it, I can't hang on to the stuff, can't think it's important. Maybe we should have cut our losses and sold the house. But it isn't easy to walk out on your past.

THE hole in the pavement outside my studio had been filled in, the red-and-white awning was gone. When I opened the studio door the air smelt dead, unused, tinged with tobacco smoke. I ran a finger over the mess on my table, drawing patterns in the dust.

There were three messages from my agent on the answering machine, each more fractious than the last. The first began jovially, 'Pussycat time.' The last was brief and exasperated: 'Where the fuck are you, Joe? The client's doing her nut.'

I opened the window briefly. The air was like iron, dark and cold, full of winter. Then I called Stonehouse to tell him about the meeting with Fernandez. He seemed curiously uninterested. 'Nice,' he said as I took him through the details. 'I say.' 'Dear boy.' 'Jolly good show.' At intervals, his end of the line became muffled as he put his hand over the receiver and talked to someone in the room. I had the impression I was boring him, that he was several jumps ahead of me.

When I finished, there was a silence. 'What happens now?' I asked.

'Nothing, probably.'

'You mean he won't pick the stuff up?'

'Hard to tell. A man like Fernandez, he doesn't rush into things.'

'He rushed into Tommy.'

'Surmise, dear boy. Can't say for sure.'

Stonehouse had the kind of English accent that makes my skin crawl. Drawling, diphthongised, full of conceit. The voice of the club bore, the claret-bibber, the anti-semite.

'You mean, after all that, he may just leave the stuff where it is?'

'Who's to tell? Perhaps he'll send a couple of his people down to pick it up. But if we move in on them, what have we got? Messenger boys.'

'It seems like an awful waste.'

'You did what you had to, dear boy. Did it well. No regrets there.'

'I was thinking of Tommy.'

'You shouldn't take these things so personally.'

'I keep hearing that.'

I pictured Stonehouse in his Whitehall office, with its mahogany furniture and view of St James's Park. The languid colleagues, the secretary bearing files and cups of tea. At twelve-thirty he would stroll across the park for lunch at the Travellers with his fellow spooks, a little gossip over coffee, a nap in a deep leather armchair in the library. The mandarin's leisurely life, greasing the wheels of state. All that Victorian gloom and faded grandeur, shrunk now into Gentleman's London, the square mile between St James's and Haymarket, Pall Mall and Conduit Street. They buy their shirts and shoes in Jermyn Street, their knitware and ties in the Burlington

Arcade, their suits in Savile Row. As if nothing had happened since the death of George V, as if the sun had never set on the Empire.

'Dear boy, you've done a super job. Can't be faulted.'

All in all, I preferred Fernandez.

I CALLED my agent and placated the client. I implied that I had gone missing for reasons no one could argue with. Without committing myself, I left an impression of doom hanging mysteriously in the air, the terminal illness of someone near and dear, so that it was impossible for them to complain. Then I called Chip, my part-time assistant, and told him there was work to do. He seemed surprised to hear I was still in business.

In the afternoon I drove out to inspect the cats. They had been brought up from the country and were now lodged in a semi-detached off Goldhawk Road, where they were being combed and primped or whatever it is they do to prepare cats for stardom. Starved, probably, so they would tuck into the canned food on cue.

The journey, which should have taken twenty minutes, took me two and a quarter hours. I knew I was in trouble the moment I drove up the slip road on to Westway. I managed fifty yards at walking pace then came to a halt. Tail lights stretched away to the horizon, three lanes of them, a gradually solidifying line of red dots leading into the sunset. The sun was a narrow slit of angry red in the black cloud and the tail lights seemed like its reflection in water. It was as if London had suffered a grand ecological disaster and its inhabitants were being evacuated on command. I pushed buttons on the radio to see if I had missed an emergency but the stations were going about their business as usual. The people in the cars on either side of me stared glumly forward. Nobody hooted, nobody gesticulated. They sat patiently waiting for something to happen, resigned, passive, at the mercy of events, refugees without a future to look forward to. I wondered where they had all come from, where they hoped they were going. It seemed strange that no one turned his head and made contact. Some small gesture of mutual recognition: We are all in this together. The inevitable had happened: London had ground to a halt and no one would acknowledge it.

Most of the time it seems a great sadness that Judy and I have no children, and when I see her holding someone else's baby or playing with a toddler my heart goes out to her. But who wants to bring up kids in state-of-the-art gridlock, in a city where nothing moves and every rush-hour is a rehearsal for the day of judgment?

It took an hour to reach the White City turn-off, another forty-five minutes to crawl the half mile to the Shepherds Bush roundabout. But there was a police car blocking the road into Shepherds Bush and when I attempted to turn left a cop wearing a luminous yellow apron over his uniform stuck his furious bull head in the window and yelled, 'Try that and I'll do yer.' His face was bright red and there was spittle at the corners of his mouth.

As I drove back up towards the Westway, it occurred to me that he was probably right. Blind rage was the only sane response.

Oddly enough, the last mile took a mere half hour. Down Wood Lane past the brightly lit hulk of the BBC Television Centre, inch by inch round Shepherds Bush, jammed in a sea of buses. When I reached the semi-detached off Goldhawk Road the cats were all asleep, each curled up in its own basket, like so many Christmas presents. Their owner was a fourteen-stone woman with tight blonde curls and the face of a dissolute six-year-old. Round and pink, with merry cheeks and sly eyes.

'They couldn't wait up for you,' she said accusingly.

'You wouldn't believe the traffic. The whole town's come to a halt.'

'It's the Christmas rush. You should make allowances.'

'Arteriosclerosis more like. A terminal case. The arteries are seizing up.'

I got down on my knees and peered at the cats. When I stroked one gently it opened its eyes and stared at me with disdain. Its eyes were pure lemony gold, the pupils mere slits of darkness. It stretched its legs languorously and went back to sleep.

'Are they always this sluggish?'

'They're not to blame. It was way past their din-dins time. I had to feed them. Cats always sleep after they've eaten.'

'Just as long as they're full of fun when the time comes.'

'You worry about your responsibilities, I'll worry about mine.'

'There'll be bright lights, heat, people moving around.'

The woman's pink face became pinker with indignation. 'My pussies are professionals, Mr Constantine. Old stagers. TV, movies, glossy ads, they've done them all.'

'Then it will be a pleasure to work with them. I'll see you at my studio tomorrow morning at nine. And please, no breakfast for them.'

She showed me to the door in silence and ignored my proffered hand.

THE traffic was lighter on the way back into town, so I made a detour to Tommy's lock-up in Kilburn. I drove slowly past the parked cars, looking for watchers. The only candidate was a blue Bedford van, parked a little uphill from the garage. Its rear windows were dark but I couldn't tell if this was because of the dim street lights or because they were made of smoked glass. I parked outside the garage, strolled casually back to the van and took a long time lighting a cigarette while I listened for surreptitious movements inside. Then it occurred to me that the police would more likely be in an upper room of one of the terraced houses, watching in comfort. I remembered all those spy and gangster films where the agents stake out a joint with infra-red telescopic lenses on their cameras and long-distance mikes for their tape-recorders. Men with two-day stubble and guns in shoulder-holsters, rooms full of cigarette butts and half-eaten sandwiches. The routine boredom and squalor of the interesting life. Better to be a bit-player in a B movie than spend my time photographing pussy-cats.

The packing-case was in the garage, exactly where we had left it. I padlocked the door again and drove home.

That evening Judy and I went to the supermarket. Usually, we take separate carts. She starts at Vegetables, I go to Dairy Products and we work inwards. There is a secret competition between us to see who can shop more efficiently. If we meet at Bacon and Smoked Meats, we consider it a stand-off.

This time Judy gripped my arm and said, 'Stay with me.'

'Why waste time?'

'I need you to help me choose.'

'Between new potatoes and King Edward's?'

'Just stay with me anyhow. Don't make an issue of it.'

I looked at her closely. She has blue eyes, a neat soft mouth, dark hair bracketing her face. A picture, usually, of composure and self-confidence, with a silky sheen to her that still turns heads, even in her middle age. Now her mouth was wavering, her eyes were shifty and she seemed ready to cry.

The supermarket was full of couples like ourselves, back from work, parading the aisles lazily, enjoying the plenitude, the muzak, a world that functioned better than the chaos outside. Some of them had children perched on the collapsible seats of their carts or trailing disconsolately behind, but at this hour most were young and intent, piling their carts with yoghourt, muesli and organically grown vegetables. There were a few old people, most of them on their own – the couples shopped earlier in the day – who lingered unnecessarily at the shelves of tinned soups and had come to get out of the cold rather than to buy. Then there were the singles, the unmarried occupants of bed-sitters, shopping for pre-cooked chicken-and-two-veg dinners, foil-wrapped lasagna and heat-in-the-bag boeuf bourguignon. Nowhere is safer than a supermarket, I thought, with its bright profusion, soft music, even light and shuffling feet. It is where we consumers come to worship, to have our beliefs confirmed. In medieval cathedrals the eye is led upward, towards heaven; we prefer the horizontal axis, the endless shelves of enticing choices. Above the fruit, meat and fish sections were modern icons, pale blue glowing loops that killed flies.

'What's up?' I asked. 'Aren't you well?'

'I don't want to find myself face to face with Hector again.'

'That's all over, sweetheart.'

'Maybe.'

I touched her hand and said, 'I'm right with you.'

An old lady burrowed past, head down, as though forcing her way through undergrowth. She tore a transparent bag off a roll and fumbled with it for a long time, trying to work out which end opened, then she studied a mound of Cox's Orange Pippins, selected three, and burrowed off again to have them weighed.

'It's an idiotic place to be frightened,' said Judy. 'I don't know what's got into me.'

'You don't choose these things. They just happen.'

'Fear and dread in Waitrose. That's a turn-up for the book.'

'No different from John Lewis.'

She worked her way remorselessly through Fruit & Vegetables, piling the cart with bags of potatoes, sprouts, onions, oranges, apples, plastic-wrapped cabbage, celery, cauliflower. She seemed to be shopping for the extended family she didn't have, or for a siege.

I stayed with her, kept close, checked the other shoppers for familiar faces.

When we reached the Cereal aisle she hesitated between Economy-Size Corn Flakes and Rice Krispies, then put both into the cart.

I said, 'We don't eat cereal.'

'Don't we?' she said vaguely. 'Maybe we should start.'

'You're letting this get to you. Now it's all tidied away you're letting it get you down.'

We wheeled the carts up the aisle and stopped at Tea & Coffee. Judy took down one-hundred-bag boxes of Jackson's Earl Grey and English Breakfast Tea.

'I think it's worse now I can put a face on Fernandez. Now I know what the threat looks like. It's given me a sense of scale.'

'He fancies you.'

'That's what scares me.'

When we drove home she kept her hand on my thigh, as though she wanted to remind herself that I was still there.

THE cats' minder and the client hated each other on sight but the cats themselves were a pleasure to work with. They trod delicately – for the first time I understood what 'pussyfoot' meant – and lashed into the food on cue.

Chip spent his time petting them when they weren't working. Chip is lanky and ill-shaven, wears a woollen cap on his close-cropped head, winter and summer, and is the only person I know who still talks about the proletariat. When I say the unions, these days, offer credit cards and favourable rates for private medical insurance, he tells me I don't understand the nature of the struggle. Politics, however, never seem to get in the way of his work. He sets up the lights and the background meticulously, takes the test polaroids, flirts with the models, is unfailingly polite to the clients, always hands me the right filter when I need it and never muddles the notes I give him on the film. Photographer's assistant is not much of a life – errand-boy, coffee-maker, dogsbody – and when I first employed him Chip made it clear that this was just a staging-post on the way to a career in photo-journalism, like an aspiring actress working as a stage manager. But recently, during coffee-breaks, I have seen him talking intently to the clients. My agent tells me not to trust him. How he would reconcile his politics with advertising is not clear.

After the shoot was over and the studio was cleared and Chip had gone off to the colour lab with the reels of exposed film, I called Fernandez. I told him I needed assurances.

'What kind of a request is that?' He sounded offended.

'I need to know we've seen the last of Hector and his pals.'

'Mr Constantine – Joe, may I? Have you been troubled in any way at all?'

'I'm not talking about myself. It's my wife who's worried.'

'Your wife is a very attractive woman, Joe. I congratulate you.'

'That's not the point.'

'But you know and I know that women sometimes get upset for no good reason.'

'She has plenty of good reasons. Hector scared her out of her wits. He chased her, hounded her. In a department store. Like some low-grade gangster movie.'

'Aaah.' He made a growling purring sound like a large cat settling, part contentment, part amusement, part threat. 'That's Hector's problem. Gangster movies are where he got his education. He's from the barrios, a simple boy, started out as a sicario and still sees himself as one tough hombre, an old-style hoodlum from Capone's Chicago. When I first employed him he was, like, crazy. He'd go into a guy's office, throw two bullets on his desk and say, "The next one goes in your fucking head." A pity. He has a certain natural talent. He has looks. These days he even has manners of a kind. What he lacks is balance. Maybe he will acquire it with age – if he lives that long.'

'Provided he doesn't acquire it at our expense.'

'What can I say, Joe? This is a serious embarrassment for me. I am a married man, a father, I understand these things. Our loved ones have irrational fears and we suffer for it. It's only natural.'

'I'm not accusing you. I just need to know that Hector and friends are out of our lives for keeps.'

'You have my word. What more do you need? I am a sincere man, Joe. I promise something, I keep the promise.'

'I believe you, Mr Fernandez.'

'Ray.'

'Ray, then.' I pictured him in his sweeping chair, against the window, London spread out below him. The arrogance of high places. 'But it's my wife who needs convincing.'

'The moment I hang up, I'll speak to the boy.'

'I'd be grateful.'

'Gratitude doesn't come into it. I'm a man of honour and you've dealt with me honourably. That's something I appreciate. A rare quality in these hard times.'

'As long as we understand each other.'

'I've got the picture, Joe. What we're talking here is imponderables, the little details that get overlooked.'

When I got home Judy was arranging a huge bouquet of flowers in a vase. Lilies, roses, exotica with spiky shapes and violent colours. 'A present from our mutual friend,' she said. 'From Fernandez. With his sincerest apologies for any inconvenience.'

'The old-fashioned courtesies.'

'They must have cost him a fortune.' She squinted at the vase, rearranged two of the roses, squinted again. Her face was flushed with pleasure.

'A business expense. He can write it off against taxes.'

'Don't spoil it for me. Just when I was taking it personally.'

The next time Stonehouse called I interrupted the flow to ask him if he knew what a sicario was.

'Picking up the lingo, are you, dear boy?'

'I don't know what I'm picking up. I just heard the word. In passing, as it were.'

'Pointless to ask where, I suppose.'

'Tell me what it means, then I'll tell you where I heard it.'

'A private in the Colombian drug army. A young contract killer, dear boy. Stalks his quarry on a motor bike so he can make his getaway in traffic.'

I thought of Hector in his tightly belted Burberry and his bookie's tout's hat. He'd come a long way from the slums of Medellín.

'Hector Gutierrez,' I said.

'You don't surprise me.'

THE rain stopped after Christmas and a pale sun rode the pale sky day after day. Frost at night, fog in the morning, chaos at Heathrow. When we walked on the heath at the weekends twigs crackled underfoot, squirrels came out of hibernation to look around, people smiled inanely at each other and shaded their eyes when they whistled to their dogs. On the reedy edge of one of the ponds near Kenwood a heron stood on one leg, staring loftily at the little crowd that had gathered to stare at him. After three weeks, pundits on the radio began to talk about drought. It seemed odd after all those months of rain but nobody contradicted them.

Judy seemed preoccupied but no longer nervous. She did her Jane Fonda exercises every evening after work and joined a weekend aerobics class at the local health club. Her muscle tone improved, her lovely backside tightened.

'Aren't you overdoing it?' I asked. 'Keep this up, you'll end up stringy.'

'I keep this up, I'll live for ever.'

'Jane Fonda had a heart attack. Anyway, I like your curves.'

'I like a shape I can control. No more sloppiness. We're in our forties, Joe. That's not old these days. The prime of life, they say. We should make the most of it.'

I admired her confidence. When I looked in the mirror I seemed permanently dishevelled. My hair – what was left of it – stuck out, my eyes were baggy, my cheeks pasty. What happened to the fit young squash player, the man who photographed the Prague

Spring and made passes at fashion models? Between marriages, of course. And what happened to the marriages? I wondered what my ex-wives looked like, what all the fuss was about? I could no longer remember a time when Judy and I weren't married. Twelve years. They seemed to have gone in no time at all and yet to comprise my whole adult life. The other day I came across a snap taken on our honeymoon. Her with her long-legged girl's body, me with a dark beard and no belly. Alien creatures, young, attractive, full of fire, smiling confidently at the camera, the turquoise Caribbean behind them. If I met them in the street now, I wouldn't recognise them, wouldn't have anything to say. Maybe ageing is easier if you can watch your children change and grow.

Fernandez had returned the key as promised. Stonehouse left us alone. There was no sign of Hector. Smiling and preoccupied, Judy did her exercises, took off weight, prepared herself for the future.

I wondered what she knew that I didn't.

PART 2

JOE

It was Geary who changed our lives. William Geary of Hardcastle and Sparks, Solicitors and Commissioners of Oaths. The bluff voice on the telephone asking if he could see me, if I could perhaps spare half an hour to come to his office. A hearty sports master's voice, full of hollow bonhomie. Not what I had expected of the annunciation.

His office was in Bloomsbury Place, ten minutes' walk from my studio. Early Victorian grey brick, big windows, spiked railings painted black. Inside it was stark and echoing. Brown lino in the corridors, no carpets on the wooden stairs, offices full of battered furniture and steel filing cabinets.

Geary was smaller, frailer, than his voice, with the stooped shoulders, grey face and collapsed cheeks of a terminal patient. He peered benignly over his half-glasses, pumped my hand with both of his, waved me to a wooden chair, then retreated behind the towers of files and papers on his desk.

'It's taken a long time,' he boomed in his disproportionate voice. 'Of course, things legal always take time. Got to get 'em right, can't be hurried. We make some small slip of the pen and God knows what the consequences might be. Not that we use pens these days, not any more. But you get my drift.'

'Not exactly.'

'Ho, ho, ho.' A Santa Claus laugh, basso profundo. 'Of course you don't. Not making myself clear, am I?' He picked up a sheaf of papers and shuffled them. The sunlight flooded in through the tall window. His half-glasses sparkled on the end of his thin nose.

'I'm talking about the will, Mr Apple's will. A regular mare's nest, if ever I saw one. Complications you couldn't imagine.'

'I probably could.'

Another cannonade of laughter. 'I was forgetting. You were a close friend, used to his peculiarities. So was I, of course. Known the dear man for years. Like to think he considered me, too, among his good friends. But friendship's one thing, the law is something else. And trying to make sense of Tommy's affairs when it comes to probate . . .'

I lit a cigarette and watched the smoke drift in the columns of sunlight. A summer indolence. Outside the window was a sooty tree and a perspective of sooty houses. A pigeon perched on a bare branch, its feathers the same blue-grey as the cigarette smoke. The sound of typing and the sound of traffic mingled with Geary's booming voice. I had expected Tommy's solicitor to be young and hungry, someone he could share his schemes with, not this ill-looking man with his noisy uneasy confidence. His protruding ears were suffused with sunlight, rosy pink, almost transparent, against his grey skull.

'Companies within companies,' Geary was saying. 'Ramifications you wouldn't believe.'

He paused significantly, waiting for me to say something.

'I'm sorry. I've lost the thread.'

'I was talking about the estate.'

'A legal nightmare, I bet. You have my sympathy.'

He shuffled the papers again and peered at them, pretending to search for something. He seemed embarrassed.

'It's your interests I'm talking about.'

'My interests?'

'Yours and Mrs Constantine's.'

I had a glimpse of Tommy in the sunlit room, hairy, overweight, full of energy and good will. I realised, for a moment, how much I missed him.

Capitalism with a human face.

'You mean we're mentioned in the will?'

Geary made a small irritated movement that rustled the papers he was holding. He peered at me sternly over his half-glasses.

'I don't think you've quite got the point.'

'I don't think I have.'

He put the papers down on the desk, squared them off, leaned solemnly forward.

'The fact is, Mr Constantine, you and your good wife are the main beneficiaries.'

'Pardon?'

'He's left you more or less everything.'

I lit another cigarette and exhaled slowly, watching the smoke twist and spread in the dusty sunlight. I studied Geary's sad face and waited for the punch-line: he's left you everything but there was nothing to leave except debts.

Geary scratched his thin hair and said nothing.

'What about his mother, his relatives? What about the ex-wives and his live-in lady? What about all the girlfriends?' I could hear my tone of voice – querulous, unsteady, unattractive. I wanted him to put an end to the suspense, to get to the bad news.

'There's a trust fund for his mother and another for a Mrs Rosie Graham, of Bournemouth – an aunt, you know. Miss Louise Schapiro is left the flat in Reddington Road and a small annuity. Everything else goes to you.'

'What do you mean by everything else?'

'That's what I was trying to explain. His accountant and I have been doing our best to sort it out. Believe me, it isn't easy. There are holding companies, shell companies, accounts in several banks. Not to mention security boxes and various goods stashed away in various places. On top of all that, the police are opposing probate,' he cleared his throat, 'pending their investigation of the circumstances surrounding his death.' He gave me his graveyard smile. 'That's how they put it officially. They mean the break-in. It's all very vexing.'

'But it boils down to something?'

'Indeed, it does.'

A seagull swooped past the tree outside the window, then veered abruptly away. The pigeon shifted on its pink nude feet and was still again.

I had a faint sense of something dawning, relief at hand, but it was hard to concentrate.

'I never expected Tommy to end up solvent. Remember what Erroll Flynn said? "If I died with money in the bank, I'd consider myself a failure." That's how I thought Tommy would be. If you've got it, flaunt it. One of those.'

'He was all of that.' Geary pulled a pipe out of his pocket, filled it carefully, lit it, tamped it with his thumb, lit it again. He coughed extravagantly. 'Can't get used to the damn thing,' he explained. 'I used to smoke cigarettes but the doctor told me to stop. Now the smell of them drives me wild and I have to make do with this.' He coughed again from somewhere deep down and wiped his eyes. 'Maybe I should just give up.'

He took a sheet of paper from the pile in front of him. 'Tommy wrote me a note when I was drawing up his will.' He smoothed out the paper on the desk and ran a probing bony finger over it. 'His mother . . . Mrs Graham . . . I've told you about them . . . Miss Schapiro.'

Booming voice and haggard face. Angel of the annunciation.

'Stuff about his wives and the money they soaked him for. You don't need to hear that. Translated into legal terms it means he's made more than adequate provision for his ex-wives in their alimony settlements. Which, God knows, is true.' A wasted smile. 'Here's the part that concerns you.' He coughed again, adjusted his glasses. '"Whatever's left goes to my friends Joe and Judy Constantine. Apart from my mother and my Aunt Rosie, they're the only people I really care about. But they remind me of the old song: 'Such nice people, with nice manners, but they've got no money at all.' So I want to leave them a bob or two, enough so they won't have to want for anything again. Also, they'll know how to spend it with style. Better than those obnoxious nephews and nieces." '

Another love letter from the grave, but this one charged with intent, written at a time when he was flourishing and a long way from death. I had no idea he wished us well in this way, impartially, not telling us anything about it. I felt confused, off balance, inadequate. I had imagined him leading the full life. Deals, bright lights, affairs, Louise, Helen, God knows who else. Now it turned out he had been lonely. Judy was right: we should have had him to dinner more often.

Geary was saying, 'You know Tommy. A sentimentalist at heart. With all due respect to him and you. So I checked with him very thoroughly before I drew up the will. By the sound of it, the nephews and nieces are a pack of wolves. But they can't contest it. So far as they're concerned, there are no loopholes.'

'In practical terms, what does this mean?'

The pigeon dropped clumsily from its branch, as though losing its grip, then gained height with a flurry of wings.

'In practical terms, once the police are satisfied, upwards of a million, a million two. Probably a good deal more. We can't tell until we've sorted it out. There will be taxes of course, a lot of them. Even so, we're talking about a substantial sum of money.'

I got up, went to the window, studied the perspective of overgrown gardens, dishevelled roofs and television aerials. Most of the houses between Geary's office and Russell Square were private hotels, full of Scandinavian tourists on shopping sprees and American scholars with research grants who spent their days turning pages in the British Library Reading Room, inhaling the musty air, half-listening to the whispers, the shuffling silence.

Upwards of a million, a million two.

'It's hard to take in,' I said. 'You see, my grandparents were rich, but me, I feel I've been short of money for two generations. Not just all my life but my parents' lives, too.'

Again the terminal patient's smile. 'It looks like your troubles may be over.'

'Or beginning. I mean, I'm a photographer, not a businessman. What am I supposed to do with these companies?'

'They can be disposed of, sold to interested parties. There are physical assets, good will, the tangibles and the intangibles.'

'In the old days, when I was with Tommy, watching him perform, I used to think that being a businessman wouldn't be such a bad thing.'

'Now's your moment, then.'

'The romance of money. But what do I know about deals?'

'There's nothing mysterious about business. It's like the races. All you need is someone to mark your card.'

'Yourself, for instance?'

A faint tinge of colour crept into Geary's grey face. Embarrassment suited him. It made him look, for a moment, a little less ill than before. 'I was thinking of Felix Abel, Tommy's accountant. He kept abreast, he knows the ins and outs.'

'And he'll talk to me for a fee, give me sound advice?'

'That's his profession. All you have to do is call him. I'll write down his number.'

I paced the shabby carpet, unable to settle. It was as if a tourniquet had been removed and I could feel the blood coursing in my veins again. Seagulls drifted and turned in the sunlight above Russell Square. I listened to the noise of the traffic, feet on the stairs, the machine-gun rattle of a typewriter. A door opened across the landing and an exasperated voice said, '*Someone* must know where the Goldman file is.'

'It's strange to think of not having money worries,' I said. 'Life won't be the same.'

Geary smiled at me and this time the expression on his ashen face was kindly. 'You'll be astonished how fast you adjust,' he said.

I PHONED my agent and told him I wouldn't be available for a while, then I called Chip and said he could use my studio if he needed it. Neither of them seemed surprised.

I was free, out of it.

I don't remember exactly when I'd lost interest in photography. Perhaps about the time I realised that taking pictures of models for fashion magazines was just a job like any other, something anyone could do on automatic pilot once they had the know-how. At that point the hype, flattery and empty enthusiasm began to seem like calculated insults to the intelligence. 'Just wonderful, darling. Those skin tones. Peaches and cream. Positively edible.' Crooning voices, flapping hands, phoney smiles. All they meant was I was giving them their money's worth and they were grateful. No need to come on like I was Rembrandt. When I was starting out I thought photographers were artists, people with an instinct for timing, light and composition, for the feeling that clings to figures and places, for the specialness of the scene, the occasion. A good picture was full of hidden meanings, heavy with the weight of appearances, the density of action. An interpretation of the world and one's experience in it, just like the other arts but more immediate, more technical, more modern. Now it was just another job. I was glad to be done with it.

I left my cameras behind and drove.

At first, I couldn't keep away from the lock-up in Kilburn. Every day I cruised slowly past. The blue Bedford van was still in place, more or less where it had been before. The curtains in the windows of the houses round about did not stir. A small surf of leaves and torn newspaper that had blown against the garage door grew undisturbed. Nobody wanted the toys from Hungary or what was inside them. It had all been a mistake, an unfortunate misunderstanding. If Tommy had been less excitable none of this would have happened. He'd have been alive, I'd have been broke.

The weather stayed fine, I went on driving. I sat in traffic jams, took short cuts through side streets choked with parked cars, worked out a back route to Heathrow, through Willesden, Brondesbury, Acton. Rows of run-down shops and sad houses, factories sending streamers of smoke into the cold air. I felt I was learning London before it was too late, before it ground to a halt. I piled tapes on the passenger seat and kept the music playing full blast. Haydn in memory of my father, Fred Astaire for my mother. I wished I could tell them the money problems were almost over, the overdrafts would be paid off

When my mother was a child she overheard her mother and an aunt gossiping about their Uncle Harry who was having an affair with a woman 'over the water'. My mother, who had hardly been out of Bloomsbury at that stage of her life, thought they meant Paris. Later, she discovered that the woman lived across the Thames in south London.

Terra incognita.

I crossed the water at Blackfriars Bridge, drove past the Old Vic, the Imperial War Museum, to Kennington, forked left towards Camberwell Green, then took to the side streets. The Mahatma Gandhi Trading Estate was beyond high-rise council housing and a railway bridge, on a long street of dingy terraced houses. Prefabricated units trimmed in ox-blood red, backing on to commuter lines from the dormitory suburbs. Trains rattling past, vans manoeuvring on the concrete area between the buildings, black children playing in the street outside. In Tommy's unit the air was dead, unused, ice-cold. There was a big work-table in the centre and boxes marked Taipei and Hong Kong lined against the walls. Everything was covered with dust. I locked the door behind me and drove on.

Herne Hill, Crystal Palace, Penge, Elmers End, places I didn't know existed. Victorian mansions giving way to 30s ribbon developments, stucco and mock Tudor. Innumerable lives, twice the population of Sweden, back-to-back, semi-detached, in houses, flats, penthouses, bed-sitters. Stacked like file cards. The houses gave out at West Wickham. I drove across a wooded common studded with gorse and twisted oaks. Pratt's Bottom, Badgers Mount. When I reached the M25 I turned north, circling London nose-to-tail at 80 mph, then south on the A1, through the familiar suburbs to home.

Our house was full of flowers, cut flowers in vases, plants in pots everywhere I looked. It was Judy's only response to our change in fortune, as though Fernandez's gesture had reminded her of what she had been missing all these years. I didn't seem able to get away from the man.

Geary had said probate might take months. Even so, I was waiting for a word. Any word. Sometimes, when I was on the road, I'd spot a telephone kiosk that hadn't been vandalised and call Judy, just to make contact. Apollo to Houston Control. Wanting to hear her voice, hoping she'd heard something. More often than not, she didn't answer. I pictured her bright office, the dazzling paper pinned to her drawing board, the neat files and ordered cupboards, the unanswered telephone filling the air with its din.

'Conferences,' she explained the first time I said I'd called. 'Suddenly everyone wants me.' A dismissive shrug, hands spread, sweet smile.

'How's that for bad timing? Now we've got money, business is booming.'

'We haven't got it yet. Better safe than sorry.'

After that, I never mentioned the times I called her and she didn't answer.

'Suddenly everyone wants me.' An innocent remark except that we had secrets we kept from each other. I thought of Judy and Tommy at the Imperial in Torquay, Helen and me in the makeshift studio in Tunis. Missions impossible, both of them. Judy and I were bonded together by the smell and texture of each other's bodies, by love, habit, goodwill, to have and to hold, etc. That didn't stop me feeling retrospectively jealous. Tommy and Judy, Tommy and Helen, Tommy and Fernandez, Tommy and his millions. Now I was Tommy's heir I felt diminished by this powerful hairy primal figure, full of appetites I couldn't match.

'What no woman understands,' Tommy used to say, 'is that sometimes it's nicer to have a not very good fuck with someone you don't know, rather than a wonderful fuck with someone you do.'

Judy and Helen.

He also liked the old Jewish saying, 'A standing cock has no conscience.'

Was that why he'd put us in his will?

Blood money.

And in the end, paid for in blood by him. Someone had been with Tommy when he died, working him over with a knife, watching him yell, expand, explode. I sifted through the new faces in my life, trying to fit them to the shadowy figures around my raging friend lashed to his executive chair. Find the right face, then nail him. That was the other part of the legacy. A favour for a favour, just like the old days.

It rained for a week and a chill wind blew from the east. The traffic ground to a halt again, so I gave up driving, bundled myself up in two sweaters and an anorak and walked the Heath, wishing I owned green gumboots, like my ex-parents-in-law. Seagulls squabbled for scraps on Parliament Hill, dipping and soaring, blown about like rags. The view over London seemed to have been reconstructed while my back was turned. It was studded with skyscrapers I didn't recognise, office blocks glinting with lights, speculative investments in Docklands, in the City. The wind blew unhindered from Russia, over the rain-sodden plains and shabby grey towns of Eastern Europe.

The days lengthened slowly and the outline of the trees became blurred, not yet green but thick-tipped, waiting to bud. Even the cold east wind seemed to smell of spring. Not long to wait, I told myself. Soon there will be no more starchy letters from the bank. Soon the manager will be inviting me to lunch, offering to advise me on my investments, wanting to be in on the act. But back home the telephone did not ring and there were no messages on the answering machine at my studio.

I wondered what plans were hatching behind my back. The police are opposing probate, Geary had said. I pictured Stonehouse and Rogers fingering through the photographs of Helen and the oriental girl and the scrawny boy. Gilt-edged investments. Better than the ones my bank manager would hustle me into. I pictured Fernandez in his eyrie, surrounded by his computers and fax machines, dictating memos into a tape recorder, moving the pieces around, London spread out below him like an expensive carpet. Against all the evidence, I liked the guy – the assurance, the lack of illusions, the dead zero reckoning. I preferred not to think of him presiding over Tommy's heart-attack.

Their go-between, their fall-guy, their poodle. If that was what they thought, so much the better. Spring was coming. It was time to put my life in order.

THE table was kidney-shaped, covered with blue baize. The club's symbol, a white conch, was painted in the centre. Beneath it were the words, The Beachcomber Club. The dealer wore a white shirt, a black bow tie, no jacket. Each time he prepared to flick out the cards he hitched back his shirt sleeves to display his nimble hands and the jewellery he wore to show them off: a gold Rolex on one wrist, a gold bracelet on the other.

The faces round the table were tribal masks, the features weighty with concentration: heavy eyelids, sombre mouths, pendulous blue jaws. Seven middle-aged men lounging indolently behind their towers of chips: black 25s, pink 100s, white 1,000s. No one seemed to be playing with less than £10,000, most had a good deal more. When their cards were dealt to them they did not bother to look until their turn came to bet. Then they cupped their hands around the cards, raised the corners briefly with their thumbs, slouching in their seats as though none of this had anything to do with them.

'High card brings it in,' said the dealer.

A fat bald man whose up card was a queen tossed a black chip into the centre. The player beside him turned over his cards. A bony-faced Arab threw three pink chips into the pot and said, 'Raise.'

The dealer pushed two black chips towards the Arab and said, 'Raise two hundred.'

The next two players turned over their cards.

A heavy surly-mouthed man studied the Arab for a minute, carefully, measuring him up. His eyes flickered from the Arab's ace to his own deuce to the other cards lying exposed on the table. Counting, calculating, memorising. Finally, he said, 'Re-raise,' and threw in a white chip.

Everyone except the Arab folded.

'Six hundred to you,' the dealer said.

'Where does this kind of money come from?' I whispered.

Fernandez smiled slyly. 'Like I keep telling you, Joe, you have a talent for unnecessary questions.'

'Look at the chips. Twenty thousand is modest. What kind of businessman is going to put his hand in his own till and take out that kind of money? Into someone else's till maybe.'

Fernandez shrugged. 'It's gambling money, is all. Not the kind you pay tax on.'

'You mean funny money? Drugs money, stolen money?'

Fernandez's smile broadened. He seemed positively benign. 'You have too much imagination, my friend. Let me tell you about businessmen. What we have here is a property dealer, two poker hustlers, an accountant (how'd you fancy him looking after your affairs?), a military gentleman who buys arms for the Gulf States, another gentleman who calls himself an international currency dealer, two Arab millionaires and a freelance heavy (retired), now doing very nicely as a bookie. These guys, they need a few bucks, they spend half an hour on the telephone and make more money than you see in a year. That's just money out there, Joe. Real money. Who needs funny money?'

His voice was low, in deference to the players. Behind our backs, three other games were in progress, smaller but no less intent.

A loud voice said, 'Goddamn.'

I turned. Fat Jack, round as an apple, sad-faced and sweating, was on his feet, staring disbelievingly at the cards exposed on the blue baize. There were no chips in front of him.

Pete the Pump pulled the chips towards him and said, 'Bad beat.' Full of sympathy, softening the blow.

'Aces have killed more Jews than Hitler,' said Fat Jack and walked out of the room.

Pete the Pump winked at me.

It was good to be back. Despite the blunt faces, the unaired bodies slumped in their chairs, there was something formal and solemn about the game, the concentration, the money casually changing hands, the ritual that flourished on a handful of words: check, bet, raise, fold. It was two years since I had played but I could feel the excitement starting up again. Behind the silence was a faint persistent susurration, a continual fast clicking noise, rising and falling, sometimes loud, sometimes murmuring, like the song of the cicadas in the Mediterranean summer. It was the sound of the gamblers playing with their chips, running them through their fingers, separating them into two columns, then squeezing them upwards and inwards so that the columns ran together like water.

Action. A world apart from my daily middle-class habits. Before Fernandez and Hector, gambling was as close as I had come to crime: dubious company, easy money, excitement, chance. A world of random events and immediate results: money won, money lost. I hadn't known how much I'd missed it.'

At the high-stakes low-ball game the man with the surly mouth and the Arab were still head-to-head across a huge pile of chips. The man with the surly mouth studied the Arab's cards and ran a column of white chips through his fingers. Then he pushed them into the centre fretfully, as though bored.

'Raise twelve,' he said.

'He's got him,' Fernandez murmured. 'That guy, he'd bet his life but not his money.'

The Arab peered at the other man's exposed cards, then picked up his own hole cards and showed them to his neighbour. He counted the chips left in front of him, shrugged and tossed in twelve whites. 'Beat seven five?' he said.

'Sixty four,' said the surly man and flicked over his cards.

The dealer pushed the chips across the table to him.

'Twenty-five grand,' said Fernandez. 'Nice and easy. That's how to make it.'

The Arab fished in his pocket, pulled out four packets of bank notes sealed in plastic and waved them at the cardroom manager. 'Chips,' he called.

We crossed into the casino and stood at the bar watching the crowds around the roulette tables, the blackjack players, the high-rollers in the baccarat game. Men in dark suits, women wearing serious jewellery.

Fernandez was smiling and at home, full of charm and good fellowship. He knew everybody by name: barmen, waiters, croupiers, the sombre gentlemen who ran things. His natural habitat.

He sipped mineral water, nibbled an olive.

'I can see how Tommy could have got himself into trouble,' I said. 'That low-ball game is huge.'

'If he was in trouble, he should have come to me. What are friends for?'

'He liked doing favours, not asking them. Everybody's Santa Claus.'

'That's not how the world works, pal. He should have known better.' Bored, unforgiving, making no allowances.

To change the subject, I said, 'It'd be great to play poker again. But I gave it up. Cold turkey.'

'Pressure from your lovely wife?'

I shook my head. 'A terrible run of cards. I couldn't afford it.'

We stood side by side at the bar, facing the casino. He was watching me stealthily out of the corners of his eyes. 'So what's to stop you now?'

'That kind of money? You must be joking.'

He sipped his Perrier, surveying the scene, taking his time. 'That's not what I hear. Word is, Santa Claus came through. You're in the money.'

I looked at him admiringly. 'How come you know my business?'

'I keep abreast. It's my business, too. Tommy and I were partners.'

'I thought his deals were below the level of your attention.'

'He'd come up in the world. He was going places, was Tommy.'

'I'm no Tommy.'

'You never know till you've tried.'

'Are you telling me something?'

He shrugged. 'We might be able to help each other. I was thinking of a business arrangement. Mutually convenient, mutually profitable.'

'I take photographs. What do I know about business?'

'That's not the point. Take a look at the board of directors of any large company. Lord Thisandthat, Sir Someoneorother-Something. What do you reckon they know?'

'You mean window-dressing?'

'That's what it's all about.'

A large soft man, dark-suited, joined us at the bar. He and Fernandez greeted each other, a four-handed handshake, full of mutual understanding.

'How's the little ball rolling for you, Benjy?' Fernandez said.

'How does it ever roll? You play roulette, you're in the hands of the gods.' American accent, a voice that seemed to start from somewhere low down, around his gently swelling belly. 'I'm losing my shirt as usual.'

'You've had your moments, as I remember.'

Benjy spread his hands despondently. 'What kind of cheap-jack operation is this, anyway? So they send a case of wine, a tin of caviar, to my hotel. Smuggle them in like they were contraband. The sums I'm losing, in Vegas they'd comp my air fare, my hotel, my girls. Fucking Brits, they got no class, Ray.'

'Don't take it personally, old friend. What they got is a Gaming Commission. Laws, rules. They pick up your tab, they lose their licence.'

'You of all people. Mr Comp himself.'

'That's how it is, Benjy. When in Rome you gotta shoot Roman candles.'

Benjy drank the whisky and water the barman had poured for him, stubbed out his cigarette and lit a fresh one. He seemed encased in gloom, like an extra layer of fat.

'Enough of London already,' he said. 'Why schlep here when I can get a better deal in Vegas or Atlantic City?'

'Don't be downhearted. Get back in there and beat the socks off them.'

'Their socks, my shirt. Whichever way you cut it, it's not a fair exchange. I'm thirteen gee to the bad, Joe. That's twenty-five big ones in real American money. And all I've had out of it is a case of fucking claret.'

Fernandez put an arm around the fat man's shoulders and squeezed him close, as though comforting an unhappy child. Benjy raised a hand in salute and wandered back towards the roulette tables.

'He's a casino operator's dream,' Fernandez said. 'A loser who doesn't know when to stop.'

'What did he mean by Mr Comp?'

'I worked in Vegas a while. A long time ago.'

'Tell me what you do now.'

'You know what I do. I'm a businessman. I'm in the world, Joe, the world of commerce. I run companies, buy and sell things. I handle delicate money and analyse the risks. Action, Joe. Just like our friend Benjy, just like the guys in the poker room. It's what makes the world go round.'

'So how could I possibly help you?'

'I like you.' Fernandez showed his perfect teeth. His dark sharp eyes were full of understanding. 'Tommy knew what he was doing when he left it all to you. You're smart, you're easy to get on with, you're clean. All you gotta do is be yourself.'

'I'm an ignoramus. What do I know about finance?'

'That's for me to worry about.'

A young woman sat at the nearest roulette table, her face lit by the overhead lamps, her soft body in shadow. Rich colouring, heavy eyes, delicate sleepy mouth. But bright with excitement, watching the smooth spin of the wheel, the little ball bouncing, hesitating, before it settled. A man stood behind her, his hand possessively on her shoulder. Two erotic presences cut off from the rest of the players, twinned, as though naked. The man in shadow, the girl with the lit face, the wheel spinning hypnotically. Pure sensuality, prolonged, out of time.

'Dix-huit, rouge,' said the croupier.

The girl reached up and gripped the hand that gripped her shoulder. She rubbed her smooth head against the man's shirt front. Both of them kept their eyes fixed on the roulette wheel.

'It's a challenge,' said Fernandez. 'A new start. You want to spend the rest of your life photographing tits and asses? With all due respect.'

'It's a worthy profession. I make a living of sorts.'

'That's what I mean. I'm talking money, Joe. More than you need, more than you can possibly spend. And all the businessman's perks: a company car, an expense account, good hotels when you travel, all the girls you can eat. Think about it.'

'I'm a man of simple tastes. What would I do with all that?'

'Enjoy. What else?'

'What's in it for you?'

'A profitable future. A partnership.'

'You've already got a profitable future.'

Fernandez finished his Perrier and set the glass carefully on the bar. The subdued babble of the casino pulsed louder for a moment, as though everyone had suddenly got lucky. Fernandez's expression was thoughtful. He brushed the air between us with his fingertips.

'I'll tell you what's in it for me,' he said. 'Peace of mind. I want to make amends to Tommy.'

As I left the casino, I saw Hungarian Mike standing at the entrance to the poker room.

'How's it going?' I said.

'Don't ask.' He leaned against the doorway. His long lined face was ashen with fatigue. 'Been up and down like a whore's skirt all night.' He closed his eyes. 'But a wheel just fell off.'

'Sorry to hear it.'

Hungarian Mike glanced in the direction of Fernandez who was standing at the bar chatting to one of the floor managers. 'Friend of yours?' he asked casually.

I shook my head. 'Tommy's. We were just having a chat.'

'I'm not curious.'

'Of course you're not.'

'I mean, why should I want to know?' His fatigue dropped, he seemed suddenly animated. 'He's not going to lend me any money, is he? And I might get my legs broken.'

'It wasn't that kind of conversation.'

He waved me away. 'Don't even tell me,' he said.

JUDY never ceases to surprise me. When I told her about Fernandez's offer I expected her to make for the high moral ground. Instead, she seemed pleased, relieved, as if a knot had been broken and she was free again. She propped herself on one elbow and smiled down at me.

'If you can't beat them, you might as well join them.'

Most of our conversations take place in bed. When we are vertical, with our clothes on, there always seems to be some duty to be performed: telephone calls to make, flowers to be watered, something to be mended or cooked or washed. We do our real talking in bed, which seems only right since that is where marriage begins and ends.

The watchers outside the house had gone but we kept the radio playing and talked in low voices out of habit.

'You don't object, then?'

'I don't see how I can.'

I studied the face that leaned over me. The faint flush of what I took to be relief, soft eyes, good smile. Seen from below, her features seemed to be weighted down with feeling, with meaning. Perhaps it had something to do with gravity.

'I thought I was going to get a lecture about drugs and gangsters and Tommy's shady dealings.'

'Too late for lectures, darling. It's a horrible mess but you're in it, I'm in it. We're Tommy's beneficiaries. All we can do is make the best of it.'

'I don't know why Fernandez wants me.'

'He has his reasons. You can be sure of that. No free lunches with him.'

'Be myself, he said. It seems a small enough charge.'

'That's the whole point.' Her face, leaning over me, was solemn. When I touched her breast she took hold of my hand and held it gently. 'If you do it, do it for yourself, for us. Don't be anybody's gofer.'

I turned on my side and propped myself up on my elbow, facing her. Like two figures on an Etruscan tomb. Monuments to sweet reason and conjugal equanimity.

'Time was we were so close you couldn't get a razor blade between us,' she said. 'Now there's something on your mind you're not telling me about. Secrets. Something to do with Tommy or Tunis or maybe with that American girl. God knows.'

'And you had a dirty weekend in Torquay.'

'That's what I mean. Our past is catching up on us. Trivial things suddenly seem important. Secrets, darling. Cocaine, police, people like Fernandez.'

'My problem is, I quite like him.'

'As long as you don't trust him. He's a killer.'

'Woman's instinct?'

'Trust me. I've always had a nose for psychopaths.'

I moved my hand back to where it had been. 'You have the nicest breasts.'

'That's not what we were talking about.'

'Stonehouse doesn't bother me,' I said. 'He's a bully and he's devious but I know his type. I'm a professional man, sweetheart. I've got a university degree. I went to art school, post-graduate, and studied photography. I read books. I'm good at my job. But when I'm with Fernandez I don't know a thing.'

She stroked my hand that was stroking her. Her serious expression did not relent. 'It's not a question of education, Joe. What's he ever read except company accounts and airport thrillers? But he's got all that mileage on him. He's been places you and I never dreamed of.'

'So how are we going to cope?'

'We stay together, we try to turn all this to our advantage. Just as long as we aren't other people's pawns.'

'And you have a plan?'

'Trust me.'

The radio playing, the corner light throwing shadows on the ceiling, the windows closed against the weather, the big house bolted against intruders, the ghosts of my childhood patrolling the empty rooms. The subtle, rousing smell of Judy's skin. The two of us face to face like we were before these strangers entered our lives.

'Lie back,' she said. 'Keep still. I've got an idea.'

She never ceases to surprise me.

JUDY

Joe is the one who is being seduced, not me. I can see him falling for Fernandez like he fell for Tommy. Me, I'm just trying to cover our backs. His and mine. Operation SOB, which also stands for Save Our Bacon.

First, it's flowers. Every day another cornucopia. After the long winter, the endless rain, the colours and scents make me dizzy. I know all he is doing is lifting the telephone, calling Harrods, but I have a picture of him armed with secateurs, ransacking hothouses, his head ticking like a bomb, his cock stirring obscurely as he handles the tender blooms.

Colour, sweetness, intrigue. Secretiveness excites the senses, reaching far back, like the smell of exotic flowers. Fever, dampness, the juices flowing.

He waits a week, then invites me to lunch at a Knightsbridge hotel. The decor is like the livery of a British Airways jet, grey and blue and silver, with a clientele to match: grey-suited, silver-haired. In my blue Louis Feraud dress I feel part of the ambient sleekness. He calls the maitre d'hotel and the waiters by their first names. They smile and bow, looking me up and down slyly, making comparisons. We linger over the skimpy nouvelle cuisine, making small talk. He tells me he misses the Arizona climate: the dry heat, strong sun, cool nights. I tell him London feels like the tropics after Aberdeen. He asks about my work and discusses a logo for his company. When I sketch out a couple of suggestions he broods over them, pretending this is a major decision, then asks if he can keep the envelope. He slips it into his wallet as though he were pocketing a billet-doux.

I wait until the coffee arrives, then say casually, 'I'm worried about Joe.'

'A fine man. Upright, sympathetic. A rare combination.' At least he has the courtesy to smile ironically.

'Leave him be. He's out of his depth.'

'That's not the impression I have. He seems like a man enjoying his luck. God knows, he's waited long enough for it.'

Again the smile, this time understanding, full of sympathy and concern. He uses his smile like an instrument, something sophisticated, electronic, miniaturised, that he can switch on and off as he needs it. Perhaps he can even smile with it.

We sit side by side on a banquette. His hand is next to mine on the table. The veins and tendons on its back are shadowed by black hairs. He has strong fingers, large and manicured. I can see his expensive watch with its diamond numerals.

'It's Hector I mean. He scares me witless. I don't want Joe mixed up with people like him.'

'What about people like me?'

'You're in charge. You call the shots. Don't let Joe get sucked in.'

'Sucked into what? I'm a businessman, Judy. Nothing threatening about that. You can check out my credentials at Company House.'

'Don't play games. You know what I mean.'

'You talk about him like he's your child.'

A waiter arrives with fresh coffee.

'Armagnac?' Fernandez asks. 'To help digest the lunch.'

I shake my head. 'I'd just sleep all through the afternoon.'

He puts his hairy hand over mine. 'I can't think of anything nicer.'

I leave my hand where it is and say, 'We were talking about Joe.'

He leans towards me, his face so close I can smell his rich breath. 'I'd like to lick every inch of your body,' he murmurs.

I feel myself blushing. My knees, my insides, are like water. 'I don't do that.' I shake my head. 'Not any more. I'm married.'

'Starting at the toes, working up slowly.'

'I don't do that sort of thing. Please.'

'I want to taste your mouth, your navel, your armpits.'

I can feel the heat of his body, the blind will power, through the protective layers of clothing between us. I take my hand away and shift along the banquette. I am still blushing when the waiter arrives with a balloon glass. A woman laughs at the next table, a high-pitched sound that registers neither amusement nor pleasure. The plate glass windows at the end of the room open on to a square with a dry fountain and six bereft lime trees. I count them twice. Six lime trees.

It was the best moment we had. There were plenty of afternoons later but none of them matched that lunch for excitement. The dry hand on mine, the expensive watch, the stealthy voice reminding me of what I had been missing in twelve years of comfortable marriage. Joe has a wiry, athlete's body and we have a great time in bed, free-wheeling and inventive. But all legal and above board, whenever we feel like it, without plotting, without guilt.

Sex without subtext. Illicitness adds another dimension entirely. Secrets, plots, intrigue are erotic in themselves. And Fernandez, too, was an illegal presence. Self-contained like a snake, full of carefully held-in violence. It would be like embracing a more dangerous order of creation.

I sit at the end of the banquette, sipping my coffee, letting my fantasies spin. I am giving him my answer, but nicely, as though this were some private joke we could share.

'I'll tell you something,' I say. 'Secrets are sexy. God knows why I had to wait till now to find that out.'

He does his smile, worldly-wise this time, the smile of a man who has been around. He takes my hand briefly. 'You don't know half.'

Outside, while the commissionaire holds open the taxi door, we exchange a social farewell kiss, slightly prolonged in mutual recognition. An hour after I get back to the studio, a taxi arrives with another basket of flowers.

After that, the flowers keep coming. No cards, no messages, just armfuls of colour and sweetness.

The next time he phones he says, 'I want to make your life beautiful.'

'The place looks like it's been painted by Douanier Rousseau.'

'I guess I should know about Duane Russo but I don't. I got other things on my mind. Like you, for instance.'

'Forget about me. I don't do that sort of thing. As I told you last time.'

'At least have lunch with me. That sort of thing I know you do.'

We meet at the same hotel restaurant and this time after lunch I discover, yes, of course, he has reserved a suite upstairs. More flowers, a bottle of champagne in an ice-bucket, a bed as big as a football field. Which is just as well.

'I make you happy.' It is more a statement than a question. We are both running with sweat but the gleam on his face is a gleam of self-satisfaction. He wears a gold chain around his neck, a gold Scorpio pendant nestling in his chest hair. He has a body like a barrel and what surprises me about it is not the hairiness but the tan. Deep and crisp and even, like the Christmas carol.

I put a hand on his thigh and say, 'Terrific.' Male vanity never ceases to astonish me. But what am I supposed to say: 'You're not a patch on Joe'? Keep Joe out of it. I'd like to persuade myself that Joe is the reason I'm here but who am I supposed to be fooling?

He runs his fingers lightly down my arm, from shoulder to elbow. 'Skin like silk,' he says.

He sees himself as a lady's man, a romantic lover. Perhaps it's one of the perks that comes to you when you hit the big time in his world.

I stroke his thigh. 'Terrific,' I repeat. 'But what I want to know is, how do you keep so tanned?'

'Never heard of health clubs, Judy? Also, I travel. Once in a while, I even get to go home to Arizona.'

He sounds lazy, we both sound lazy, trying not to be bored, trying to keep up the interest now we've finished.

We have an understanding, that much is agreed. What I'd really like is a promise, an assurance. I want him to say, 'Sure I'll look after Joe, keep him safe, keep his hands clean. We have a deal. Don't even think about it.'

I touch his cheek and glance at the wristwatch I haven't taken off. His five o'clock shadow is there at four.

'I've got to go.'

I tell myself, all I'm doing is covering our backs. Joe's and mine. But I feel terrific.

JOE

The next time I drove past the Kilburn lock-up I looked for the blue Bedford van and couldn't find it. I parked outside the garage, car window open, music playing. A bright windless day, almost warm. There was no sign of the leaves, the scraps of newspaper and clouded plastic that had drifted against the garage door.

A gang of boys was skateboarding down the hill. They side-slipped round the corner at the bottom, jumped the kerb, pirouetted. Drumming wheels, excited shouts, jeers, laughter. Then they trudged back up the hill to repeat the performance. Someone was hosing the winter grime off his car. Someone else was clipping a privet hedge. The long hibernation was ending.

I studied the scene in my rear-view mirror. A battered red Ford Fiesta double-parked outside one of the terraced houses and a young couple began unloading their week's shopping. The woman, bending a little with the effort, carried four Sainsbury's bags indoors. She wore a chiffon scarf over her head to cover her hair curlers. The man dumped two more plastic bags on top of a cardboard box and heaved them sullenly out of the car. When the woman came out of the house she shouted at him, 'The boxes are full of breakables. Don't just pile things on them. How many times do I have to tell you, for Christ's sake?'

'Fuck you,' said the man. He wore jeans and a baggy sweater. He needed a shave.

Two crying children watched them from the doorstep.

Saturday morning.

I climbed out of the car and looked up and down the street. Nobody took any notice of me. Casually, I unlocked the garage door. Casually, I swung it up and over.

The packing case had gone.

I felt outraged. Judy and I had found it, brought it to London, stowed it safely away. Then we had informed the interested parties. Responsible citizens, doing our duty, keeping our side of the bargain. Stonehouse had been impressed, Fernandez had thanked me. Then both of them seemed to lose interest. I remembered Stonehouse's bored voice on the telephone talking about messenger boys, the anonymous envelope containing the garage keys wrapped in a tissue that had been slipped through our letter-box the morning after our meeting with Fernandez. The game had moved on elsewhere, and no one had bothered to tell us.

The skateboarders came thundering down the hill again. One of them did a slide turn and came to a halt in front of the garage. He paused, arms spread, holding his balance, the front of the skateboard lifted in the air like a drawbridge. He looked at the Sony boxes, then at me. A crafty, urchin's stare.

'You giving them tellies away, mister?'

I banged down the garage door and fastened the heavy padlock. Not that it would do any good.

As I drove home, outrage gave way to something more nebulous, more plangent. I felt disappointed, left out. It was as if the purpose had gone out of my life along with all the newcomers. Policemen, civil servants, businessmen, gangsters. The whole freakshow seemed to be waving farewell. The game's changed and we've gone on without you, they were saying.

I was going to miss them. Stonehouse and Rogers with their hints and threats: handling drugs and stolen property, aiding and abetting, pornography; the implication was they could set me up at the Old Bailey as an accessory and I would go down for years; could but wouldn't, because they needed me. Fernandez with his profound know-how, silky violence and seducer's charm. Helen with her youth, Aunt Rosie with her ramrod back and walking stick. The components of an interesting life. Better than fashion photography.

There was a parking space in front of our house. As I backed into it, I glanced into the rear-view mirror. A red Ford Fiesta was turning into Glenloch Road.

Maybe I was still a player, after all.

WHEN I phoned Stonehouse he told me to meet him at an address off Hill Street. A mews house with window-boxes and chintzy curtains. The young woman who opened the door looked like both my ex-wives rolled into one: an English rose with burgeoning hips, candid blue eyes, set jaw, a don't-let's-be-sentimental-darling manner. What Stonehouse's mob would call 'good breeding stock'. I followed her domineering backside up the steep stairs.

The drawing-room had sporting prints on the walls, floral covers over the armchairs and sofa, silver candlesticks and a carriage clock on the mantelpiece, a small Regency table with a bowl of flowers on it and assorted trinkets.

'This is Langton Green,' said Stonehouse.

Langton wore a blue blazer, a button-down collar, loafers with tassels on them. He was large and long-limbed and his handshake was like iron. A whisky face, cross-hatched, thick-nosed, but with an athlete's ruddy glow to it. The kind of man who covers miles on the tennis court. Unstoppable.

'Ollie's told me about you,' he said. The accent was mid-western, gritty and unreconstructed. Unlike his appearance. 'You've done great things.'

'The packing case has gone,' I said.

'Nothing to worry your head about,' said Stonehouse.

He flopped into one of the deep armchairs, Langton into the other. I settled uneasily on the sofa. The English rose came in with a tray. Silver coffee pot, silver milk jug, bone china cups and saucers.

'You do yourself proud,' I said.

'Family stuff.' Stonehouse flapped an arm airily. 'Got to keep up appearances.'

'Why didn't you tell me it had gone?'

'What you don't know can't hurt you.'

'Who's got it? Fernandez or you?'

'It doesn't matter. It's not the point any more.'

'It matters to me. I'm pig in the middle. If Fernandez took the stuff, that's fine. It's your problem. But if you got bored and moved in, I'm in deep shit.'

'You worry too much.'

'Easy for you to say. You don't have to deal with Fernandez on a day-to-day basis.'

Stonehouse hooked an arm between his legs and scratched an inner thigh. A sign that he was interested. He cocked his head, showed me his lined face, his cold pouchy eyes. 'Day-to-day?'

'He's made me an offer. A business proposition. Him and me in lock-step, marching towards a profitable future. He wants me to take over where Tommy left off.'

Stonehouse flapped his free hand, tried a crinkly smile. 'He's not serious, of course.'

'Never more so. Solemn's the word. The riches of the world can be mine. Plus an expense account and a company car. I felt like Jesus on the mountain top.'

'I like it,' said the American. He was sunk in his chair, legs crossed comfortably, one tasselled foot beating time to some inner rhythm.

'I'm glad you see the joke,' said Stonehouse.

'No joke. Our friend here has potential. We know it, now they know it.'

Stonehouse smiled again, a real smile this time, as though the penny had dropped. 'It might work, at that.' He nodded complacently.

'Don't mind me,' I said. 'I'm only here for the coffee.'

Stonehouse eyed me critically. 'It's not what I imagined,' he said. 'But if they want him, they want him.'

'Forget tough guys,' said the American. 'Hectors are two a penny. The world has moved on since the old days.'

I looked from one to the other and wondered what I was doing there. Nodding heads, knowing smiles. The cosy English room with its expensive silver and neutral taste. A county family's *pied à terre*, somewhere to put their feet up and sip gin and tonic after a hard day at Harrods and Fortnum and Mason. They were leading me on, waiting for me to respond. I drank my coffee and said nothing. The jug was Georgian, the coffee instant.

'Time was,' Langton's eyes were colourless and watery, 'when the Mob ran Vegas, you'd find the strangest people in the strangest places. Tony Spilotro, remember him?'

Stonehouse nodded contentedly. 'From Chicago.'

'Number Four on the totem pole. He worked for Milwaukee Phil Alderisio, who worked for Joe Aiuppa, who worked for Tony Accardo. An old-time hoodlum, Spilotro, a widow-maker. Guess what? He ran the gift shop at the Stardust. So what's he doing with embroidered jackets and personalised coffee mugs? The guy who ran the gambling operations, chairman of the executive committee, was Lefty Rosenthal, ex-baccarat dealer and small-time bookie for the boys. But the guy at the top, Allen Glick, the chairman of the board, he was a nerd from nowhere, clean as a hound's tooth. His job was to putz around, run the hotel, play the big shot and keep his back turned while they skimmed the take.'

He licked his lips, leaning back in his enveloping chair, enjoying himself. His foot tapped like a metronome.

'Times change,' said Stonehouse.

'Damn right they do. That's why we have a Gaming Board, state investigations, federal probes. These days the casinos are owned by multi-nationals and run by little men in grey suits.'

'Like Glick?'

'Nothing so colourful. Accountants, company men, guys with computers. Glick was something else. He wore sports shirts and tartan pants, drove a Mercedes, lived out the Californian dream.

The big house, the fifty-metre pool, the company jet, the razor-wire on the fences round the grounds.'

On cue, as though this were an act they had rehearsed, Stonehouse asked, 'Where did they find him?'

The American spread his hands wide. 'That's the mystery. I talked to a lawyer once. He told me he had this dream. They study the high school year books and they pick out a hundred guys who look smart and clean, like Allen. Then they watch them through college or law school and they narrow it down to ten, then to two. Finally, they pick one guy and they tell him, "You're it. We're gonna set you up in business. You get a nice cut, you leave the rest to us." Just a theory, right, a daydream, but it makes a kinda creepy sense.'

'You're trying to tell me something,' I said. 'Why the parables?'

'Guys like Glick are redundant, is all. These days the big boys don't rate the rough stuff. They leave it to the blacks, the Puerto Ricans, the South Americans. The founding fathers have gone legit. They're all company men. What they're looking for is respectability.'

The windows were double-glazed, shutting out traffic sounds, footsteps, London coming and going, the great swarming mass. The only sound was the clock on the mantelpiece, quietly ticking. I listened for the English rose but heard nothing. I pictured her perched on a high stool in the kitchen, headphones clamped around her helmet of blonde hair, watching the spools turn as they recorded our conversation.

Stonehouse reluctantly withdrew his hand from between his thighs, took out his pipe, his leather tobacco pouch, his lighter with the angled flame. 'What you lack is perspective,' he said. 'Langton here is trying to fill you in. The general outline, the broad sweep.'

'Here's the gist of it.' The American picked up a black attaché case that stood by his chair, opened the hinged top, sorted through some papers and withdrew two closely typed sheets. 'Fact is, you're tailor-made, Joe. An upper-class boy, college educated, a career of a kind in what these days is considered a respectable profession. But come down in the world, right? Grandpappy was rich but pa died broke.' He glanced at the sheet of paper. 'The estate paid eight pence in the pound. Correct me if I'm wrong. And you were left holding the baby. Expensive tastes and no real money. A hard hand to play. But happily married. Wife with a career of her own. A lawyer's daughter. Just what the doctor ordered.'

He stared at me, his eyes misty with understanding. I stared back and did not answer.

'And just the right touch of sleaze.' When he smiled his raddled cheeks seemed to shatter. 'Questionable deals with your pal Tommy, club poker with professional gamblers. It's a perfect profile. You've got a taste for the underlife, Joe. It kinda turns you on, right?'

'What makes you think you know so much about me?'

A wide gesture with the hands, the bluff eyes twinkling with sympathy. 'You think I could do this kinda work if I hadn't been there myself? I share these feelings you have. It's an interesting world out there.'

Stonehouse puffed his pipe and said, 'No criticism implied, dear boy. The simple fact is, you could help us more than you know. With very little effort. Join the club is all we ask.'

'Go along with Fernandez,' said Langton. 'Do what he wants. And maybe make yourself a lotta money on the side. It's a good deal whichever way you cut it.'

I got up from the sofa and walked over to the window. Down in the mews a chauffeur was polishing the bonnet of a Rolls-Royce. A steady spiralling movement, over and over. Fourteen layers of paint, a deep rich sheen, gleaming in the pale sunlight. A postman passed on his midday round. The chauffeur looked up and said something but I couldn't hear the words through the double-glazing. They both laughed.

'You want me to put my head in the noose for you,' I said.

'Routine stuff,' said Langton. 'Nothing to it.'

I wandered round the room, picking up the scattered knick-knacks, peering at them, putting them down. I assumed the microphone would be hidden somewhere I would never find it.

'Do I have a choice?' I asked.

Stonehouse said, 'We're all friends here.'

I paused in front of the empty fireplace, looking down at him. 'That's not the impression I got from our earlier meetings. The way I construed it was there are all sorts of charges you could bring: drugs, pornography, handling stolen property. A whole bookful. As our friend here says, correct me if I'm wrong.'

Stonehouse squirmed in his deep chair, sniffed the back of his hand and looked away. 'I may have exaggerated for effect.'

'That's not the point. The point is, now you're asking me to cosy up to a known criminal.'

'I wouldn't put it in quite those terms.'

'What terms would you put it in if things go wrong and I'm left holding the can? I can see myself set up at the Old Bailey, facing ten years in the Scrubs, with you and Rogers and a hanging judge on the other side.'

Stonehouse put his hand between his thighs and tried to tie himself into a knot. His body seemed made of a more pliable material than the rest of us mere mortals. Space technology, minimum weight, maximum flexibility. He blushed like a schoolgirl but when he glanced at me – on and off, a flicker of light – his cricketer's eyes registered distaste. Don't push your luck, they said.

He said, 'That's not how things are arranged, dear boy.'

'I need assurances. Cut and dried. Preferably in writing.'

The American had been watching me, amused and benevolent. He turned his florid face to Stonehouse. His eyelids drooped. 'I don't see we have a problem here.'

'Quite,' said Stonehouse. 'Absolutely.'

'You drop the charges,' I said. 'You get off my back.'

'Dear boy. It's all been a terrible misunderstanding. I'm devastated.'

I braced my shoulders against the mantelpiece, enjoying my moment of power. 'There's another thing,' I said.

Stonehouse's eyes narrowed but he went on smiling. 'You have only to name it.'

'Tommy's lawyer says the police are opposing probate.'

'That's Rogers. Never knows when to stop. I'll talk to him.'

'I can't live with all these loose ends. I've got a tidy mind. Mess confuses me. It's only natural.'

'I'm truly sorry.' Stonehouse unwound himself. He leaned forward in the chintz-covered armchair, all earnestness and good will. 'I'll clear it up straight away. Rogers will do what he's told. Never fear.'

'A clean slate. A new beginning.'

'Anything you want,' said Stonehouse.

THE Jaguar crawled east along Commercial Road surrounded by buses, delivery vans, long-distance lorries bound for Dover. The sun shone but the air was grey with diesel exhaust. Riley tapped his fingers on the steering wheel and exhaled irritably, humming some tune I couldn't catch. Hector lounged beside him, profile tilted, smiling at his own slow thoughts.

I sat in the back with Danny, trying to remember the dream that had woken me that morning.

A woman, but no one I knew. Oval face, smooth as a pebble, without a line or a sag or a weakness. Clear blue eyes, the mouth quiet and closed. The face was beautiful but ominous. It hung in the air, bodiless, isolated, picked out by light. I could no longer remember where she came from or what she was doing in my dream. All I knew for sure was she signified harm, she had unlimited powers of evil. I woke feeling someone had put a hex on me.

Dark bearded faces on the streets, women wearing saris under their overcoats, crumbling cinemas advertising Indian films. I studied Hector's profile. His mouth was sulky and downturned, the upper lip slightly overhanging the lower, the chin small and neat, pebble eyes, sleepy lids. A slightly womanish profile, the petulant girl who would turn nasty if crossed.

'Look at the colours. It's the fucking tropics out there.' Danny sprawled comfortably in the back seat, leather jacket unzipped in the car's purring heat. 'No after-hours drinking clubs in Whitechapel and precious few betting shops. Your Pakis are like your Jews, family people. They keep to themselves, they don't like outsiders, they work unsocial hours to turn a penny.'

I studied his pock-marked face, ready to take offence. 'I'm a Jew,' I said. 'Not paid-up, not practising. An atheist when it comes down to it. But once a Jew always a Jew.'

'A lovely people, always admired them.' He smiled, not missing a beat. 'I suppose it's because I'm a family man at heart. Not married as yet but it's what I aspire to.'

His smile was unexpected, wide and slow and warm, quite different from Hector's photogenic grimace.

'You don't have to tell me about lapsed,' he said. 'Myself, I was raised by the Jesuits. You know how it is: theirs for life. I still feel a twinge, even now. A hankering after spiritual values. Mental discipline, the purification of the body. That sort of thing.'

'This isn't the kind of conversation I expected to have, in the circumstances.'

'I've always had a philosophical turn of mind,' said Danny. 'You have to take the opportunities when they come.'

Riley stopped the car outside a laundromat and left the engine running while Hector and Danny went inside. I watched them through the plate glass walking slowly past the white machines, the wire baskets of folded sheets, the harassed young women with toddlers. Old ladies in out of the cold stared mesmerised at the clothes turning, the suds sloshing, in the recessed windows of the machines. Soap opera. An Indian in jeans and cardigan waited gloomily at the back. They talked to him for a couple of minutes, standing either side of him, so close their shoulders almost touched his. Then they all turned and went through a door marked 'Private' in cut-out plastic letters. Hector was carrying a black leather case that opened at the top, the kind commercial travellers use. When they got back into the car he placed it carefully at his feet. As we drove off, Danny leaned forwards and gave the Indian a friendly wave. The Indian stared at him woodenly.

They repeated the performance several times: at laundromats, video shops, corner groceries and newsagents.

'Small change,' said Danny. 'You own properties, you have to collect the rent.' He settled himself into his extravagant leather jacket, like a bat preparing for sleep.

'I don't know why I'm tagging along.'

'Maybe Mr Fernandez thought you should see the assets.'

'I'm not impressed.'

'This is just a company within a company. Add them all together it comes to something.'

I watched the street names, trying to make a connection. When I was in my teens my father decided he was interested in the family history and went down to the Public Records Office to see what he could find. What he found was a young man called Tucker who looked like a rabbinical student, thin and dark and hungry, but was in fact a genealogical researcher who knew what to look for, where to look for it and, unlike my father, could read Hebrew. Tucker went to Bevis Marks and searched the records, he checked the census returns and ploughed through the Miscellanea volumes of the Jewish Historical Society of England. He went to Somerset House and came back with copies of ancient birth certificates, marriage certificates, death certificates which set out in meticulous copperplate the addresses and occupations of remote ancestors. General dealers, tailors, pen and quill cutters who lived in places called Fleur de Lis Court, Three Tun Alley, Gravel Lane, Mulberry Court, men with illiterate wives who made their marks on the marriage certificates. The first wave of English Jews, Spain to Amsterdam, Amsterdam to London, Whitechapel to Deptford, Deptford to Bloomsbury and Regent's Park. Then the next flood, fleeing the pogroms of Eastern Europe. Now the Indians, Pakistanis, Bengalis. The great slow-moving river of London. All those races churned together, all those lives.

The Constantines' link with the past was a decrepit factory in Stoney Lane, a rackety place where girls sat at sewing machines turning out the not quite smart enough dresses that were sold in the family shops. 'Exclusive lines,' they called them, probably because no one else would stock them. I was taken there once when I was very small. I remember a creaking ancient lift, the chattering girls who made a fuss of me and two disdainful teenage boys who trundled around the racks of dresses. The factory closed while I was still at school and after that the firm bought in their goods from other manufacturers, though even that didn't stop the slide into bankruptcy. Now I was back, touring the same streets in a chauffeur-driven Jaguar with two sharply dressed hoodlums. Try as I might, the place meant nothing.

Occasionally, I got out of the car and followed them inside. They had a rhythm going, a double act based on hints and nuances. No threats but the pervasive intimation of threat. No arguments, either. They simply leaned together, one on either side, bearing down, voices low and reasonable, stating the facts. Shoulder pressure, strategically shifting weight, soft voices making clear statements. We are reasonable people and we have an agreement. Nobody, in the end, gave them any arguments.

The tenants were resentful but subdued and surprisingly polite, as though feeling their way in this alien environment. Family groups behind the counters, husbands and wives, small children, unmarried uncles and aunts, posed between the shelves of cigarettes, sweets and chocolate bars and the racks of newspapers and magazines. Cherrywood pipes, boxes of throwaway lighters and pens gathered dust under the glass-fronted counters. There were packets of writing paper and envelopes, exercise books and comics, battered copying machines, freezers full of ice-cream and soft drinks. The shop windows were plastered with cards advertising old bicycles, washing machines, fold-away beds, rooms to let for professional ladies and gentlemen, babysitters, dog-walkers, masseurs, yoga-teachers. The wives wore bright saris and kept the books, the men shuffled around in corduroy carpet slippers. Profits counted in pennies, building slowly as coral.

Hector used his smile but only as a gambit. He'd flash it on as he went in, a shark's grin, promising mayhem, then he'd flash it on again, scenting blood, at the first hint of resistance. But Danny smiled as if he meant it, clapped the shop-owners on their shoulders, shook their hands warmly. 'Just business,' he seemed to be saying. 'Nothing personal. No hard feelings.' They smiled back gratefully and shook his hand but always handed the money to Hector. He nodded when he took it, made an entry in their rent books, another entry in a ledger he carried in his black case.

Back in the street, the schools were emptying. Dark-skinned boys in blue blazers and dark ties, girls with neat white blouses and grey skirts under their open coats. Danny studied them, his face serious and respectful. 'One thing's for certain,' he said, 'they're not staying long in these parts. Look at the little buggers with their satchels full of homework. Next stop the university, accountancy, the law. If the Irish had that sort of determination, with our gift of the gab, we'd be running the world, not digging ditches.'

Hector fingered the gold chain around his neck and looked at him sideways. A slit-eyed look.

He's not of our world, I thought, not when you come down to it. Danny recognised the schoolkids and their ambitions, the families squeezing a livelihood out of the little shops; he registered the carpet slippers and shiny trousers, the penny-pinching, the dogged effort. It struck a chord. I could talk to him. But Hector came from a place without mothers and fathers. He surveyed the scene and all he saw was so much meat. His animal reactions were strong. He smelled trouble, resistance, threat, where the likes of Danny and I noticed nothing more than, maybe, vague unease. But for him, the rest was just background blur, out of focus, below the level of his attention. Profile tilted against the brightness of the windscreen, petulant upper lip, receding chin, he was the thing itself with no antecedents.

'You got a wife and kids?' I asked him. 'Someone to go home to in the evenings?'

'Never got around to that stuff, man. The boss keeps me too busy. And I reckon there gotta be better ways of spending my money.'

'It's not all changing nappies and clipping coupons.'

'That's what they like to say. That's how they con you into it.'

Danny winked at me and said, 'You're missing out on the finer things, Hector old lad. What are you going to do for company in your old age?'

'I wasn't planning on having one.'

'That's me boy.' Danny was delighted. 'Ever the optimist.'

It was late afternoon when we got back to Long Acre. Danny and Hector went straight into Fernandez's room with the leather case, I lingered in the outer office with Helen. Both the monitors on her desk were switched on. One of them was filled with columns of names and figures. On the other, a woman, carrying a file in both hands, like an offering, was walking briskly down the corridor outside.

'Been getting the grand tour?' Helen asked. Her teeth, when she smiled, were small and even. The glow from the screens made her skin unnaturally pale.

'Not as grand as I expected.'

'Don't be taken in. That was just a facet. Not even. Just a corner of a single facet.'

The picture on the monitor switched itself automatically to the lift doors opening. Two beer-bellied men got out, talking animatedly. The cameras tracked them down the corridor to another office.

Helen had a pile of continuous stationery on the desk in front of her. She peered at it and tapped figures into the computer. The columns shifted and jumped, seemingly of their own accord.

Pale skin, pale hair. In Tunis, with the little oriental and the hairy youth, her whiteness had seemed startling, almost freakish. Here the flickering monitors washed her out, made her look exhausted.

'You been doing this all day? You look beat.'

'Somebody has to keep the figures coming. The boss has been having one of his long lunches.' She made a vague gesture with her hand and I caught her scent, faint and far off, a tremor in the air. She was watching me, as though expecting a response.

'I wouldn't have guessed you could work one of these things.'

'I just type the stuff. The wizard who juggles the figures is your friend Karl.'

'You mean the Kraut, the poet of the revolution?'

'Poetry doesn't pay the rent.'

'Find someone to mind the store and I'll buy you a long lunch any day.'

She typed more figures into the computer and the columns performed their silent dance. I watched her from the other side of the desk. When she turned the sheet of paper she was copying, she leaned slightly towards me and whispered, 'Just be careful in there.'

Hector and Danny came out of Fernandez's office, rolling their shoulders, lighting cigarettes, as if just dismissed from parade. 'He's all yours,' said Danny.

Fernandez, too, was slumped in front of a computer, deep in his encompassing chair. The desk lamp made a pool of light in the shadowy room.

'Everywhere I look in this office there are people tapping away at computers,' I said.

'You see me tapping, pal?' He waved me to his side of the desk. 'I don't even know how to type. Two-fingered, it takes me a working day to pick out my own name.'

When I leaned over his shoulder I smelled talc and cologne and soap. Maybe this was some American secret, to smell permanently as if you've just stepped out of the shower. Or was that what executives did after a long lunch? He made me aware of my own staleness.

There was a brightly coloured graph on the screen in front of him, little rectangles along its base, blue and red, marked with commands: Help, Tools, Send, Get Current Data, Show Report, Return.

'They got it figured out,' he said. 'The word is bosses hate computers and don't understand them. Also they think it's infra dig to punch a keyboard. So whatta we got? A computer any asshole can use and no keys to punch. Make yourself comfortable, Joe. You're an executive now, so take a look at the ultimate executive toy.'

I pulled up a chair and sat down beside him. The lights of London were at my back, stretching away to the orange glow on the horizon. There were five jagged lines on the graph, three ascending, two descending, all in different colours.

'This here is a problem we just solved with one of our subsidiaries,' he said. 'Do-it-yourself supermarkets, five of them, all near the M25. The graph shows two are losing money, so we want to find out why.' He touched one of the coloured rectangles at the bottom of the screen. The chart disappeared and the monitor filled with lists – paints, brushes, ladders, cement, wallpaper lined, wallpaper unlined – each followed by a string of figures. One of the figures was in red.

'Sweets,' he said. 'They're losing on candies. Now look.' He touched the screen again and another set of lists appeared. The figure in red was also for sweets. He touched the screen and said, 'Now we compare them with the other stores.' More lists came up, a dazzling sequence. In each, sweets were positive numbers. Fernandez was watching me sideways, grinning, pleased with himself.

'So we've isolated the problem: everyone is making good money out of candies, but these two stores are losing on them. At that point we send in a guy to find out what's going wrong. In this case, we already done the legwork and we know the answer. One schmuck had the candies stacked too high, above the sight level of the kids. The other, would you believe it, had them at the entrance instead of the checkout. So a guy goes in with his family on Saturday morning, and already he's feeling guilty about the brushes and screwdrivers and all the other junk he's going to buy and never use. At that point you think he's going to listen when the kids say they want a Mars bar? We got assholes managing stores that shouldn't be running hot dog stands.'

'Where does the information come from?'

'It gets keyed in straight from the electronic cash points. I can go on drilling down to find out which line of paint goes best, which brand of brushes. You name it, it's all here at a touch.'

'And no keyboard.'

'Forget keyboards. A touch screen is all you need. Next thing, they'll be voice-activated. You'll be able to choose how you want the questions asked: male or female, stressed or unstressed.' He did an accent. 'Good morning, Mr Fernandez. Which company are you interested in today?'

'I'll stick to Helen.'

Another sidelong look. 'You do that, Joe. That's one classy girl.'

'There's a computer on her desk. That mean she shares the company secrets?'

'No way. It's edited so that certain people have access to certain sections. I'm the only guy with an overview.'

'Edited, voice-activated, access. You've got all this lingo, Ray. How come a man like you is so deep into computers?'

'Information is life-blood, the new way of the world. Why do you think Gorbachev hammers on about glasnost? Because he wants to drag Russia into the late twentieth century is why. That means computerising the joint. And you can't have computers without openness because computers talk to each other, they exchange information.'

He swung his deep chair around and faced me. His apathy had dropped away, his face was bright and perspiring. 'I'm good with figures, that's how I got where I am. I could work out the sums, see the connections. That made me useful. These days computers do that stuff for you.'

'So why aren't you out of a job?'

'You gotta know the right questions to ask, the places to look, the connections. In the old days, you had a problem you asked middle management. "We'll look into it," they'd say. "We'll get back to you." It took them two days, then they lied to you, gave you the runaround, because they were protecting their own asses, their special areas of power. When computers arrived, everyone asked, What'll happen to all the secretaries, the bookkeepers? Now we know. The lower grades are doing fine; it's middle management that's out of a job.'

'Do I get to play with your toy?'

'Karl could teach you.'

'The poet.'

'He's smarter than he looks.'

'And he has access?'

'Nobody has total access except me. He could teach you the rudiments.'

'I don't think I could handle the responsibility.'

'It's just business, Joe. A boxful of companies. Profit and loss. Nothing secret. The pieces mean what they say they mean.'

'But only you know them all.'

'The overview is something else. It's useful to our competitors, it influences the price of the shares.'

'Did Tommy have an overview?'

'Tommy was a business associate, not a partner. You worry too much about Tommy.'

'He was a friend.'

'My friend too. You reach a certain age, these things begin to happen all the time. Friends die. Age, Joe. Nothing to be said in its favour.'

I eased back in my chair and looked out of the window. Night was beginning to settle over the town, a great field of lights, glimmering like flowers. Judy would be home by now, puttering around the kitchen, sipping a drink, wondering where I'd got to. Checking out Greensward Properties, darling, a subdivision of Landfall Enterprises. It didn't feel like a day fretting over lighting and camera angles. It didn't feel like work. If I asked her what sort of a day she'd had, she'd shrug and say, 'The usual.'

'I drove around all day, watching Batman and Robin do their thing. Is that all there is to the executive life?'

'Just easing you in,' said Fernandez. 'Showing you some of the bits and pieces.'

'It's not what I imagined. And there are things I could do without.'

'What things?'

'Hector, for example.'

'He's a good boy.'

'He's got a nice smile. But you ever looked at his eyes, Ray? They're like pebbles. Nothing in them.'

'He doesn't have our advantages. He comes from a very deprived background.'

'You're saying that with a straight face? A man who tells me he's worked in Vegas. "Deprived background." Am I supposed to believe my ears?' The left side of his face was lit by the desk lamp, the other side was in shadow. I waited for a smile to crack but nothing happened.

'We have delicate investments, Joe. Restaurants, night clubs, betting shops, mini-cab companies.' His voice was slow, slightly bored, as if explaining to a backward child. 'We're dealing with an unreliable class of people, so we need representatives who can make themselves understood.'

He studied me thoughtfully, waiting for a reaction. When the smile finally came I felt relieved.

He stretched and rocked back in his leather chair, making it creak softly. 'Next time I'll get Helen to drive you around,' he said.

JUDY

I don't know what to do about Joe. He seems more seduced than I am. Full of sidelong references, hints I'm only half supposed to pick up, like a child with a guilty secret he's dying to tell. Men talk, the tough world of business. He comes back buzzing with excitement, talking about computers, the miracles of information technology. Fernandez shows him the keys of the kingdom and tells him nothing at all.

You like me, Joe? Just as well. I spent the afternoon fucking your lovely wife.

Always the same hotel. The British Airways livery is appropriate – blue paint, polished granite, polished steel – it feels like we're airborne, off somewhere in suspension, the sea like sheet metal far below, engine noise, bottled air, lassitude, the drinks at peculiar hours to keep you going, moments of broken sleep, the adrenalin rush of take-off and landing. Who said sex is always intimate? This is sexy because it's impersonal. I know next to nothing about my lover. Body hair, unseasonal tan, expensive aftershave, a murmuring American voice in my ear. He might as well be the executive in the next seat co-opting me into the Mile High Club. The curtains are drawn, the room is sound-proofed. We could be hanging in space, a beaten path of moonlight on the sea below.

Intrigue has added a new dimension to my life. I want to capitalise on it and work out a plan, something to get us out of this mess. Maybe Fernandez is the way out. At the start he was all orders and macho authority: do this, do that, put your hand here, turn over, kneel down, stand up. Now he burrows into my breasts and lets me call the shots. I spread his legs, climb on top of him, kiss his neck. 'You're full of surprises,' he says. I tell him it's my northern inheritance. 'Viking blood,' I whisper. 'Pillage and rape.' He asked me once about Joe and me but I didn't reply. Jealous, I thought. That's a start. The trick is to get him hooked, soften him up.

Stonehouse is tougher and trickier. I call for an appointment, expecting to be summoned to Whitehall. Instead, he gives me an address in Mayfair. 'My little pied à terre,' he calls it. Otherwise known as a safe house, I suppose. I wonder if he intends to make a pass but there is a big-hipped Sloane to open the door and make the tea. His minder, his chaperone. 'Miss Loveridge, my assistant,' he says, simpering. 'Couldn't survive without her.' She plunks the tea-tray down in a bossy way, then makes herself scarce, flowered skirt swishing. Her face is elongated, like her boss's, but pale and plump, with the beginnings of a second chin. She is brisk and efficient now, alert to Stonehouse's every whim, but in a few years' time she'll be a frump and her husband will wonder what he ever saw in her.

Stonehouse is wearing a Bertie Wooster tweed suit, subtle autumn browns with a green thread, rumpled and expensive. He flops in the armchair like a broken doll, long legs twisted together, arms all over the place. A fragment of cotton wool clings to his jaw where he has cut himself shaving. He is lanky and sharp-eyed and faintly unsavoury.

He flaps a hand, preparing for small talk, but I come in swinging. 'Why are you pushing my husband around?'

He brushes back his thin hair, fumbles in his pocket for his pipe, feigning surprise and dismay. 'Dear lady?'

'You're making him mix with terrible people.'

An expansive gesture, a lop-sided smile that is intended to be disarming. 'We're not *making* him do anything. He's a free agent. I have the impression he rather likes the company he's keeping these days.'

'That's not what he tells me.'

'Does he always tell you everything?'

'It's one of those marriages. Close.'

'I don't doubt it. But even the most devoted couples keep things back.' He glances at me quickly, then looks away. 'Do you tell *him* everything?'

He can't know, I think, but blush all the same.

'You've got some kind of hold over him,' I say. 'Maybe that's what he doesn't tell me.'

'Not him exactly. His friend the late Thomas Apple. How much has your husband told you about Apple and his deals?'

'Tommy was my friend, too. A hustler is all.'

'He hustled in very shady areas.' He raises a hand and begins to count off on his bony bitten fingers. 'Stolen property, drugs, pornography.' He shakes his head, registering schoolmasterly disapproval. 'That's not your ordinary hustling businessman, Mrs Constantine.'

I sit still in the chintzy room to attend to this. A carriage clock chimes, a single high note marking the half hour. 'That's the first I've heard about porn and stolen property.'

Stonehouse flaps his hands. 'So you see, he doesn't tell you everything.'

'What Tommy did doesn't make Joe guilty.'

'That's just what Joe said. We agreed to differ.'

'And for that you're turning him into an informer?'

'You make it sound like Northern Ireland. Nothing so dramatic. He hears things, he tells us. In exchange, we drop the charges. Forgive and forget. It's a good deal, not much to ask.'

'If this comes to court, what guarantees will you give that Joe isn't going to be prosecuted?'

'He has our word.'

'I said guarantees, something in writing you can't go back on.'

He gives me a wolfish smile. 'You have an unnecessarily low opinion of us.'

He rubs his cheek with his bitten fingernails. He has the hands of a working man, not a civil servant, large and muscular and battered. Perhaps he is a fanatic gardener, a delver and grubber, a man who spends his weekends with earth clogging his nails, digging and forking, tending the shoots, putting down fertiliser, spraying and weeding. He would use and discard us without a second thought. Betrayal, for him, is a way of life, a philosophical principle. This dignifies his aggression. By doing Joe down he reinforces his idea of himself as a man of principle, working for the greater good, weeding the garden of society.

'My official word,' he says.

'Will that help if things go wrong? He's mixing with drug-dealers, gangsters. It's terribly dangerous.'

Again the sidelong, calculating look. 'You've mixed with them, Mrs Constantine. You know they're perfectly containable.'

What can he possibly know? I think. Is the whole of London wired for sound? But if I go that route I'll end up paranoid, crouched unspeaking in a corner, arms hugging my breasts, eyes flickering like strobes, left and right, right and left.

'I've met them,' I say. 'That's why I want Joe protected.'

'I thought you objected to my watchers. Or that's what you told me.'

'We objected to your intrusion into our private life. The microphones and the phone taps, people following us when we went about our domestic business. Keeping Joe safe from those bastards is something else again.'

'He might not agree. You'd better ask him.'

'And there's another thing. If Joe's doing dangerous dirty work for you, I expect him to be rewarded, enormously well rewarded.'

'There's a thought.' Stonehouse leans back comfortably and looks me up and down. He seems amused and faintly roused, like a bully no one argues with. 'Joe seems happy enough. We've already withdrawn our objections to probate on Apple's estate. You're about to inherit a lot of money.'

'It may not happen. Meanwhile, my husband isn't working. He hangs around Fernandez, reports to you and lets his professional life slide.'

'You drive a hard bargain. Harder than him.'

'He's an assimilated Jew. I'm an unreconstructed Scot.'

'You're a lady of many talents, Mrs Constantine. He's a lucky man.'

'You haven't answered my question.'

'I'll have to talk to my masters. Off the record, I'm sure we can come to a satisfactory arrangement.'

Outside, the swirl and din of traffic are amazing. There is a green haze over the trees in Berkeley Square. The air feels soft, almost warm at last. He'd throw us to the wolves without a thought, but at least I'm not going to make it easy for him.

THAT night I dream I'm being hunted. Running down forest paths, crawling through undergrowth, hiding, running. They are all after me – blacks, wrinkled and heavy as rhinos, uniformed whites wearing black berets – all of them heavy-mouthed and corrupt. I keep running although I know I have no chance of freedom. But the running itself exhilarates me; it makes me realise I am young again. Throughout it all, I feel I am involved in a powerful plot that is slowly unravelling. But I wake up before it is revealed. My heart is beating from the exertion and I am wet with sweat. Fear or menopause, a premature hot flush? In my dream I am young, effortlessly running and running. I curl up against Joe, put my arms around him and fall asleep again to his slow breathing. In the morning I can still feel the excitement of the chase, the release of energy, the frustration of the unresolved plot.

I cancel lunch with Fernandez and spend the day at my drawing board. Joe calls at two.

'How's it going?'

'How it always goes. Where are you?'

'On the road. Getting the tour.'

'With the beautiful blonde?'

'With the three musketeers. Today it's mini-cabs.'

'Why don't you do some work?'

'I'm being paid twice what I made as a photographer.'

'That's not an answer.'

'I've had it up to here with photography. All is vanity, saith the preacher. But money is nice.'

'Is that what you phoned to tell me?'

'I phoned to hear a friendly voice. I got the wrong number.'

'I just think you should get off your arse and do some real work.'

'I'm off my arse. I'm being driven round town in a black XJ6.'

'Then why phone me to complain?'

He hangs up. When the telephone rings twenty minutes later I let it ring, thinking, I should have an answering-machine. It might be someone important, it might be a commission.

That night we stay on opposite sides of the bed, back to back. I fall asleep thinking about the curtained hotel room, thinking it's Joe's fault I wasn't there, thinking maybe the dream will recur and this time I'll follow the plot to its end.

INSTEAD, the plot comes to me. Ten-thirty in the morning. The wind from the south-west, boisterous and warm. The roof of the Round House gleams dully in the sun. Scudding clouds, seagulls soaring and wheeling. Rush hour is over, pedestrians few. All morning I have been thinking about my father. Square hard body, heavy jaw, washed-out eyes, the mop of hair that started straw-yellow, went white, then yellowed again in old age, as though stained by his chain-smoking. A bruiser's body and a fighter's face, blunt features, bitten mouth. I remember moments of dizzying violence when he was young and vigorous and I was a child. The crack of his hand against my mother's face. Sobbing, swearing, drunken forgiveness. I remember crouching with her in the corner of my locked bedroom while he bayed for vengeance outside the door. Sober he was frosty and full of rectitude, the lawyer, the churchwarden.

Not easy to love, though easier than my victimised mother, with her resignation and down-turned mouth, forget-me-not eyes and passion for Chopin. Stifling afternoons with her at the piano, rivers of sugary music filling the room, Aberdeen rain outside. I felt used, sucked dry by her unvoiced needs, faintly unclean and full of feelings a child shouldn't feel for a parent: sorrow, pity, contempt. In another century, she would have pined away like the Lady of Shalott, wasted by a Romantic consumption. Instead, she gleefully buried the old man, then joined the Women's Institute and went into good works. Jam-making, distressed gentlefolk, save the rain forests, harvest festivals.

Not good stock, when you come down to it. Not a flash of warmth or generosity between them. No wonder I like the Jews.

The long-distance lorries are lumbering in from the north. Refrigerated lorries loaded with meat and dairy produce, giants hauling industrial equipment, petrol tankers, brand names in bright colours streaked with mud.

I don't know how long I follow him before I realise who it is. The belted raincoat, the tweed hat at a sporty angle. He walks with a swagger, swinging a large briefcase. I increase my pace to keep up. Halfway to Camden Market, he veers left down a side street. When I reach the turn he is going into a shabby workman's cafe. On the opposite corner is a furniture shop. Young marrieds' stuff, stripped pine cupboards, tables and chairs, country-kitchen style, tending to unsteadiness. I pull open drawers, examine price tags and keep an eye on the cafe door.

Five minutes later Hector comes out, walking briskly, all business and job satisfaction. A black Jaguar is parked fifty yards down the road. He climbs in and the car drives off immediately.

The air in the cafe smells of frying oil, close and warm. A dumpy woman in a white overall sits at a table near the back, crying noisily. The young man who serves my coffee is pale and unsteady. The cup rattles when he hands it to me. Then he hurries out to the kitchen. I hear confused male voices, loud but tremulous, tenor and bass, operatic. The young man comes out again followed by an older man holding a wad of paper towel to his face. There is blood on his neck and shirt, bright patches of blood on the paper he holds to his cheek. His face is unnaturally white, as though all the blood in his body were soaking away through the embossed paper.

'I'll tell them I cut myself shaving, for fuck's sake,' he says.

The younger man says, 'Who's gonna believe . . .'

'Whadda they care? They seen everything before.'

The woman gets up and stands close to the wounded man. 'Show me,' she says.

The man looks at me apologetically and shrugs. He lifts the wad of paper. His face is cut from ear to chin and his cheek is open like a flower, pulsing blood. I look away embarrassed, not wanting to intrude.

The woman gives a little cry, 'Enrico,' and crumples at the table again.

'Bastard,' says the young man. 'I kill the bastard.'

The older man steadies himself on the edge of the counter. 'You won't do anything,' he says wearily. 'Just get me more paper. Lots of it. I don't want to bleed all over the taxi.'

I am sweating, light-headed, suspended between shock and curious secret stirring which I realise is excitement.

I have had a glimpse of something hidden. The blood line runs from Hector to Fernandez, who sits behind his desk, touching his computer screen, keeping his hands clean. There is a mystical connection between the rose blooming on the man's cheek and my groaning lover in the hotel bedroom with his thick body hair and the astrological pendant around his neck. Everything connects. There is no coincidence. I daydream about my violent father and violence erupts into my shuffling life. Fernandez with his chain of companies, all of them legal, registered, paying corporate taxes, PAYE, VAT, NIC, a myriad of bureaucratic details, batteries of lawyers and accountants to take care of them, specialists to feed the computers, tailor the programmes for his needs, keep the machines going. But the bloodline runs straight from him to Hector. The rest is decoration.

I swallow my coffee and leave before the taxi arrives.

Birds blowing about the sky, lorries lumbering in from the north.

I wonder if my husband has watched Hector at work. A macho turn-on. According to Stonehouse, Joe was deeper in with Tommy than he ever let on. But this is another order of activity. Impossible that he could have kept it from me. The excitement would have burst him.

'Another magical mystery tour?' I ask him that evening, keeping it casual.

He shakes his head. 'I spent the day in the office. Exploring the wonders of information technology. Then I walked home. All the way from Covent Garden. I wanted to clear my head.'

'Did you?'

'I'm exhausted, if that's what you mean.'

I touch his face. 'How exhausted?'

He smiles back. 'Come to bed and I'll show you.' Making his peace, as he always does in the end.

We eat our evening meal slowly and drink a bottle of wine. Upstairs, we close the curtains, undress without hurry, make love without hurry. It's good to be back.

'This is the only place we meet,' Joe says.

'We should do it all the time.'

'At our age?'

'You know what I mean. Often. Much more often.' I hold on to him, still shaky from the morning's events.

Later, in the shadows, I say, 'You know what he does, don't you?'

'Who he?' Joe's hand is between my thighs. He is on the edge of sleep.

'Hector, who else? He uses a razor, Joe. He cuts people about.'

He rolls over and props himself on one elbow. 'You're dreaming.'

'I saw him. In a cafe off the Chalk Farm Road.'

'And you saw it happen.'

'I saw him go in and come out. Then I went in. The owner's face was sliced open. Like a fig, Joe.'

He leans over me, saying nothing. The wind is still blowing boisterously in the streets. I watch the shadows of the tree outside move on the ceiling.

After a little I say, 'What worries me is, do you know about that stuff and aren't saying?'

'I've had whole days with them doing the rounds. Of a boredom you couldn't conceive. He and the Irishman have an act going, Mr Nice Guy and Mr Nasty, like New York cops in a buddy-buddy movie. I stopped taking them seriously. I thought they were play-acting. All talk, no action.'

'Now you know.'

Loud young voices from the street. A snatch of drunken singing. The wind breaks up the sounds and carries them away.

'I know something else, too,' he says. 'Someone used a knife on Tommy.'

I put my arms around his waist and squeeze close. 'It doesn't bear thinking about.'

'Eyeball to eyeball with that bastard. What a way to go.'

I squeeze closer and say, 'I'm sorry.'

Joe is staring at the window. His face in the shadows is lined and serious. 'I keep thinking about him. I didn't know how much I'd miss him.'

'I'm sorry.'

'He must have felt so damn lonely,' Joe says. 'No wonder his heart burst.'

'They're bad medicine. You should get out, go back to what you know. It's not like you even need the money, thanks to Tommy.'

'That's the point. We owe him. I want to pay him back.'

I turn away to the shadows on the ceiling and Joe's sad set face.

'Our trouble is we're not ready for this kind of stuff,' I say.

'We lead ordinary lives. We can't take it in. That man in the cafe with a face like a split fig. The strange thing was, he seemed the calmest person there.'

Joe leans back against the pillows. When he finally speaks his voice is weary and remote. 'I'm not going to let it go. Tommy wasn't just a friend. Our parents die so we take on other figures to replace them. An element here, an element there. It's like a shadow-show, everything shifting and merging. Tommy adopted us, took us on, took care of us. The least we can do is even the score.'

I thought the violence had gone from my life when my father died, but now it is back again, spilling over. I begin to cry, but silently, and Joe doesn't notice. We lie side by side in the darkness, holding hands, while the wind blows outside and the shadows run on the ceiling. Joe's breathing deepens and slows and the tears stream down my face, wetting the pillow. I wonder what plots will enter my broken sleep tonight.

PART 3

JOE

How long now since Judy began to change? Weeks? Months? Something lazy and replete about her in bed, a kind of submarine slow-motion lassitude that I didn't recognise. When I first sensed it I thought her mind wasn't on what we were doing. She's bored, I thought, and was offended. I was right but for the wrong reason. It took time to see she was in some kind of sexual trance, off in a sensual dream, not caring who her partner was. Which meant I wasn't the only one.

One morning I left home early, drove into town in the rush hour pack, ate a slow breakfast in a workman's cafe in the city, then drove back to Chalk Farm and parked up the street from her studio. Just after midday, a taxi drew up and Judy came out, elegantly dressed, carefully made up, dark hair shining. I followed the cab at a discreet distance to a plush Knightsbridge hotel. She said something to the doorman as she went up the steps and he came away beaming, as though they were old friends.

For the moment, I saw her through his eyes, as a stranger. An attractive woman, I thought. I could go for her.

I sat outside with the car window open and the radio playing, smiling at the traffic wardens as they came and went. Judy came out at half past four. She seemed to move languidly and even from across the street I could see that her face was smooth and flushed. The doorman eyed her covetously. She was anybody's woman, everybody's woman. I was following her cab back to the studio when I realised I should have stayed behind to see who came out after her. Perhaps I didn't want to know. Perhaps I knew already.

I was surprised not to feel jealous. When my other wives had strayed I was deranged with jealousy. But that was because our love life was never much good and I was tormented by the idea that they were getting from someone else the satisfactions I seemed unable to give them. With Judy that didn't apply. It would be different for her with a lover but I didn't think it would be any better. That night in bed I found I was trying to break down some barrier in her neither of us had known was there. I wanted to wake her from her trance, to make her acknowledge my existence. Or that's what

I told myself. The truth was, the knowledge that she had spent the afternoon with another man turned me on. As the poet says, 'The desires of the heart are as crooked as corkscrews.'

Afterwards, on the edge of sleep, she held on to me and mumbled, 'I *do* love you.' As if I had confronted her with it.

The next day Fernandez sent me out on tour again, but this time Helen came with me. I drove her to Clerkenwell, to a goldsmith's workshop at the top of a flight of rickety stairs, a chaos of old tools, flickering gas jets on the work benches, newspapers on the floor. The goldsmith was an elderly man in a brown apron, with thick glasses and a cigarette glued to the corner of his mouth. He and Helen talked together in low voices, heads close, then we drove back to Long Acre.

We went out again the next day, to Dalston, touring slum properties ripe for development. Two days later, Fernandez asked me to drive her up to Birmingham, to a shabby casino, its walls covered with purple drapes, and six disconsolate customers at three o'clock in the afternoon. We were met by a red-faced man in a pin-striped suit, who greeted us like we'd known him for ever. Helen handed him a fat manila envelope and they went upstairs, leaving me to play 50p roulette at an empty table. Ten minutes later she came down holding a different envelope and we drove back down the log-jammed motorway to London.

Her job as a receptionist and secretary seemed to be on hold. Fernandez was throwing us together as he must have thrown her and Tommy together. We drove around, more or less pointlessly, ate lunch, drank in pubs at the end of the day. Within a week we were in bed together. Since Judy had taken a lover, it seemed the least I could do. Helen's body was slim and smooth, infinitely pliable. Feeling her against me, under me, over me, I seemed to shed years. Yet it was a curiously passionless exchange. She treated sex like eating, a natural function, nothing to make a fuss about. It was one of the things she'd learned young and was good at, like tennis or swimming. She was deft, precise, soft-mouthed, even tender, since tenderness was one of the necessary skills. When I looked in her eyes I saw only a kind of sportsman's concentration. I wondered if she took something before she fucked, something to unlock the gates or simply to get her through it. Sometimes we went back to her room in the afternoon. She drew the curtains, lit candles, turned on the hi-fi, anointed her body and mine with Johnson's Baby Oil, the full production. We slithered together like eels, a high-pitched attenuated ecstasy, near screaming-point, endlessly prolonged. After it, we were emptied-out and remote. She lit a cigarette, turned on the television, filling the room with people and noise, while I showered carefully to wash away her smell. When I kissed her goodbye I could sense her relief as well as my own. I was always glad to get home.

Oddly enough, she made me want Judy more, though Judy, too, seemed off in some different private place, full of sadness. I could feel my life unravelling around me.

There were times when I was sure Helen recognised me. A momentary questioning gleam, then it was gone. One afternoon, between the sheets, sweating and tired, I said, 'I've seen you before, you know.'

'How before? Where before?' She didn't sound interested.

'Tunis.'

She giggled. 'Christ, those were the days. You'd be amazed the pills I swallowed in my youth.'

'No, I wouldn't. I saw you.'

'How saw? I didn't see you.'

'In close up. I was behind the camera. I've had a thing about you ever since.'

'And now you've got me.'

'That's right. Now I've got you.'

'Well, I hope it's not a disappointment.' She kissed me lightly, then rolled over on to her back and stared dreamily at the ceiling. 'That's when Tommy and I first made out. I guess he was worried about me. He only came along because he reckoned I was too stoned to manage the journey by myself. My minder. A dear man. Going to bed was his idea of taking care of you. He had a limited view of the world but he was a sweet guy. That's why I loved him.'

'We both loved him.'

'I guess that's why we're here.'

Her blonde hair gleamed in the candlelight, gleamed and flickered. With her shadowy quattrocento face and delicate limbs she could have gone places, done what she liked. She seemed too young to have settled for so little.

'Why did you do the pictures?' I said.

'Ray asked me to. As a personal favour. And when Ray asks everybody jumps. You know how it is.'

'So Tommy gave them to Ray?'

'Something like that.'

'And what did Ray do with them?'

'Search me. Maybe he kept them as a memento. To remind him of old times.'

'He's another of your admirers, then?'

She sat up in bed and turned on me fiercely. 'Why don't you leave me alone, for Christ's sake. You guys are all the same. You're less interested in the girl than in who's been there before you. It's like all you really want to do is fuck each other.'

'You don't need all this.' I touched her face. 'You should go home to California.'

'It's too late. I told you that the first time we met.' She got out of bed and went across to her dressing table. 'Hey,' she said, 'you want a joint?'

I shook my head. I watched her as she busied herself with a cigarette paper, her and her naked image in the mirror, front view and back view simultaneously. A beautiful girl from any angle.

'You know what I want in this life?' she said.

'A handsome husband and a hundred grand a year?'

'Boy, are you out of date. An executive job is what. An office of my own, a company car, a briefcase full of papers to take home at night.'

'To hubby and the kids?'

'That's as may be. It's my place in the system that matters. Something to fill the hours, fill my head.' She went across to the window and pulled back the curtains. The candles looked pale and dusty in the afternoon light. 'I need a proper place to live,' she said. 'I hate this crummy room with the cooker and the mini fridge in an alcove. I want my own genuine American kitchen, with machines and marble tops, the whole schmeer.'

She stood there naked, one arm extended, the other cocked on her hip. 'Can't you just see me, Joe, arguing the clauses of a deal, beating you down on the fine print? Miss Career Girl. Clothes by Nicole Farhi, shoes by Kurt Geiger, perfume by Penhaligon.'

She made me feel old and shabby, with my middle-age paunch and shop-soiled adultery. 'What do you need that stuff for?' I asked. 'Right now you could conquer the world.'

'That's the whole point, see. I want to do it the hard way. With my clothes on.'

'What's to stop you? Ray trusts you, gives you delicate work. I've watched you, head to head with those difficult customers. And Ray's a hard man to please.'

'Ray's a crook. Just for the record. In case you didn't know. In case you were getting sentimental and buddy-buddy. He's a man with a mission, a firm sense of purpose. If you want it, take it –

but make sure you go for the jugular. One of those. I'm the other kind of American.'

'What other kind?'

'A drifter. Out of the great empty heartland. Except I come from California. I got itchy feet but now I've seen the other side of the coin and I'm learning.'

It occurred to me that adultery wasn't worth the effort. I was getting sucked into Helen's life, with its plots and subplots, when all I'd intended was a subplot in my own. She had unfinished business with her remarried father who sent her cheques and her remarried mother who had other children to think about. Envies, jealousies, obscure aspirations. I'd thought of her as marrying rich, then day-dreaming secretly of the wild times she'd left behind. She saw it all in direr shades, a choice between career girl in London and go-go dancer in Topeka, Kansas. She squatted on the end of the bed, puffing solemnly at the joint. Even her beauty seemed sad, her lovely breasts, smooth shoulders, tilted chin. All that wistfulness, all those unresolved ambitions.

'I still think you should go home.'

'Don't nag me, Joe. If all you mean is we should stop, that's OK by me, too. We've hardly started, anyway. I'm not in your hair, Joe. I can take a hint. You don't need to put six thousand miles between me and your precious marriage.'

'It was you I was thinking about. Honest. My marriage can take care of itself.'

'That's what I like about older men. They make love slowly, then they worry about you. You and Tommy both. You got to hand it to Ray. He's no worrier.'

'I wish you'd let go,' I said. 'Nobody's after you, nobody's trying to call it off. I just think you're in over your head.'

'When the waters close, I'll wave. That's a promise.'

I stood under the shower, washing her off me, then put on my clothes. When I came out of the bathroom the television was on and she was propped up in bed, the tin of dope and the packet of cigarette papers on the covers in front of her. She had snuffed out the candles and the room smelled of burnt wax. Clothes and magazines scattered over the floor, an orange cushion, a box of tissues. Coffee cups, make-up, bottles of perfume on the dressing table. The litter of her daily life.

I sat by her on the bed, watching the headlines of the early news programme, then I kissed her and went home to Judy.

THE atmosphere in the car was festive. I sat in the back, my thigh pressed against Helen's. On her other side, Fernandez tapped a Gucci shoe in time to Frank Sinatra.

> Don't you know, little fool, you never can win,
> Use your mentality, wake up to reality . . .

Hector, in front, smiled his aloof smile. Riley forebore to sniff and wipe his nose as he barrelled the Jaguar, like a blunt instrument, down the fast lane.

'Listen to that sound,' said Fernandez. 'In-car CD. A small step for the Japs, a giant step for mankind.'

'A day in the country,' I said. 'It feels like a school away match. A gift from nowhere.'

'We work hard, we deserve a break,' said Fernandez. 'Helps promote the team spirit.' He hummed along with the tape. 'That Cole Porter's the greatest. It reminds me of the old days. I listen to that stuff, so help me, I get all choked up.'

'I love you when you're sentimental,' said Helen, and laughed.

'No shit.' Fernandez laughed with her. 'Listen to Sinatra's voice. Sweet as sugar, smooth as silk. And with that little come-on edge to it. I knew Frankie back when, before he put on weight and his tubes got like sandpaper. You got through the bodyguards and the bullshit, he was one helluva guy.'

When the tape finished Fernandez made Riley play it through again.

We were off the M4 by then, into the wide rolling countryside around Newbury, the empty hills from which Jude sighed towards Christminster. We drove through a white wooden gateway in a white wooden fence, down a long curving drive, past a Palladian house, into a yard surrounded by stables and outbuildings. There was stabling for twenty horses, smelling of horse sweat, manure, hay, but scrupulously clean, the stone floor gleaming with fresh water. Expensive horses shivered in their stalls, shifting nervously from hoof to hoof, while grooms smoothed their shining coats with curry-combs.

Fernandez was off in one corner of the yard talking to a tall thin man in a hacking jacket, jodhpurs, gleaming boots. His brown felt hat was cocked at a rakish angle. His face was long and delicate and lined, sensitive as a borzoi's. He was wearing string gloves and, as he talked, he counted off items on his fingers. Fernandez listened intently, head bowed.

Riley stayed with the car but Hector hurried across the yard to a gate in one corner. He seemed excited. Helen and I followed him slowly.

The gate opened on to a broad sweep of hillside. Hector was leaning against it.

'Look at those motherfuckers go,' he said. His face was intense, with a brightness in the eyes I'd never seen before. Longing, craziness, love.

A line of horses was racing across the hillside, long legs pounding and blurring, manes flying, flanks stretching and gathering, the great muscular necks extended. A muted thunder of hooves. The jockeys, perched on their backs, seemed not to belong to this show of power, superfluous baggage.

The sun shone, the larks sang, a hawk rode a thermal high above the hill top.

As the brilliant horses pounded towards us, Hector shook his head, smiling as though he really meant it. 'Ave Maria purissima,' he murmured.

A hundred yards short of the gate the horses slowed to a walk. They came towards us, shaking their heads, blowing air out of their velvet nostrils, flanks steaming in the mild sunlight. Hector tagged on to the lead horse like a small boy, following it into the stables, deep in conversation with the jockey. Helen trailed after them. I leant against the gate, listening to the larks.

Soft voices behind me. I heard Fernandez say, 'What about Archer's Triumph?'

The tall thin man said, 'Not with the weight he'll be carrying.'

Two more horses came galloping across the flank of the hill, smooth as running water.

Fernandez leant against the gate beside me. 'You got some lovely horseflesh,' he said to the other man.

'The sport of kings,' the thin man replied. 'I've always thought that kings meant the horses, not the people. We're a graceless lot in comparison.'

A couple of hundred yards out, the jockeys eased their mounts to a canter, then a walk. When they passed us the air was sharp with horse sweat.

'The Queen's Arms still do a good lunch?' Fernandez asked.

'As long as you keep away from the complicated stuff. Stick to steak and chops, you'll do all right.'

'Join us?'

'Love to, old boy, but I'm a bit pushed. Got to check out my charges, see that they're up to snuff. His nibs is due in early afternoon, along with his advisors, his bodyguards and at least two of his wives. He ought to get Rolls-Royce to build him a charabanc.'

He strode off with long lithe steps, swinging his gloved hands.

'Best man in the business,' said Fernandez. 'Nothing he doesn't know about it.'

'I didn't realise Hector was so hooked on horses. He's like a child in a toyshop.'

'It's an addiction. That's where all his money goes. Believes anything a jockey cares to tell him.'

'Life is full of surprises. I had him figured for one of those paranoid types who believes nobody. Someone who nurses his mean streak and waits to take offence.'

'What's bugging you, Joe? I thought you were enjoying our little day out.'

'Maybe I'd feel better if someone would tell me what I'm supposed to be doing.'

'You're supposed to be having a good time. Sniffing the fresh air, loosening your collar. And at the end of the day, you'll have some interesting bets to place, if that's your fancy.'

'So why do I feel left out?'

'Maybe you're like Hector, one of those paranoid types.'

'Too many loose ends, Ray. They make me anxious.'

'There you go again. Ease up, can't you? Admire the horses, enjoy the scenery, partake of the hospitality. A good steak and a glass of wine. You'll come away feeling like a million dollars.'

'What about the shipment, Ray? I'm still waiting for you to tell me about it.'

'Jesus, you never let up. The shipment was nothing. A crate of fucking toys. You saw them yourself.'

'What did you do with them?'

'Nothing. We let them be. It was the principle that mattered. You restored my faith, Joe. I'd been waiting for a man of principle.'

'As a man of principle, I've got news for you: the garage is empty.'

'So?' A deep shrug. 'The police want them, they can have them. Give them to their kids next Christmas. They've become an irritation, a distraction.'

'Tommy would be glad to hear that.'

'You harp too much on Tommy.'

'I want to know what happened to him.'

'You know what happened. A heart attack.'

'It was provoked. There were people with him. Hector, for instance.'

'You've got a thing about Hector. He's a good boy.'

'He's a thug, a killer in a Burberry.'

Fernandez shrugged. 'Why should I fool you? Tommy and I had a difference of opinion. I sent Hector round to speak to him.'

'Hector and his knife.'

'The lad got carried away.'

I let that hang in the air a moment. The larks sang, the day was still and fresh.

'I can't work with him,' I said. 'Every time I see him, I think of Tommy.'

Fernandez turned. He studied me carefully, face closed, giving nothing away. 'Something on your mind?' he said finally.

The sharp smell of horse sweat lingered on the air. The hawk rode its thermal in great sweeping circles. Vengeance is mine, saith the Lord.

I looked Fernandez in the eye. This was, after all, the moment I had been waiting for.

'If you want me, he's got to go,' I said. 'An eye for an eye. Your friend for mine.'

He turned away, facing up the hill again. 'I don't know if I can do that.' He spoke slowly, weighing his words. 'My muchacho. We go back a long way. OK, he's impulsive, he gets excited. But he's a man you can trust. You say, "Do it," he does it.'

'He killed my friend.'

'Not on purpose. Hector's problem is, he overreacts. He rapes too easy, flies off the handle.'

'Take it or leave it.'

Fernandez looked me up and down without pleasure. 'You're operating in mid-air,' he said. 'But I'll think about it. Just don't push your luck.'

Over lunch they talked horses. Newmarket on Wednesday, Goodwood Friday. Hector was still on his high, full of what passed, in him, for goodwill. 'If the going's firm, it's gotta be Venturesome. They start overnight, they can't beat him.' And so on.

I drank too much, a private celebration, and dozed most of the way back to London, Helen's smooth thigh against mine. Each time I woke, I saw Hector's face in profile, the overbite, neat features, pebble eyes, but everything still softened a little by the day's excitement, by the sound and smell of thoroughbred horses. When we got to the office Fernandez took my hand in both of his and said again, 'I'll think about it.'

EVERY Thursday evening at six, I met Stonehouse at the little mews house off Hill Street and gave him the sweepings of Fernandez's computer. Sometimes Langton Green, the American, was with him, sometimes not; sometimes they seemed interested in what I told them, mostly not. They took notes, but dutifully, more to show me I was wanted than out of conviction.

But when I told them about Hector and my ultimatum there was a sudden stir of attention. Green leaned forward, square head cocked, watery eyes alert. Stonehouse displayed his yellow smile and twisted his arms together appreciatively. 'Bloodthirsty little bastard, aren't you?' he said.

'First Tommy, now Hector,' said Green. 'I like it.'

'Tit for tat, is it?' said Stonehouse. 'Guts for garters. Poor old Hector.'

I was disconcerted by this show of animation. They were like a music-hall double act. I sat tight, studied the tips of my shoes and said primly, 'I don't know what you're talking about.' It seemed important not to get caught up, not to let them condescend to me.

Langton leaned back comfortably and grinned. His teeth, in his veined and shattered face, were startlingly white. 'We're talking about the hard men,' he said amiably. 'You tell them you want rid of somebody, they tend not to worry about the small print. Rid is rid.'

'That's not what I meant.'

'What you meant doesn't matter. It's how he reads it. The way I see it, Hector isn't much longer for this world.'

'Nothing's for free, of course,' Stonehouse said thoughtfully. 'My guess is he'll want you in at the kill. To prove that he means what he says, that he can keep his side of a bargain. Also to prove he's serious. He'll want you there to see what happens when they lose interest, when they decide you're no longer useful to them.'

'Build a few bodies,' said Green. 'That's how you get on in their world.'

'You're trying to put the wind up me,' I said.

'No such luck, old boy.' Stonehouse unravelled his arms and settled back comfortably, stretching his long legs. 'You've moved up a class, Joe, up into the world of real events where your every wish is fulfilled. You get exasperated and say "Drop dead." Bingo, you've got a corpse on your hands. These people don't have time for idle gestures. And they're not long on patience. Someone gets in their way, they dispose of them.'

The afternoon light flooded in, yet the room felt sealed as a tomb. The double-glazing kept out the street noises but the silence was heavier, thicker than that. Only the clock ticking busily on the mantelpiece. Not a sound from Miss Loveridge in the next room, Miss Loveridge with the big hips and long face. Maybe the place was soundproofed, an isolation cell in the heart of Mayfair.

'Is that what happened to Tommy?' I asked.

Stonehouse shrugged. 'Maybe yes, maybe no. It looked like a mistake but Fernandez wouldn't have cared much either way.'

'Tommy was getting cute,' said the American. 'He was getting on the boss's nerves.' He got up, walked over to the cold fireplace and studied the clock, the silver knick-knacks on the mantelpiece, his back towards the room. 'They ransacked your friend's office,' he said. 'Went through it with a fine-toothed comb. It seemed kinda disproportionate at the time, considering the size of the shipment. My guess is, they were looking for something else.' He turned and faced me. 'Has Geary come up with anything?' he asked.

'Only with what you'd expect. Warehouses stuffed with trash: teddy bears, artificial flowers, remaindered books. Computer games in lock-up garages, television sets with funny brand names. A few thousand quid's worth. A nice little windfall, I'm not complaining, but not enough to go to war over.'

'What about equities in Fernandez's companies?'

'Not that he's told me. The real money's all in property. A semi-detached in Neasden, a couple of flats in Bromley, four shops in Watford, a big house in West Hampstead cut up into bed-sitters. That sort of thing.'

'I'd swear there's something else,' said Green. 'Look around, keep your eyes open.'

'Tommy wasn't stupid,' I said. 'Except about women. He wouldn't have tried out his fancy footwork on Fernandez.'

Green pressed his shoulders against the mantelpiece and flexed his knees, as though trying to lift the thing on his back. He grunted slightly, a small pleasurable noise, a powerful man, spoilt by booze, chafing against petty restrictions. 'You'd be surprised how fast people lose their sense of proportion when serious money's involved,' he said.

'Serious enough to send in Hector,' Stonehouse said. 'Serious enough to kill for.'

'My wife saw Hector carve someone up for nothing at all,' I said. 'The owner of a workman's cafe. He rapes easy. Fernandez's very words.'

'All the more reason for Fernandez not to send him in,' Stonehouse said petulantly. 'Show some sense.'

'If I'm supposed to be keeping my eyes open, what should I be looking for?'

'God knows.' Green strained against the mantelpiece again. 'Share certificates maybe. Some kind of company Tommy and Fernandez set up together.'

'Offshore, of course,' Stonehouse said.

'Why are you telling me this?'

'You're his heir.'

'Why not ask Geary or the accountant?'

'This is official business,' Green said. 'We don't want to spread it around.'

'You muddy the waters, you find nothing,' Stonehouse said.

They had their double act off so pat it sounded rehearsed. I got up and walked to the window. A line of angry clouds, driven by the wind, moved across the house tops. The day was gathering itself to rain, although the sunlight still poured in. A spring shower to freshen the streets and lay the dust. The endless rain of the previous winter was a vague memory, as of some youthful unhappiness, long outlived, something that returns as a puzzle, something to be nostalgic about. How did I get into that? Was I ever that young?

'It doesn't match what Fernandez told me,' I said. 'He says it was a matter of principle between him and Tommy. The shipment had disappeared. He felt cheated, outsmarted. That's not something he'd take to kindly, not from a small-time hustler like Tommy. He felt angry so he sent Hector round. That makes sense to me. But then there was a muddle and things got out of hand. Everything was predictable except the outcome.'

'And you feel inclined to take his word against ours?' Stonehouse said.

'Two volatile ingredients, Tommy and Hector. But Tommy had a bad heart. What more do you need for a disaster?'

'There was something else going on,' Stonehouse said. 'All the evidence points that way. Trust me. A deal, an arrangement.'

'And Tommy outsmarted him.'

'He got cute,' Green said. 'It was in his nature. A fatal flaw. The one temptation he could never resist.'

'Tommy's world was full of temptations he couldn't resist,' I said. 'He hired a secretary, the next thing you knew he was romantically involved. He propositioned them, he proposed to them, some of them he even married. Louise, Helen, all those unforgiving wives. He was a one-man band, Tommy, mouth-organ strapped round his neck, violin in his hands, cymbals on his elbows, drums worked with his feet. The noise was unstoppable. He wanted everyone to love him and applaud.'

'Dear boy,' Stonehouse said placatingly. 'You knew him for years, so who are we to contradict you? All we ask is, keep your eyes open and stay in touch.'

Evening was coming on. Outside the sealed box of the house the noise of the city seemed overwhelming. The swish of car wheels on the wet streets, horns tooting, snatches of conversation and music, patter of rain drops, the wind gusting round corners. I turned up the collar of my jacket against the rain. In a lighted window two men faced each other across a desk. One listened impassively while the other talked with his hands, elaborate arabesques, explaining, apologising, selling, plotting. Tight young leaves glinted on the trees in Berkeley Square. A commissionaire stood in the portico of the Clermont, an outsized umbrella at the ready. I walked slowly up to Piccadilly, wondering what Stonehouse had been trying to tell me. Hector dead at my say-so. Pathetic. The world is not ordered like that. People like me don't hold the keys to life and death. He was winding me up, trying to put the frighteners on me. As for the offshore company: maybe, just for once, he was asking, not telling.

JUDY hadn't bothered to switch on the lights. In the silvery evening she looked about twenty. Jeans, T-shirt, running shoes propped on the coffee table, showered and powdered after her aerobics class, full of the righteous virtue that comes from strenuous exercise. I poured two drinks and flopped down on the sofa beside her.

She held her drink up to the window's light and said, 'I shouldn't be doing this, not when I've been working to get it off. But what the hell.'

'I've been thinking about Tommy,' I said. 'Tommy and Fernandez. I seem fated to play straight guy to crooks. What is it about me that inspires this trust, sweetheart? It sure isn't the face I see when I shave. The lines and pouches and bloodshot eyes. Too much booze and nicotine, not enough sleep. It must be some aura I give off, the spiritual equivalent of body odour.'

'I'll tell you about your aura, if you don't know it already. Diffidence, boredom, dissatisfaction. You look chronically under-used, Joe. You look like someone waiting for a kick-start.'

'You mean our friend the poodle? Thanks a lot.'

'Don't be so touchy. It's your hidden assets that turn them on – the public school, university stuff. You're a cultured man, darling, educated, all the things they're not.'

'You're forgetting the sleaze factor. I'm an easy mark. There's all that money sloshing around in the system and I've never understood why I shouldn't have a share of it.'

The evening was deepening minute by minute. The room brimmed with shadows.

'The truth is,' I said, 'it didn't come as any great surprise when they told me Tommy had been dealing in stolen goods. Not that he'd ever breathed a word. It's just that it felt too simple. But I told myself that's how it is in the business world. Money breeds money. Unto him that hath shall be given. All you need is a foot on the ladder. That's what Tommy did for me. From then on it was simply a matter of avoiding awkward questions.'

'And doing him favours in return?'

'Few enough in the circumstances. Considering what he did for us.'

'I don't think I want to know about your favours.'

The photograph Rosie had given us was on the coffee table. I picked it up. Tommy and me in the good old days, laughing into camera, arms around each other's shoulders.

'He was a lovely man,' I said. 'We owe him more than favours. We owe him us.'

'It would have happened anyway.' Her voice was mournful and resigned. I wondered who it was she was seeing, who and why and how much she'd given up for him, or thought she'd given up. Her marriage, my marriage, our marriage. Built on a rock. In the end, what did a little adultery matter?

' "The poor benefit of a bewildering minute",' I said.

'What's that supposed to mean?'

'The orgasm. Seventeenth-century style. It comes with that education you think is so sexy. Tourneur, Middleton, one of those. I don't remember.'

'Meaning us?'

'Who else?'

I turned the photograph around. It was a cheap frame, the kind you buy in any department store.

'The joke is,' I said, 'the one straight thing in my life is this marriage of ours. And it was engineered by our crooked friend.'

'The one straight thing.' She sounded bored. 'You kid yourself, darling. That's why you get on so well with crooks. You like to imagine yourself as this devious hustler kept on the straight and narrow by your righteous little wife. Don't project your super-ego into me, Joe. I've got problems of my own.'

'You want to tell me about them?'

'Confession time, is it? Dr Constantine, I presume. You sit in the armchair, I'll lie on the couch. Then maybe we'll swap places and do it over again. Come on, Joe.' She looked away towards the pale square of the window. 'Not after all these years, thanks.'

Her tone surprised me. Anger and grief. There was a big bowl of freesias on the coffee table, releasing their sweet and heavy scent into the darkening air. Fernandez, I thought. Everywhere I turn.

'What we have here is a slight hiccup,' she said. 'A brief disturbance in the smooth curve of our marriage. We'll get over it.'

'What we have here is too many strangers in our life. It used to be an exclusive arrangement. You and me against the world. Now look at us.'

She turned her shadowy face towards me. 'Give them up,' she said. 'Go back to what you know.'

I shook my head. 'There's unfinished business.'

'If you mean money, we don't need it. We always got along before. Now there's the Apple fortune, whatever that means.'

'I was thinking of Tommy. He's lying up there in that hideous cemetery and the people who put him in the ground are walking around as though nothing had happened.'

'What are you planning? A duel with Hector?' Her voice was low but heavy with contempt. 'Choose your own weapons. Like cut-throat razors. You wouldn't stand a chance.'

'Let the police have him. I don't want anything fancy.'

'Stonehouse would turn him, use him for his own purposes, then give him a fat pension.'

'There's always Rogers. Rogers of the Met.'

'Rogers does what he's told. You're living in dreamland, Joe. What's happened has happened. Our job is to save our own hides. Like Tommy would have done.'

We were each defending Tommy in his own way. Tommy the saviour, the generous friend, the victim. Tommy the survivor, selfishness incarnate. Somewhere along the line we had lost touch with him, he was receding into the past, completing his death. Judy was right, of course. Revenge would make no difference to him now; it was just a way of repaying a debt. Nothing like a death for making you realise how much you care for someone. If Tommy were still alive, Judy and I would be locked in our private world – the jobs, the evening weariness, bed. Instead, the house was full of flowers and both of us were making love to strangers.

'A simple question of justice,' I said. 'It seems a small enough thing to ask.'

'It may turn out bigger than you expect. There are layers upon layers. And these are very determined people.'

'Stonehouse's American friend called them the hard men. But all I'm after is Hector. He's the one who's responsible and he's a mere foot-soldier. Fernandez talks about him sentimentally – my muchacho, he says – but at heart he doesn't give a damn. If he could clear it all up by handing Hector to Rogers, he wouldn't hesitate.'

Judy had turned around on the sofa. She sat facing me, her legs tucked up under her, her eyes hooded in the darkness. 'Maybe you're the sentimentalist. You think you've become indispensable. What if he decides it's you who's the irritation?'

I thought about that for a moment. 'There's something missing,' I said. 'Something they couldn't find when Tommy died. He needs me to find it for him. God knows why. But until whatever it is turns up, I think he's going to have to behave himself with me.'

Silence. She brushed her hair from her face and shifted in her seat. I could smell her faint scent on the air. 'Sometimes I think I'm losing you,' she said. 'I don't know what you want any more.'

I laughed. 'Times change,' I said. 'I used to think, if I had it all to do again, I'd like to be a musician, spinning all that loveliness out of thin air. Now I think I'd like to be a rich American. East coast, upper class, with an apartment on Fifth Avenue overlooking the park, a big old house in Connecticut, and endless reserves of money. It's a sign of age, of the failure of ambition. I want the good life, the easy life. Stylish, restrained, unperturbed.'

Another silence. Finally, she said, 'You've given up.'

I got up and switched on the lights. The room jumped into focus, full of detail and colour.

'Let's get drunk,' I said. 'Let's get drunk and take it from there.'

'THE holding company is called Feats Ltd.' Felix Abel's office was like a study, its walls lined with novels, biographies, histories of World War II, jumbled in with books about tax law and accounting. 'One of Tommy's little jokes.'

We sat on buttoned leather sofas, facing each other across a coffee table. Piles of books and papers everywhere, a comfortable chaos. Felix Abel was compact and self-contained. Neat beard, clever eyes.

'It developed from his first company, FEA Ltd. He told the bank FEA meant Free Enterprise Associates. He told me it stood for Fuck 'Em All. So when it came to a holding company Feats was a natural: Free Enterprise Associates Trading Services, a.k.a. Fuck 'Em All Together in Spades.' A brief barking laugh. 'That's why I was so fond of him. He brought a little life even to accountancy. Geary feels the same. Tommy had a buzz about him. Everything brightened up when he walked through the door.'

'The good ones always go first,' I said. 'The people with most to offer, the ones with appetite. It's the general rule.'

'And the rest of us hang on in our dismal way. There's a grey principle ruling the world and we're part of it.'

He didn't look grey. Ruddy complexion, powerful neck, his chest bulging under the well-cut jacket. His suit was the only grey thing about him.

'I don't understand about companies.'

'You don't have to. Tommy bought and sold things, did deals, invested in property. That's all you need bother about. For Tommy, a company was a ghost, a consensus, an abstraction. It had no physical reality apart from pieces of paper. Where multiple companies are concerned, forget about goods and services and things you buy and sell. At that point a company is a financial convenience, an arrangement for shifting money around. Tommy collected them like schoolboys collect stamps.'

'What did he use them for?'

'Making money disappear, what else? A company that's making money acquires a company that's losing money. It's a kind of balancing act. The object is to save taxes, keep all the balls in the air, keep the cash circulating. Tommy was terrific at that stuff, all sleight of hand and dazzling footwork. He treated it like poker, a game of skill and judgment. But none of that need concern you, unless you want to go the same road. Which I gather from Geary you don't. So there are goods that we're disposing of and properties that you can keep or sell as you decide.'

'What about a business partner called Fernandez?'

'His name turns up in some of Tommy's deals.'

'No partnerships? No joint companies?'

Abel shook his head. 'He's just a name, a man Tommy did business with occasionally.'

'Could there be a company you don't know about?'

'Here and in the States companies have to be registered, they have to file accounts, list their shareholders. If Tommy and this Fernandez were in partnership I'd have the details.'

Behind Abel's head, outside the window, there were flowering cherry trees against an overcast sky, bubbling masses of pinky white. 'I've an office in town,' Abel had told me on the telephone, 'but I only use it for formal meetings. The real work gets done at home.' I had walked across the heath to his house in Highgate, where there was a wife in the kitchen with two small children, as well as secretaries and assistants. A large golden retriever had followed me into the study and sprawled down like a splendid rug next to the coffee table. When I stirred it with my foot it lumbered to its feet and lay its soft domed head on my knee. It closed its eyes when I stroked it and its mouth opened a little. It was smiling.

So was Abel. 'You're not convinced,' he said.

'The police think there are papers missing. They think Tommy and Fernandez set up a company for some deal. An offshore company, probably.'

Abel shrugged. 'The police know how to check all the obvious records. It's possible Tommy did things without consulting me. It's also possible they're just fishing.'

'Put it another way,' I said. 'There's something I don't understand about Tommy's legacy. There's the bits and bobs, the deals, the usual Tommy hustle. That's been sold off for a few thousand. Maybe Tommy would have trebled that, more, perhaps, with his flair. But it's not a fortune. Then there are the properties. They represent a lot of money, but the rents don't amount to that much. It's a long-term investment, solid back-up, the kind of thing banks appreciate. I don't want to sound ungrateful. To me as a freelance, self-employed, it's more money than I ever dreamed of. But somehow I can't help thinking there's a discrepancy.'

Abel raised his eyebrows, held his peace, waiting.

'According to Fernandez, Tommy was playing in a huge poker game. Thousands of pounds washing around the table every night, fortunes won and lost. Apparently, he was doing OK, but he was playing against pros and in the end there's only one way the money will go. What I don't understand is, how did he manage it?'

Abel smiled indulgently. 'What we have here is the essential Tommy Apple. Acting out a fantasy, as they say. He always wanted to be a major player. That's the role he saw himself in. His destiny. Of course he didn't have the money to throw around, but he did it anyway. Sometimes there was a slight problem of cash flow, a hiccup, that's how he saw it. Needless to say, I didn't approve, but then I wasn't consulted.' A downward wave of the hand, a kind of blessing. 'I couldn't help admiring him. That sort of gesture was part of his appeal.

Larger than life, unwilling to accept its limitations. You get what I mean.'

'Unless he knew there was other money available. Ready cash, funny money, stuff he didn't tell you about.'

'It's possible. In fact, its mere possibility would have been enough. Tommy always liked betting on the come. Isn't that what they call it in poker?'

The dog opened its eyes, its jaws sagged ecstatically. It was laughing now from the sheer pleasure of being caressed.

'Tommy wrote me a letter before he died,' I said, 'hinting that he had a really big deal going down. The kind of deal that would set him up for life. Serious money, not just properties in the suburbs. I assume it was something dodgy or he'd have mentioned it to you.'

Abel pursed his lips disapprovingly. 'He didn't, I assure you.'

'But just suppose the deal went through and there really is something missing, where would it be? A numbered Swiss account? A set-up in the Cayman Islands or the Bahamas, that sort of thing?'

Abel shook his head. 'Smart money doesn't go that way any more. Not since all that drugs cash started sloshing around in the system. Too much pressure from the States. My guess, and it's just a guess, would be Panama. The last of the tax havens. It's against Panamanian law to reveal the names of shareholders or associates and there's no system of filing accounts to a register of companies.' He smiled at the dog and said, 'Is he annoying you?'

'Does it look like it? Go on about Panama.'

'It means secrecy, impermeability. Something else, too. What you have is a kind of alternative currency. Physical possession of a bearer share certificate gives the holder absolute power over the funds of a Panamanian company.'

'I'm an innocent,' I said. 'Translate that for me into lay terms.'

'It means finders keepers. If you have the company's share certificate, you have the company's money. A bill you can cash in for so many thousand dollars.' He paused, licked his lips, made a brisk dismissive gesture. 'Not that I would know, of course. As Tommy's accountant, I only dealt with the kosher side of his affairs. If there were funny share certificates, he'd have kept them in a safe, well away from me. For my sake as much as for his, you understand. I have my professional code of conduct to consider. He was too good a friend to compromise me.'

'Supposing it existed, what would it look like, this Panamanian share certificate?'

'Nothing special. A printed sheet of paper with a border around it. No crests or fancy writing. Just a certificate stating the name of the company, the number of shares and their value, dated and signed by the company president and secretary. A curiously undistinguished-looking document, considering what it might be worth.'

'For a man who doesn't know about these things you're doing fine.'

'I have to keep up. You never know what you're going to need in an emergency. There are all sorts of tricks I don't know about officially. Dummy IOUs, for example, to conceal ownership, profitability, taxability. Maybe that's what's gone missing. Some innocent sheet of paper, signed and dated and worth a fortune. Like I was saying, when you're dealing with interlocking companies, you're dealing with pieces of paper, significant pieces of paper. That or electronic money, figures on a computer screen shifting from terminal to terminal around the globe. A kind of second atmosphere, an alternative ether. You switch on a radio, you get music if you're tuned to the right frequency. It's the same with computers. There's money moving everywhere all the time, if only we could tune in. Blessed be the hackers for they shall inherit the earth.'

He clicked his fingers and the dog slouched over and settled comfortably at his feet. He bent to stroke it, ruffling its silky fur the wrong way, then smoothing it down.

'I was a Marxist when I was young,' he said. 'I went into accounting because I was good at figures and I didn't want to upset my mother. She was ill and I was the only son. I thought, Right, I'll do it, but only for people who need it. Writers, painters, freelancers, people in marginal jobs. But I had a knack and the next thing I know my books are full of Tommy Apples. Twenty-three years later, my mother, bless her, is still alive and I'm paying a fortune in nursing home fees. Without the Tommies I couldn't afford it. But my daughter by my first marriage is a Stalinist, living in a kibbutz and sharing out the money I send her for birthdays and Christmas because she believes property is theft. Me, I'm becoming just like my old mother: I worry about my other kids growing up and getting serious jobs.'

FERNANDEZ had given me an office next to his and fixed it up with all the appropriate executive gear: two telephones, a computer terminal, a tape recorder, a set of streamlined pencil holders and boxes in brushed steel, everything necessary to make me feel I had a real function in the business. There were also machines – a telex, a fax – that chattered out messages about contracts and deliveries. After the first couple of days I stopped reading them. Identical machines delivered identical messages all through the office. Fernandez invented papers for me to sign and telephone calls to make, but mostly I sat at my desk staring out over the panorama of central London and wishing I were back in my studio, setting up the lights and working out camera angles. Helen brought me cups of coffee at regular intervals, always coming closer to me than was strictly necessary to include me in the zone of fragrance, a young girl's perfume, she moved in. Otherwise, she was formal and distant. The fact that I had once photographed her, puzzled out ways of lighting the elusive smile and elegant breasts, seemed more of a link than the mere fact of having slept with her. She belonged to my real life, which had very little to do with the office or her bed-sitter in Westbourne Terrace.

The afternoon after I saw Abel, I called Judy and told her I'd be home late, don't wait supper. She didn't seem particularly interested. When the office closed I went to a bar in Covent Garden where most of the other customers looked too young to be drinking legally. They made me feel like a foreigner, a visitor from the country of the middle-aged. I watched them over the evening paper – white wine and lager in enormous quantities; pale drinks and pale faces – then crossed the road and ate a hamburger in a restaurant with wooden tables and loud piped music. At eight-thirty I went back to the office.

The reception room was lit by the closed-circuit television monitor on Helen's desk. In monochrome, the empty corridor outside seemed ghostly. I went into my office without turning on the lights, drew the curtains and switched on the computer. The bright symbols appeared on the screen. I touched them and got a set of graphs, touched again and the graphs were replaced by pie-charts. The group's quarterly figures predicted a hefty deficit. I brought the companies up, one after the other: properties, restaurants, casinos, car hire, laundromats. There were no names I didn't recognise and the figures were all green, comfortably in profit. The only figure in red was 'Sundries. 3,600'. I touched it. The machine bleeped and a message appeared on the screen: 'No information available'.

Sundries. A multitude of sins.

I stared at the screen a long time before it occurred to me that the figures were in thousands. Three point six million. An insane sum to write off in terms of office equipment, company cars and entertainment. And if I probed further on the computer

I'd probably find all those itemised and accounted for. 'Sundries. 3,600.' The computers were linked and the same figures must be available to the head office in America. No wonder Fernandez was twitchy.

Tommy's big deal.

The room was silvery dark, illuminated only by the computer screen. When I lit a cigarette my enormous shadow jumped on the wall. It was possible that 'Sundries' was a tax dodge, a device still to be worked out. But I didn't believe it. Tommy was there in the darkness, a grinning presence, triumphant. It was what he had wanted all his life: to put one over on a multinational, to pull off the big one. And he wasn't around to enjoy it.

Tommy, you stupid bastard, you got it all right except for one detail: they are who they are.

I watched the shadows, waiting for an answer. The only sound was the humming of the fan inside the computer.

Three point six million. The pieces shifted and reassembled. I hadn't been thinking clearly enough. The packing case contained maybe fifty train sets. An engine, a tender and two carriages to a set. Each piece contained a package of pure uncut coke. In all, anything between twenty-five and fifty kilos of the stuff. In street value that was a huge amount. Even three point six million, though what did I know? Yet Fernandez pretends it doesn't matter. He talks about principle and offers me deals. He talks calmly, indifferently, as though the packing case were already safely stowed away after its unscheduled detour to Bournemouth and Kilburn.

So why the deficit?

Because the people the drugs were meant for had paid and Tommy had gone off with the money.

I stared at the computer screen: 'No information available'. Abel was right. There had to be a company somewhere, some innocent piece of paper, signed and countersigned.

I switched off the computer and the darkness closed in. Tommy disappointed me. Streetwise Tommy, who knew all the angles, had seriously thought he could take the money and walk away. Something must have happened to his sense of reality. A lesion, a short-circuit, some fatal disruption of the machinery. It didn't fit with my image of Tommy flailing around the squash court and gargling in the shower, going upstairs always two steps at a time, wheeling and dealing. Tommy with his appetite for food and women and business, his cunning and speed off the mark, his network of friends. He had seemed aggressive and hard-edged, a man in charge of his life. Of our lives, too; by sheer bull-headed persistence he had backed Judy and me into a corner where our vacillations made no sense and marriage was the only choice left. A big man, dangerous to others, beneficent to us. But when real money arrived he couldn't handle it. I felt let down.

A faint light came though a gap in the curtains, the sodium glow of London. The wind sighed past the window. 'No information available.' It would be available, of course, on Fernandez's terminal, assuming I could get into it without a password.

I stubbed out my cigarette and moved carefully across the room. The cold light of the closed-circuit monitor made the reception room seem brighter than my room. I glanced at the monitor as I passed behind Helen's desk, crossed to the door of Fernandez's office, then came back quickly. The camera no longer showed the corridor. It was focused on the lift doors. Someone had pressed the button to this floor. The doors opened as I watched and Fernandez came out, deep in conversation with Karl, leaning towards him as they walked, heads down, intent.

I moved quickly back to my room, not running in case I blundered into something, leaving the door ajar so they shouldn't hear it close or feel its vibrations lingering on the air. A single band of light lay across the desk. Maybe I should sit down, switch on the reading light and brazen it out. But I had no excuses ready and my mind was blank. I crossed to the window while a key scraped in the lock of the outer door. The curtains were heavy flecked wool, reaching to the floor. I got behind them and squeezed into the corner, trying to hold my breath. I wondered if Fernandez would notice the cigarette smoke and decide to look around.

The outer door opened, the lights went on. Karl was saying, 'Fascinating, but not our problem. We followed your instructions to the letter.' Clipped voice, careful enunciation.

'You hear me arguing?' A deeper rumbling note.

'You choose to do business with the Jews, you know what to expect.'

'Take it easy. Let's hear what Phoenix has to say.' Fernandez's tone was placatory, not like a boss to an underling.

The door to his office closed.

I stood in the narrow space between the curtains and the plate glass window. The great mass of Centre Point loomed in front of me, behind it the Post Office Tower. The sky was moonless, starless, enormous, filled with fast-moving orange clouds. I concentrated on the sounds in the office, waiting for the door to be flung open and the room to be flooded with light. I wanted a cigarette, I wanted to move about, I wanted to get the hell out. I tried to remember if there was a closed-circuit monitor among the battery of machines on Fernandez's desk. Maybe he had brought out the cut-glass decanter and they were sipping brandy together in comfort. The relationship between them seemed skewed, as if Karl were calling the shots. A clipped neat voice stating terms and conditions.

I moved slowly along the window and laid my ear to the wall that separated me from Fernandez's office. A faint murmur of voices. I could distinguish the bass from the tenor but I couldn't hear the words. The wind tugged at the building, the scudding clouds seemed quite close. I wondered what they were plotting in there over their drinks. I could picture the leather and steel furniture, the glint of cut glass, but the talk eluded me. Arguments about Tommy, about payments, about some arrangement Fernandez had made. Fernandez and Karl and the people at head office in Phoenix. A significant piece of paper worth three point six million. Sterling or dollars? Not that it mattered at that altitude. I couldn't see the connection with Karl and his safari jacket and steel-rimmed spectacles. The revolutionary poet and computer wizard. Another anti-semite. But casual, offhand, an anti-semite as a matter of course. Fernandez had sounded embarrassed by what he said, like a father with a bad-mannered child. I remembered the fat roulette player at the Beachcomber. Fernandez must have spent a large part of his life with Jews; he had the same worldliness, the same robust cynicism.

The door of his office opened. Fernandez was saying, 'Like I told you, you don't have a thing to worry about.'

Then Karl's voice, light and pedantic, 'My colleagues have unpredictable temperaments. They're not as reasonable as I am.'

'Believe me, you're home and dry. You heard head office. Everyone agrees it's not your problem, right? If anybody's ass is on the line, it's mine.'

'As long as we understand each other.'

The outer door closed. A heavy sigh, then slow footsteps as Fernandez walked back into his office. I waited for the sound of the door closing but it didn't come. A brief silence, then the murmur of his voice on the telephone.

I pushed the curtain aside. The lights from the reception hall laid a shadowy track across my office. I moved softly to behind the door and listened. The words came in waves, broken by attentive pauses. It was like listening to the sound of the sea in a seashell.

'No way he got it out of the county ... Naw, naw ... We

dropped on him too fast. He didn't have time to ... You think I'm sitting here on my butt doing nothing? ... Sure I got an idea ... Don't even think about it ... Plus a certain incentive, right ... What have I got to lose? Three point six is what. As if you didn't know ... Trust me, you hear ... Yeah, no problem, I got the guy right here, the office next to mine. He farts I know about it ... Sure ... OK ... The point being, you got the crazies off my back. I appreciate that ... Right, I'll get back to you.'

Another racking sigh, then silence. It was too late, I realised, to get back to the window. I waited behind the door, unmoving. My throat tickled and I wanted to cough. When I swallowed the noise in my ears seemed immense.

After what seemed a long time, I heard a chair creak, the clink of glass on glass. Another silence.

'Screw 'em,' said Fernandez loudly.

Brisk steps across the reception hall. The lights went out, the outer door closed. I sidled round the door and watched him on the closed-circuit monitor. The camera angle made him look crab-like and top-heavy. The camera held on him until the lift doors closed, then refocused on the corridor outside.

His office smelt of cigarette smoke and alcohol, warm and comfortable. When I switched on his computer a message appeared as I had known it would: 'Password please.'

Not that it mattered. All it could tell me was a name. Fernandez had no more idea where the company papers were than I did. Less, probably.

JUDY had forgotten to close the curtains. I stood outside for a moment, watching her move to and fro. Friends' paintings on the walls, shelves full of books, vases of flowers, the yellow glow of the lamps, shadows in the corners. She has a knack for taking places over. Her jacket tossed on to the sofa, her shoes kicked off on the carpet. I watched her go over to the hi-fi, full of purpose, concentrating. What's it to be? Faintly through the window came the sound of Ella Fitzgerald singing 'They Can't Take That Away From Me'. Softly, Judy began to sashay around the room, eyes closed, smiling like a cat. She seemed to shed years as she moved, a shapely woman, fighting her weight, keeping her age at bay. Twenty years old again, while the music lasted. The sudden view, I thought; one of the perks of marriage. She takes over rooms, trailing her scent, her pieces of tissue, like she has taken over my life. A generous woman, full of fight but never mean-minded, critical without being censorious. It was impossible to imagine a life without her. Helen was young and exciting but domesticity was erotic in a different way. I wondered if Judy felt the same about me when she was with her lover.

She went on dancing when I came in and we danced together until the song ended, just like old times, but when I told her how I had passed the evening her face tightened and her tongue probed her cheek. Storm warning.

'I think you make me sick,' she said carefully. 'Behaving like it's some stupid game. You could have got yourself into deep trouble.'

'It's Fernandez who's in deep trouble. He needs me to find that piece of paper. Hearing him on the phone, I felt kind of sorry for him.'

'When you heard them coming you should have switched on a light and faced them out. Said you were putting in overtime.'

'A likely story. He has to invent things for me to do as it is.'

'You could have thought of something.'

'The fact is, I was enjoying myself.'

'I knew you'd say that. They killed Tommy. What makes you think you're immortal?'

'Because they need me for the time being.'

'They needed Tommy and much good that did him.'

'Tommy had a dicky heart. They didn't reckon on that.'

'Would you cope any better if they set Hector on to you? It's your arrogance that gets me, your blind bloody arrogance.'

'Don't get worked up. Nothing happened.'

'No fault of yours.'

She put her stockinged feet on the table and stared at the photograph of Tommy and me. 'I'm beginning to think I don't like your friends,' she said.

'*Our* friends, remember?'

'I think the time's come when I want to disown them. Fresh start, clean slate, new day, that sort of thing. We can't go on being grateful to Tommy for the rest of our lives.'

I picked up the photograph on the coffee table and studied it. Tommy and I both looked absurdly young and optimistic. Unrecognisable. 'Three point six million,' I said. 'What an asshole.' I put my hand on her thigh and asked, 'What would you do with three point six million?'

'Idiot question.' She sat quiet a moment, considering the choices. 'It's drugs money, dirty money. I don't want to touch it. Also it's too much. We have a decent life, so why should we change it? Tommy's left us as much as we'll ever need. And even if he hadn't, I couldn't cope with being seriously rich. Nor could you.'

'Exactly. Even Tommy, Mr Big Shot, couldn't handle it. It ruined his sense of proportion. Killed him in the end. What we have to do is give it back, then they're off our backs.'

'Unless they decide you know too much and want you out of the way.'

'What do they know I know? Fernandez thinks I'm an innocent, a man of principle, whatever he wants to call it. Tommy was a competitor, a hustler with an eye on the big time. Me, I'm just some nebbisch who does what he's told. If I hand him the share certificate, all he'll do is revise me downwards in the stupidity scale. He's in trouble already. Why risk more by getting cute with me?'

'How can you hand him something you don't have?'

'All I got to do is find it.'

'You make it sound so bloody simple.'

I woke in the night and lay listening to Judy's quiet breathing. She turned and muttered something I couldn't hear. The wind blew in the street outside. The curtains billowed. 'Vespa,' she said, in a clear light voice. I took her hand under the covers. She was back in a time before I knew her. Judy on a Vespa, like Audrey Hepburn in *Roman Holiday*, threading the traffic, skirts billowing.

I went downstairs to the kitchen and poured myself a glass of milk. I stood by the open fridge door, watching the eerie shadows over the sink. Then I went into the living-room. Time to begin, I thought.

JUDY

Rogers has a hutch of an office, brightly lit. Joe says he's a bully, full of self-righteousness and disapproval. With me, he is efficient and low-keyed, almost diffident. Maybe he is shy with women.

What I don't tell him is why I am here. Fernandez and me in our Knightsbridge time capsule, curtains drawn, bedside lights on, ice melting in the bucket around the half-drunk bottle of champagne. Fernandez standing by the bed, looking down at me. The first time we met, in his office with Joe, he inspected me like I was a commodity for sale – packaged meat – checking the quality, the weight and shape, the sell-by date. A cool appraising buyer's look, the customer and the whore. I felt my insides flow, my knees become unsteady. Now his expression is soft and devoted, doggy.

'You're different from the others,' he says. 'No lacquered hair, no pancake make-up, no frilly underwear. You are what you are. A classy woman. I love those neat white panties of yours.'

'Two pound something a shot from Marks and Sparks. You buy them in packets of three.'

'They're real cute. Or maybe it's who's wearing them that counts.'

He crosses to the chair where he has left his clothes, sits down and pulls on a sock. He always starts with his socks when he dresses.

'Listen.' His voice is hoarse and a little unsteady. It seems to come from further down his throat than usual. Silence. I wait while he pulls on his second sock. 'Listen, if anything happened to Joe . . .' he picks up his shirt . . . 'would you marry me?'

My mouth is dry and it's hard to swallow. I wait, hearing my heart thump, trying to breathe. Finally, I manage, 'Nothing's going to happen to Joe, for Christ's sake.'

'Sure, sure.' He pulls on the shirt and knots his tie, taking his time. 'But if it did?'

It's important to keep my voice steady. 'We have a great time, you and I. But that's all there is to it, Ray. Great times. You're married, I'm married.'

'Just suppose.'

'Just suppose is for kids. But you're a lovely guy all the same. Don't ever doubt it.'

He comes over to the bed. He is wearing his socks, his shirt and his tie, but no underpants as yet. What sort of a man puts his socks on first? Apparently, he does not see himself as ridiculous. When he kisses me I kiss him back sweetly. For the first time since all this began, I am terrified.

I mention none of this to Rogers. I tell him about the fortune that's gone missing, the phantom company, about Karl. He takes notes and seems pleased.

'Why Budapest?' I ask. 'What's so special about Hungary?'

'Apple had commercial contacts there, people in the import-export business he could trust.'

'Tommy had contacts everywhere. Contacts were his speciality. He had a collection of business cards as big as the Oxford dictionary. A fat volume with plastic leaves. He showed it to us once when we went there for dinner. He boasted that he never threw a card away unless the person he'd got it from gave him a new one. The rag trade in Portugal, scrap iron in Bulgaria, he always knew the man to contact. That's how he made his money.'

'We've got the book. We're sifting through it. If the British Library had a commercial section, they'd pay a fortune for the thing.'

'You haven't answered my question: why Hungary?'

'Because of what you might call your customs interface. They're not looking for drugs from Eastern Europe.'

Rogers's office is stripped bare: grey steel desk piled with papers, grey steel filing cabinet against the wall behind him. The only ornament is a framed photograph on one wall: fifteen burly men in shorts and hooped shirts; beneath them, in gothic letters, is written 'Metropolitan Police R.F.C. 1978–79'. The man seated in the middle of the front row is holding a rugger ball. Rogers stands behind him, looking young and unforgiving.

He watches me now from under his bushy blond eyebrows. When he smiles the muscles in his jaw flex with the effort.

'Why have you come to me? Not that I'm not grateful and all that. We need what you've told us, need all the details we can get. But why have you come, not your husband?'

'Because I'm worried about my husband's safety. It's too much money. They could do anything for those sums. And Joe doesn't take it seriously. He treats it like a macho joke, a test. He seems to think he's playing with *them*, not the other way round.'

'And you have reason to think otherwise?'

'It's common sense. They only need him as long as they think he's useful. They don't owe him any favours. And anyway, they're not in the favours business.'

'So you came to me instead of Mr Stonehouse.'

'I don't find Stonehouse easy to talk to.'

The jaw muscles flex again. This time it's a grin, not a smile. 'Those Whitehall manners. They take some getting used to.'

I smile back. 'With Stonehouse I don't know who I'm talking to. All that gifted amateur stuff. I find it bewildering. Anyway, this is a matter for the police. One man has been murdered already.'

'Manslaughter. The cause of death was heart attack. Officially.'

'Whatever you want to call it. The bottom line is he's dead. I don't want that happening to my husband.'

'Point taken, Mrs Constantine. All you have to do is keep us informed.'

'Informed about what?'

'About your husband's movements, meetings, occasions when things could take a wrong turning.'

'It's not that sort of a marriage, Inspector. We don't keep tabs on each other.'

Rogers's jaw flexes again to produce what is supposed to be a patient smile. 'But you talk, yes? In the evenings, when day is done.'

'By then it's too late, isn't it?'

'But if something big was coming up, he'd tell you in advance?'

'He might.'

'Then you call me. It's not much to ask.'

'A propos big, Joe has this thing about Hector Gutierrez. Because of what happened to Tommy. He keeps saying he wants to even the score. It's a sort of obsession. Now he's asked Fernandez to get rid of him.'

'Symmetry,' Rogers says. 'I can appreciate that.'

'Except that Stonehouse says it's a request open to misinterpretation.'

'That depends on what your husband meant in the first place.'

'He meant get rid of him, send him back to wherever he comes from, find him another job.'

'Fernandez would have trouble taking it that way.'

'I gathered. According to Stonehouse, Hector is about to run out of time and Fernandez will want Joe to be there when it happens. As a sort of lesson.'

'That's how Fernandez would think. A lesson about power, about behaviour.' Rogers leans back in his chair and studies me.

Cold blue eyes but the expression is sympathetic. Then he seems to remember himself and the big smile comes back, the voice turns enthusiastic. 'We get our timing right, it's us who could do the teaching.'

His eyes are cold but he looks, for the moment, young and gung-ho. Maybe he is trying to impress me with his competence, maybe this is his way of flirting. More likely, he is a man who knows what he's about and enjoys his job. I realise I like him, whatever his motives. I want him on my side. I even like the way he flexes his jaw muscles, the Jack Palance he-man trick. He is probably about my age but he makes me feel comfortable, maternal. I look at his bony face and scrubbed cheeks and wonder what kind of mother he had. Like mine probably, nothing to boast about.

'We don't want your husband doing anything rash,' he says.

'*You* don't want. What terrifies me is he's beginning to think he's a hero. When I asked him why he hid behind the curtain like Polonius, instead of switching on a light and facing them down, he told me he was enjoying himself. The truth is, he's bored. Photography bores him and now this new thing, playing the businessman, bores him even more. If there's some kind of showdown, God knows what idiocy he might perform. Just to break the monotony and make himself feel he's alive.'

The noise of the place gets to me. I had expected something formal, hushed, perhaps a little secretive. Instead, there is all this din: telephones ringing, footsteps, loud voices. Rogers appears not to notice it. His expression is sober and intent.

'You make him sound like a very depressed man,' he says.

There is no accusation in his voice but I find myself apologising. 'He's middle-aged and his life hasn't turned out the way he wanted. No great glowing success and no money to make up for the lack of success. Not because he lacks the talent but because he's never used himself properly. He stands in his own way. He's too modest. It's one of his nicest qualities but it's also a sickness.'

'I'm sure you're not to blame,' Rogers says soothingly.

'Why are you sure? I have my own work, I do my own job. Maybe I should have given more time to him.'

'But it's a good marriage, all in all?'

'That's what I always thought. Now I'm not so sure. Maybe he's pushing his luck in order to get a reaction out of me.' The strange place seems to be getting to me. This is a policeman I'm talking to, not a marriage counsellor. 'I don't even know why I'm telling you all this,' I say.

'The more we know, the easier it will be to help.' He seems faintly embarrassed. 'What matters is to stop your husband doing something foolish.'

He gives me his private number, the direct line, writing it down on a sheet of official paper and handing it to me solemnly, like a love letter. 'You and I,' he says. 'We can see this thing through, no trouble. It'll come out all right. Not to worry.'

'With a little help from my friends,' I say, giving him a wan smile.

But when I am outside again in the swirl of London all I can think of is my inadequacy. I'm not much of a wife, I lack the old-fashioned virtues, I should take better care of my husband. Not that Joe would thank me for saying so. He sees himself as a free agent making his way among obstacles. These days I figure as just another obstacle.

It is time to stop these unholy alliances, to stop kidding myself. I pretend I'm sleeping with Fernandez to save Joe's hide, like Joe tells himself he sleeps with Helen because I'm bedding someone else. All lies. Joe has had a thing about that girl since he first set eyes on her, and I've had a thing about Fernandez. Helen's youth, Fernandez's brute authority. The smell of violence and power, the flat-eyed detachment. Everything I don't get in my marriage. I seem to have a taste for the perverse. Carefully hidden, even from myself. And now it turns out Fernandez has a taste for the ordinary, for an ordinary woman with an ordinary marriage, for Marks & Spencer underwear and not much make-up. What a let-down. I pictured him as a man with floozies on the side, spending his life with other men, giving them orders, making them jump. But smoothly, quietly, a man with so much power he does not need to flaunt it. Oiling the wheels with money, making deals. The world of executive decisions, power lunches, permanent five o'clock shadow. He made my domesticated life seem dingy and forlorn. Now he says he wants to marry me and I'm disappointed. Unless it's just a ploy to frighten me.

The pieces are slotting together and I still don't know what part I'm playing. Long stop, maybe. The figure at the edge of the field who pulls off the miracle last-minute catch. Some hope. Joe has had other wives, blurred presences as far as I'm concerned. I can rehearse their bad points – his version of their bad points – but know nothing of their virtues, if they had any. Am I becoming another figure in his landscape. Does he talk about me to Helen?

He comes back early, while I am in the garden cutting flowers. Fernandez's exotica are withered and gone. I cut tulips, early roses, to fill the empty vases.

He pours drinks and slumps into an armchair. 'I can't go through with it,' he says. 'I see Hector peacocking about and I feel sorry for the little prick. What do I want with guns and knives and the power of life over death? It's not our world, sweetheart. We're not cut out for violent death. We're going to die like everybody else – slowly, inconveniently, of some smelly disease. If we're really lucky, we'll keel over with heart attacks, like poor old Tommy.'

'Poor old Tommy. I was wondering how long it would take you to get round to him.'

'I note the dry tone,' he says. 'Thanks.'

'I thought your mission these days was to even the score.'

'I've changed my mind. Tommy must look after himself. Greed got him in the end and he behaved like a fool. The prospect of all those millions softened his brain. The Tommy we knew was someone else. He got superseded by Fernandez's Tommy, who was just another grasping hustler. The worst kind of Jew, as my old dad used to say. The type that gets us all a bad name.'

'Is this Jewish anti-semitism I'm hearing? Our kind of Jew, their kind of Jew. That's quite a turnaround for a devoted friend.'

'I've seen the creature at the centre of the maze and I don't want any part of it. I'm not vengeful enough, indifferent enough.'

'What makes you think you can walk away now?'

'Fernandez doesn't want to lose Hector. They go way back. He feels protective. And why should he want the complications?'

I arrange the flowers, easing them apart, giving them space. The scent of the roses brings the early summer indoors. Joe is smiling in a self-satisfied way. Now he has made a decision the problem ceases to exist. His complacency irritates the hell out of me.

'You're assuming Fernandez is like you, a liberal at heart, Mr Nice Guy, a softy. Where did you get that idea? If he's taken an executive decision, he'll go through with it. He has his position to think of, his authority. Here and back in the States with his bosses. He's not like you and me. He makes a decision, he doesn't draw back. Consequences don't bother him, as long as they work against other people, not him.'

'I thought you'd say something like that.' His smile has gone. He leans forwards, talking in a low voice. 'I've played it out in my head again and again. I see it happening in a warehouse somewhere behind King's Cross. Pentonville Road, Caledonian Road, York Way, part of that urban sprawl. Heavy traffic but no pedestrians. Shops selling motor spare parts, builders' materials. The place itself unused, musty and cold, a couple of naked light bulbs, grimy floors. Maybe a long table down the middle where whatever work they did was once done. And packing cases scattered all over, like the one we collected from Bournemouth. Danny would be there and probably Fernandez, to show who's boss. Maybe Karl too, because now we know Karl is someone they want to impress. Hector in his Burberry and foolish tweed hat. They'd have pulled out one of the packing cases, perhaps the one filled with wooden trains, the one that started all the trouble. Fernandez says, "Open it up." The point being to make it look like a drugs killing. Hector jemmies off the top, flexing his muscles, showing off as usual. Then Danny reaches into that batwing leather jacket and pulls out a gun. A gun with a silencer that makes it look clumsy and unbalanced.'

His voice, as he speaks, has become quieter and quieter. I have to lean forwards to hear him. I wait. The scent of the roses is heavy on the air. His eyes are dreamy, elsewhere. Suddenly, a quick embarrassed smile.

'At that point, whichever way I figure it, the gun is turned on me,' he says.

We sit in silence while the light fades and the brilliant red of the tulips drains away.

'People like us don't get involved in thrillers,' I say at last. 'We lack the necessary resolve, the hard outlines. The others, the ones that are good at it, they don't have private lives. Maybe they have faceless wives at home who eat alone in the evenings and leave hubby's dinner in the oven. Kids they see at weekends, if they're not working. You and I, we're not like that. What we have is this marriage. Everything else is on the side, a way of passing the daylight hours.'

'I'm glad to hear it. I had the impression that this holy marriage of ours was beginning to fall apart.'

'Because we're trying to play their game. It's not that we're outclassed. We just don't know the rules.'

He shifts in his chair, then turns slowly and looks at me. 'Give him up,' he says. 'Whoever he is.'

His back is to the light. I touch the edges of his face, trying to make out his expression. I run my fingers over his mouth. He does not move.

'It's over,' I say. 'There was nothing there to give up. An idea is all. I got it wrong.'

He looks at me wide-eyed. I can make out that much in the fading light. He was just guessing. A stab in the dark and it hit home. Or rather, he tells himself he was just guessing. He has known all along. After twelve years, how much can you hide?

'I don't want this to be like my other marriages. All that shabby deception.'

'It isn't. You know as well as I do. I don't have to prove it. It was a mistake. Not even. The fact is, I thought I could help us. *Us.* You have to believe me.'

He shrugs. 'After all this time, who else have I got to believe?' He raises his glass. 'A drink to us, for better or for worse.'

'You're my best friend,' I say. 'Among other things.'

'That's a truth.'

We clink glasses and drink in silence. But finally, I have to say it, 'There's always Helen to consider.'

'Helen's nothing. A kid. Tit for tat.'

'Twenty-three-year-old tits for tat. The trouble is, I don't trust you, Joe.'

'You don't trust *me.* That's rich. There wouldn't be a Helen if I hadn't thought I was losing you.'

'You're a romantic, Joe. That's what I don't trust. You get involved.'

'And you don't?'

'Only with you, with us.'

Another silence. Then he says, 'We shouldn't be wrangling like this, not if we're best friends. We both got it wrong and now there's something more important to worry about.'

The room is dark. I get up and switch on the lights.

'Like life and death,' I say.

WE go jogging now the mornings are fine, leaving the car in the park on the lower heath, trotting across the causeway between the ponds. The trees are full of early morning light. The slog to the top of Parliament Hill makes us pant and sweat but the aerobics classes stand me in good stead and after a couple of days my legs no longer ache too viciously. From Parliament Hill we strike off cross-country, over the open sweep towards Kenwood, then back down the long avenue of lime trees, across the rolling ground behind the pond to the car. Sweating, out of breath, feeling good.

On really warm days we finish with a swim in the pond. The water is amber and chilly and tastes of mud. When we come out we glow from head to foot, as though newly born, full of mindless well-being. On the way home we stop at the baker's in South End Green and buy warm bread for breakfast. If you have taken exercise, a discreet amount of self-indulgence is permitted.

Jogging is our excuse for not starting the day with sludgy muesli.

One morning I notice that Joe has a bulky object in his tracksuit pocket. It drags at the fabric and bounces awkwardly on his hip. I drop back to study the effect as he runs. A steady thump thump against the tyre of middle-age fat around his waist. He touches it occasionally, as if for reassurance.

The object is there the next day and the next. On the fourth morning I ask him what he's carrying.

He puts his hand defensively on his pocket, looks sheepish and says, 'I was hoping you wouldn't notice.'

'Of course I noticed, I'm your wife, remember?'

'I don't see the connection.'

'It's there, believe me. I notice more things about you than I do about me. All the little irregularities. That's what marriage is about.'

The expresso machine on the stove begins to steam and stutter. I cut the warm loaf and help myself to marmalade. Joe prefers Gentleman's Relish. I push the white and black jar towards him, then go and fetch the coffee.

When I come back there is a small revolver on the kitchen table. Flat, blunt-nosed, efficient-looking.

'The American gave it to me. The one with the name like a village, Langton Green. Stonehouse is fixing the licence.'

'Did they say why?'

'The general impression I got was, things are tough all over. Specifically Hector. In case something goes haywire.'

'You don't know how to use it.'

'They took me out into the country and made me practise. It's not as hard as you'd think. You point it like you point your finger.'

'And you're going to point it at Hector?'

'Only if I have to. Only in self-defence.'

'I hope I'm not around to see it.'

He spreads the paste carefully on his bread, takes a large bite and chews pleasurably. 'It's just in case things get out of hand,' he says.

'It looks like they've got out of hand already.'

We eat in silence. The bread is delicious, creamy in texture, with a crust that crunches when I bite into it.

'Better to be prepared,' he says between mouthfuls. 'Who wants to go naked to the conference table?'

When I phone Rogers later in the day he is non-committal. 'I see,' he says. 'I see.'

'I wish I did.'

'It could be for the best, in the circumstances.' Then he adds in an aggrieved voice, 'But I'm surprised Stonehouse didn't see fit to tell me.'

My husband is toting a gun and all that concerns the police is interdepartmental rivalry.

The revolver has introduced a new element into our lives, a seriousness. Before it, death was not on the agenda. My parents died, of course, but both had beaten their allotted three score years and ten and by the time they went there was no love between any of us. I mourned what they had been, not what they had become, and was secretly glad not to have to pretend to feelings I no longer had. Tommy's death was shocking, a twentieth-century happening, random and mindless, like a violent mugging for small change. But I felt no decline in myself. I might still have a baby; a new beginning was possible.

The revolver has put an end to options. It signifies chaos, mayhem. Hector's death, Joe's death, my death. We could all get blown away at any moment and Joe goes around with the means of our destruction in his pocket, dragging his jacket out of shape. In the evenings I can't take my eyes off the thing.

Louise comes to dinner, picks at her food, talks about the Cambridge diet.

'I'm on the market again,' she says wryly. 'Time to get myself into shape.' She leans her heavy breasts on the table, runs painted fingers through her mop of hair. 'Not that I begrudge you,' she says. 'You knew Tommy much longer than I did, and anyway I've got the flat.'

'What will you do?'

'Sell the place probably, go back into the schmatte trade, buy myself a partnership.'

She watches Joe balefully as he refills her glass.

'I know the business,' she explains. 'I've got friends from way back. The truth is, Reddington Road's getting me down. It's too big, too lonely for me on my own. All those red brick mansions and no one around when you get back at night. Muggers' paradise.'

'You'll get a fortune for the place,' Joe says.

'Fortune. I prefer we shouldn't talk about fortunes.'

'We had no idea,' I say soothingly. 'We hadn't even seen much of him recently. It turns out this was something he planned years ago.'

'I'm not holding it against you. It's just that it makes me feel used. I'd always thought, maybe if I don't push it he'll settle down, we'll make a go of it. Now it turns out I was just another temporary all along. He wasn't taking me seriously.'

'He didn't take himself seriously. He'd given up on his private life. I suppose that's why he fixed on us.'

Louise's painted mouth turns down at the corners and the lines around it deepen. I can see her a quarter of a century on, Louise at sixty, gossiping over coffee and cream cakes with her friends, women with heavy rings on their fingers, diamond brooches and dyed hair, with husbands who spend their evenings playing kalooki at the club.

'So why the continual hustle for money?'

'That was his game. He wanted to be a winner.'

'I feel shut out,' Louise says.

Her future is mapped out in the lines around her mouth. The husband with a head like a fringed cannon ball, the children, the ritual quarrelling, the gossip, Tommy just a blurred image from her indiscreet youth.

'She's a devious bitch,' Joe says after she's gone. 'Trying to work on our guilt. Hoping we'd split the pot with her probably. She put in two years with Tommy and got an annuity and a half-million-pound flat out of it. And we're supposed to be embarrassed.'

'You sound like her. Why don't we just forget the money. Who cares who's got what?'

He takes the gun out of his pocket. It is black and business-like, disproportionately small for its power. 'I should have shown her this. I should have said, "You want Tommy's legacy, you can have it." '

The gun is sleek and compact and self-contained. It has presence and authority, a figure in the household, like the child we've never had.

'Put it away. It gives me the creeps.'

Joe switches on the television. 'What we need is a late-night thriller, Lee Marvin or Robert Ryan, someone threatening who knows how to handle these things. Someone whose perceptions aren't changed by them.'

'Why don't you give it back? Tell Stonehouse it's not your style.'

'You mean it's not your style. I find it kind of reassuring.'

'I wish I could make you understand this isn't a game.'

'That's what I'm getting at. It's a real situation and we're real players. That's why we need the gun.'

Feet up, immovable in front of the television set. His smugness is back tenfold now he has the revolver. Which he scarcely knows how to use. There is no sign of extra ammunition in the house, so I assume he no longer practises with it. Unless he is seeing Stonehouse on the sly, slipping off in the afternoons to some fenced-off government enclave and shooting at tin cans. Somewhere not too far from town, like Camberley, where they are used to soldiers and the noise they make.

You point it like you point your finger.

Rather him than me.

'It may make you feel good but it scares me to death. Just keep it out of my sight.'

Joe puts the little revolver back in his pocket, then turns up the television in time for a burst of gunfire. I leave him to it.

IT is summer now, real summer, hot and dry. We swim every morning and some evenings we drink beer on the pavement outside pubs, being young with the young. But mostly we sit outside in the garden, enjoying the evening air, the big old house at our backs.

The old-fashioned house has old-fashioned features like French windows that once opened on to a conservatory. But the family fortunes had begun to decay when Joe was very small and the house had decayed with them. All that is left of the conservatory is a square of glazed tiles that used to be its floor. A few years after the war the conservatory collapsed for no apparent reason. It simply toppled under its own weight, weakened by bombs, V1s and V2s, by the weather, by age, by lack of care. It happened one morning when Joe's mother was soaking in the bath. She heard a vague muffled thump, like heavy artillery in the distance, and the water swayed around her in the bath. Two minutes later, the doorbell rang. The only other person in the house was Minnie the cook but Minnie never answered the door, supposedly on principle – because cooks were paid to cook, not to perform ordinary domestic chores – but really because she was too deaf to hear it. Mrs Constantine wrapped herself in a towel and padded downstairs, leaving wet footprints on the carpet. The neighbour's child was on the doorstep, shivering with glee.

'Mummy said to say, something's happened in your garden.'

What she found when she opened the French windows was a tangle of broken glass and wood, splintered lattice-work and furniture. She laughed till she cried, then she just cried.

'My beautiful conservatory.'

Eventually, the rubble was cleared away but nobody ever got around to filling out an insurance claim. Now we have money again I have plans for a new conservatory but in the meantime we sit out there on fine evenings, listening to the poplars rustling together at the end of the garden, the tiled floor a reminder of Constantine fecklessness.

There is a passage along the side of the house, past the kitchen door, the tradesmen's entrance in the good old days, where the milkman and the coalman and the man from Harrods made their deliveries. Now only the dustmen use it when they collect the bins. The old door at the street end sags on its hinges and in autumn leaves collect on the cracked uneven concrete.

Friday evening and we are outside, sprawled in deckchairs on the decrepit platform of tiles, the last light fading behind the poplars, the evening concert turned up on the radio, the French windows open at our backs. I am not surprised when they appear quietly at the corner of the garden, three shadowy figures, a thickening of darkness. Maybe I have been waiting for them.

Fernandez is in front, leading the way. He holds up his hand to us, a placatory gesture, and the others shuffle to a halt behind him. Danny and Hector, dressed for summer in T-shirts and bomber jackets.

'We rang the bell and no one answered,' Fernandez says.

'It's the music,' Joe replies.

'So I heard. And we saw the lights. That's why we came around the side.'

Joe heaves himself out of the deckchair and starts towards the French windows. 'Have a drink now you're here.'

It is strange to have them in our sitting-room, among the familiar things. Fernandez seems put out by the books and pictures. He sits stiffly in the armchair, cradling his drink, knees together, back straight. The other two remain standing, one either side of his chair, like acolytes. Danny peers around the room, grins at me cheerfully and says, 'Grand.' Hector watches Joe, wooden-faced.

'Why haven't I seen you this week?' Fernandez is talking to Joe but he glances quickly at me, then quickly back. He smiles pleasantly.

'I've had things to do at the studio.'

'At the studio?' Another smile, slower this time, indicating disbelief. 'I thought all that was behind you.'

'I can't just leave it flat. I have clients, an agent, an assistant, all sorts of ends to tidy up.'

'You should have called.' Again a flickering glance in my direction, on and off.

Joe looks at me shrewdly and laughs. 'I never knew you cared.'

Fernandez puts his drink on the coffee table and spreads his hands, palms up. 'I begin to wonder about you, Joe, whether your heart is in this new work of yours.'

'Funny you should mention it. The truth is, I don't see what I'm doing with you except wasting time. Your time, my time.'

Fernandez clasps his hands together for a moment, as if in prayer: 'I thought we had something going. A relationship. I thought I was giving you a new lease on life, saving you from boredom.'

He is still talking to us both but now he looks only at Joe. He has made his point and Joe has picked up the clue.

'Oh my,' says Joe.

Hector has moved away into the shadows at the back of the room. He picks up a round ivory powder box that belonged to Joe's grandmother, examines it, puts it down. Then he leans against a bookcase, hands in his jeans pockets, watching us from a distance, girlish mouth set in a tight smile.

I suppose they had to come here sooner or later. The family home Joe has never managed to leave, for all his surface sophistication, his comings and goings. They have come to join the other ghosts, the crumbling fabric, the fucked-up family history, parents, sisters, old servants, all dead and gone. We should have sold the place when we had the chance, moved somewhere new and started over. But Joe is rooted to the spot, as though hypnotised. The boy who couldn't leave home.

Fernandez has taken up his drink again. He swirls the whisky around in the glass, making the ice cubes clink. 'I don't think you're being altogether straight with me,' he says lightly.

A chill descends. Nobody speaks. I feel Joe beside me on the sofa, a bristling tension. He eyes the three men, waiting for the next move. But when he finally speaks he manages to sound relaxed, all pals together. 'Hey, I'm the man of principle, remember? I found the packing case for you.'

'Not that I'm not grateful,' Fernandez says. 'But the game's moved on since then.'

'What game?'

'Tommy's game. His big coup, the schmuck.'

'I don't know anything about it.'

Fernandez sips his drink and leans back comfortably. His dark eyes are moist with understanding. 'Let me spell it out for you. We did a deal with certain people, unsavoury people, unreliable people with short fuses. You know how it is. Tommy was the middle man. The money went through him and he was supposed to get a percentage for his efforts. A generous percentage. Instead, he tried to walk off with the lot.'

Joe laughs. 'That sounds ill-advised.' I sit upright beside him, gathered up in myself, waiting for the punch line.

'What got into him?' Joe sounds as though they were discussing some troublesome child.

'Greed,' says Fernandez. 'Greed and chutzpah. A fatal combination. He spun me one of his bullshit stories. He said there's been a delay, the money hadn't come through on time, so he'd removed the goods to safe keeping.'

Hector levers himself upright and moves off around the room. I can hear him behind us, picking things up, putting them down.

'Of course, we knew better,' Fernandez says. 'He was playing for time. A couple of days to tie up the loose ends and get the hell out. Hector found the tickets. To Papeete, for Christ's sake. He was the last of the romantics, was Tommy. Starting over again on a tropical isle.'

'Tickets?'

'One for him, one for Helen. But we were ahead of him, of course. Helen works for me.'

Just in case Joe has forgotten.

'Pathetic,' says Joe. 'I can see why you lost patience. What I don't see is where I come into the picture.'

Fernandez sighs. 'Greed,' he says sorrowfully. 'It'll be the death of us all.' He looks at me fully for the first time, a long slow tender look. 'Tell him, Judy.'

They are putting on this show for my benefit, acting cool to impress me, to show me who is boss. Their conceit knows no bounds. I can feel the colour rising to my cheeks – but in anger, not embarrassment. If I had any sense, I'd walk out and leave them to it. I start to get up but at that moment there is a rustling sound, a sharp explosion of breath behind me. Hector has lunged forwards. He grabs Joe's hair with his left hand and jerks his head back. In his right hand is a flick knife with a stiletto blade, long and elegant, sparkling in the lamplight. Everything seems to be happening in slow motion and great detail. Hector's eyes are gleaming with excitement.

A thin red line opens on the side of Joe's neck, grows fat and spills over. Big drops of blood drip down into his collar.

'Stop him,' I yell.

Fernandez is watching, glass clasped in both hands, knees pressed demurely together. He glances at me and smiles faintly. He is making a point for my benefit.

'Hector,' he says. 'Restrain yourself.'

Hector doesn't move. He has Joe's head pulled back. The knife rests lightly against his throat.

'Let him go.' I try to keep my voice down but I can hear the rising note of panic. Hector turns his gleaming face, shows me his teeth and runs the tip of his tongue over his lower lip. Joe rolls his eyes towards me and does not move. His jaw is clenched tight.

'The share certificate.' Fernandez leans forwards. 'Let's not screw around any more. We know you've got it.'

'Get him off.' Joe speaks carefully, trying not to disturb the knife at his throat.

Fernandez nods and Hector moves Joe's head forwards. The knife stays where it is.

'I suppose this turns you on,' I say to Fernandez. 'Who're you trying to impress?'

He looks at me without sympathy, then motions to Hector, a fractious impatient gesture. Hector lowers the knife and lets go of Joe's hair.

Joe presses a handkerchief to his bleeding neck, then looks at the bloodstains on it with astonishment. 'He hurt me.' He sounds puzzled.

'Nobody wants this.' Fernandez's expression is solemn and concerned. 'We're all friends here. Let's keep it that way. Why don't we have another drink and talk business?'

Joe goes over to the cupboard and picks up the bottle. He moves stiffly, like a man in shock. The muscles of his jaws are working. When he tips whisky into Danny's glass the Irishman grins at him and shrugs. Hector has retreated into the shadows at the back of the room, the knife still in his hand.

Joe hesitates before he replaces the bottle. His eyes flicker around the room. I know what he's looking for. The gun is in his jacket pocket and his jacket is slung over the back of a chair in the kitchen.

He sighs and sits down beside me on the sofa, takes the handkerchief from his neck and examines it again. 'I don't believe this,' he says.

'It isn't what I intended, nothing like it, I promise you.'

'The man's an animal.'

Fernandez displays one of his smiles, this one slow and warm-hearted. 'I'm genuinely sorry. But this thing's been going on too long. We're all on edge.'

'Tell me what you want then.'

'You already know.'
'Tell me anyway.'
'The payment was made into a Panamanian company. Tommy was handed a share certificate, negotiable, like a bearer bond.'
'What makes you think I know where it is?'
The question, or Joe's tone of voice, seems to reassure Fernandez. He stretches languidly and glances at his watch. 'You're a poker player, Joe. You know how it is. Instinct. Sometimes you can read a guy's hand as clearly as if he had all his cards face up.' He sips his drink, leaning forwards, watching Joe carefully and smiling his smile.
'Don't screw around, Joe. Just give me the fucking thing.'
Joe holds the stained handkerchief to his neck. His eyes are bright and the muscles of his jaw are still working. 'What about our deal?' he asks.
'Which of our many deals are you referring to?'
Joe jerks his head slightly in the direction of Hector who is standing by the open French windows. I can see rose bushes behind him, white garden furniture in the darkness.
Fernandez shrugs. 'A deal's a deal.'
I get to my feet and move towards the kitchen, saying, 'Anyone want coffee?' Nobody takes any notice. While the kettle boils, I stare at the telephone. If I call Rogers, the telephone in the sitting-room will light up and they'll be in here immediately. I pour my coffee and sling Joe's jacket over my shoulders, feeling the reassuring weight of the gun. When I get back no one has moved. Joe and Fernandez lean towards each other, one either side of the coffee table, like two chess players.
'I don't have to go anywhere,' Joe is saying. 'It's right here.'
'You mean you've got it on you?'
'I mean it's staring you in the face.'
There is a lamp on the coffee table between them and next to the lamp is a terracotta head of myself when young, sculpted by a friend at art school. The face is tender and hopeful and vulnerable, and I no longer like it. It reminds me how far I have travelled in the last few years. Next to the head is the smiling photograph of Joe and Tommy, the two musketeers. Fernandez picks up the photograph and turns it on its back.
'Right on,' says Joe.
I sit down beside him on the sofa, close enough for him to feel the gun in the jacket between us. He smiles and squeezes his leg against mine.
The back of the frame is sealed with Sellotape. Fernandez picks

at it impatiently, hunched over and intent. Angled shreds of tape peel off the edges. *Greed, It'll be the death of us all.* He clicks his fingers at Hector and holds up his hand, palm upwards, while he goes on picking at the tape.

'Knife.'

Hector hesitates, then lays the knife sullenly on his upturned hand. Fernandez does not look up. He keeps staring at the framed photograph as if it might disappear if his concentration lapsed. He cuts delicately around the frame, then hands the knife back to Hector. Very carefully, he lifts off the cardboard back and takes out a sheet of paper, turns it over, examines it.

'Son of a bitch,' he whispers. 'You had it all along.'

'I only found it a few days ago. I was going to give it to you. I swear to God.'

Fernandez looks at the paper, then he looks at Joe. He laughs expansively. 'You're a character, Joe. I reckoned I'd seen everything but, so help me, you're a one-off.'

'I'm a man of principle, remember?'

Fernandez smiles indulgently. 'You know something? I think I'm disappointed.'

'Suit yourself.'

Fernandez shakes his head. 'You've got a fortune right here, the kind that could set you up for life.'

Joe smiles ruefully and shrugs. 'What would I do with a fortune, Ray? I'm not the type.'

Till death us do part, I think. When he was young and ambitious I was swept along in his wake. It was a terrific ride, full of appetite and hope. I loved him for his impatience, for the fire in his belly. Now the fire has gone out and he's no longer trying to impress anyone, not even himself, and I think I love him more. A modest man with modest aims. What were we hustling for, all those years?

I watch Fernandez's hairy hands as he folds the paper neatly and slips it into his pocket and wonder why I ever wanted him to touch me. Hooded eyes, heavy mouth, dark jowls. He gets to his feet wearily, his little paunch hanging over his belt. Danny is at his shoulder, an indolent presence, smiling happily. They turn to Hector who has drifted away and is standing by the door into the hall.

'Well now,' says Fernandez.

There is a new tension in the air, bristling and edgy.

'You all right, son?'

Hector nods. 'Never better, boss.'

'That's good, because what we've got here is a little problem. The thing is, Hector, you're supposed to disappear. Mr Constantine here disapproves of what you did to his friend and he wants rid of you. "Get rid of him", those were his very words. Pretending he means find you a job somewhere else, get you out of his sight. But you and I know what he means, don't we, old pal? He means ice the bastard but do it somewhere I don't have to look.'

He turns to Joe. His face is lit by anger, purified by it, like a man who has shed a great burden. 'I know about you, Joe Constantine, don't think I don't. You support the right causes, you sign the right petitions. Save the whales, save the rainforest, viva Nicaragua, save the fucking workers. You and the rest of the self-righteous liberal mob. Just so you can sleep easy at nights with your pictures and your music and your books. Let other people hustle for money. You're superior to all that, aren't you?' He pauses. Indignation makes him tremble. 'I don't buy that shit, Joe. I can see right through you. You're a vindictive little prick at heart. You want Hector's balls on a plate, not because he hurt your friend but because he disturbed your peace of mind, your cosy domestic idyll. So you hand me the money and say, "A deal's a deal," expecting me to do your dirty work for you. Well, I've got news for you, friend. I'm a man of principle, too. I believe in loyalty to my own. Isn't that right, Hector?'

Hector bares his teeth in the lamplight.

Fernandez leans towards me and puts a hand on my shoulder. 'Come with me, Judy. He's not just a loser, he's a creep, a coward. You deserve better.'

They are all looking at me now. Joe's mouth is tight, his eyes are wide and dark.

I shake my head.

Fernandez shrugs. Then he touches the edge of my face and smiles, a real smile finally. 'Light of my life,' he says.

He and the Irishman go out the way they came, through the garden.

There are moments when the house goes quiet and I can feel the presences that keep Joe tied to the place. Like voices just out of earshot. I strain to hear the words but it does no good.

Hector has stayed behind. He watches us, lips rolled back over his pretty teeth.

Joe takes no notice of him. He eyes me gravely. Sadness, disappointment. It's no use saying, I was only trying to help, or even, What about Helen? It's too late for the usual domestic squabble, the mutual recriminations, the inevitable stand-off. *Light of my life.* Who would have thought someone as streetwise as Fernandez could come up with an old-fashioned phrase like that? But then, he's always had a knack for making me feel good. For a moment I see myself as mistress of an adobe palace in Phoenix, swimming laps in the Olympic pool before breakfast. But of course, his wife would get all that.

Hector ambles over to where we are sitting, the knife balanced lightly in his hand. The smile is still fixed on his face, the murky eyes glint with pleasure.

He stands over Joe and says, 'Just you and me.'

I feel Joe's hand slide into the pocket of the jacket between us. He inches forwards on the sofa, preparing to stand.

'It had to happen sooner or later,' he says.

'You better believe it.'

Joe grins. He is trembling with excitement but when he speaks his voice is light and easy. 'You've always been the fly in the ointment, Hector. For me, Fernandez was never a problem. I like men who know their way around. It's something I lack, a quality I admire. Also he's got a lot of charm, if you don't mind being manipulated. Likewise Danny. I'm a sucker for Irish blarney, the gift of the gab, the tear in the bluff blue eye. But you're something else, Hector.'

'What am I, mister?'

The knife is level with Joe's face. He stares past it, up into Hector's grinning face. 'You're the spider in the cup,' he says. 'You're what it all comes down to in the end. The irreducible brute element. There's no way around you.'

'You're way over my head, man.'

Joe pats the air between them. 'Don't be offended. All I'm saying is, we were meant for each other. You know what's wrong with me, why I can't make a go of things? It's because I've never believed in happy endings. The good marriage, the little nest egg, the comfortable life. My wife here, she's an optimist. She thinks things will work out, we'll live happily ever after, and all that stuff. Not me, Hector. I've always known there was someone like you waiting for me. The crock of shit at the end of the rainbow.'

The knife twitches in Hector's hand. 'Don't get cute,' he says. 'It's a fine line you're treading here.'

Joe holds up his hand in a gesture of peace. 'Don't misunderstand me. All I'm saying is, it was only a matter of time. We were bound to finish up like this.' He turns to me. 'Just look at her, will you? Observe the wide eyes, the trembling lips. See her leg pressing against mine. She's telling me to shut up, you see, to stop provoking you. You know why she's doing that? It's like I said, because she's an optimist. She thinks if I keep my mouth shut and sit tight and don't get you mad, you're going to walk out of here, walk out of our lives, along with the dope and the violence and her friend and mine, Ray Fernandez, with those hairy hands she finds so attractive. Then, bless her, everything will be back where it was, cosy and intimate, just like she always wanted. But that's not how it is, right? You and me, Hector, we've got unfinished business, haven't we?'

Hector is swaying slightly to some demented inner rhythm. His upper lip is still rolled back in a rictus of mirth but his muddy eyes are not quite focused.

'One thing I want to know,' Joe goes on in the same light taunting voice. 'Are you here because Fernandez told you or are you working on your own account?'

'Call it personal,' says Hector. He leans suddenly forwards and there is a flicker of brightness as the knife arcs through the air. I hear myself scream. Joe's cheek opens from ear to chin in a terrible grin.

He gasps and lifts his left hand to his face. Then he raises the gun, still in the jacket pocket, and shoots Hector point blank in the stomach.

Hector looks at him astonished. He makes a low growling keening noise and lunges forwards again unsteadily. Joe is on his feet now, blood streaming down his face, the gun levelled in the trailing jacket. He twists away as Hector comes at him and fires again. Hector staggers and keeps on coming. The knife goes into Joe's upper chest, below the right shoulder. He grunts as if he'd been poleaxed and drops the gun.

Hector staggers back and sits down heavily on a chair, holding his abdomen. There is blood all over his jeans, his face is drained, his eyes are wide in astonishment.

Joe is on the floor, rolled into a foetal position, blood everywhere. I go down on my knees beside him and pull the little gun out of the jacket pocket.

Hector manages a wasted smile. 'Now the cunt's getting into the act,' he informs no one in particular.

I point the gun at him, holding it in two hands, straight-armed, like they do in the movies.

Hector gets unsteadily to his feet and stands swaying, the knife loose in his hand. 'He shot me,' he says in a puzzled voice. 'The little creep shot me.'

'What did you expect?' I say.

He stares at me and the ghost of a grin comes back, although there are bubbles of blood at one corner of his mouth and his face is like ash. He wavers uncertainly towards me, holding the knife at waist level.

'Gimme the gun. You're a nice lady. You don't do that stuff.'

He inches forwards and I move back, trying to keep the gun steady.

'Come on,' he says. 'You and me, we don't have no quarrel.'

My back is against the wall. I steady myself as he comes closer.

'Come on,' he repeats and makes a drunken grab for the gun.

When I pull the trigger the revolver jumps in my hands.

Hector sits down heavily, blood all over his T-shirt. He shakes his head in disbelief. His face twists with pain, then slowly relaxes. He looks at me with an expression of profound disappointment, lets go of the knife and rolls over on to his side.

'You're all the same,' I tell him. 'You push and you push. In the end, something has to give.'

JOE

The first time I woke, Judy was sitting by the hospital bed, holding my hand. There was a presence at the back of the room. Seated. Someone I didn't know. It was all very vague. I drifted back to sleep.

The next time I woke, Rogers was in Judy's place, bulging out of his ill-cut suit, too fit and solid for the bright sterile room. The presence resolved itself into a burly young man on a chair against the wall, a notepad on his lap. He scribbled furiously when I answered Rogers's questions. After a few minutes, a nurse came in and shooed Rogers out. The young man stayed where he was. He did not speak.

There was a clock on the wall with a hand that jerked forwards minute by minute, but they gave me injections to make me sleep and at first it was hard, in the windowless room, to know which hour was which. After a while, I learned to tell the difference between day and night by the noise in the corridor outside.

My face ached, my chest ached, it hurt me to breathe, but at least the drugs made me sleep.

I timed my day by Judy's visits. Her face was pale, there were lines around her mouth, her eyes wandered. She sat by my bed in silence and held my hand. When I asked her what was happening she blinked and shrugged. 'Everything's back to normal.' Gripping my hand as if one of us were in danger of falling.

After Rogers's second visit, the burly young man with the notebook disappeared.

Rogers came again a couple of days later, telling me things now, no longer asking questions.

'They just faded away,' he said.

His soothing bedside manner surprised me. He held up a hand, ticking the players off on his stubby fingers.

Fernandez had driven straight from my house to Heathrow and taken the first flight west. He had what he was after. No point in hanging around.

Danny had vanished. Dublin probably but who needs him?

Helen followed the next day. TWA to Los Angeles. One-way.

Her passport was in order and there was no reason to detain her.

Riley was now sitting at her desk in Long Acre, answering the telephone and waiting, presumably, for some accountant from the parent company to come and wind the business up.

As for Karl, he had left two days before Fernandez paid me a visit. 'We assumed he was linked with a terrorist organisation,' Rogers said. 'Buy drugs, sell them to buy arms, that sort of thing. But he's not famous enough to have his picture up in German airports and Interpol has no trace of him. Personally, I suspect he was nothing more than a messenger boy for a bunch of Kraut gangsters. He came on like he was a political idealist. You know the line: contributing to the decline of capitalism by feeding its vices. In fact, he was a greedy little opportunist. The terrorism was just an act, a fantasy. It went with the lousy poetry.'

A ship of fools, I thought. They swim into my life, bells jangling; they turn it upside down, then sink without trace. I felt cheated.

As the pain subsided and my injuries healed, I realised Rogers was telling me something else. Telling me it was over, telling me to mind my own business. He seemed uneasy, a little shifty, and I couldn't make out if he was embarrassed by these disappearances because they spoiled his efficient image or if he was acting under orders. He'd let them slip away because the authorities did not want publicity. But it was no concern of mine and I was glad to see the back of him.

It was not until his final visit, the day before I left hospital, that I asked him why I hadn't seen Stonehouse.

Rogers straightened his back. The bedside manner dropped away. 'This is strictly a police matter,' he said. 'A man has been killed. There are possible criminal charges to answer. There is also the question of an illegal firearm.'

'It wasn't illegal. I got it through Stonehouse. I don't understand why he hasn't been here.'

Rogers looked at his shoes.

'Mr Stonehouse has taken early retirement.'

The shoes seemed to fascinate him. They were Oxford half-brogues, buffed to a high military shine.

'Cultivating his garden? Tending the thatch?'

Rogers cleared his throat. 'He seems to have gone abroad.'

'You're trying to tell me something.' I wanted to smile but my face hurt.

He shifted his bleak gaze to the window. 'Mr Stonehouse has been a great problem to me,' he said. 'Always under my feet in that Whitehall way of his. Never quite as helpful as he seemed. It was his men on duty the night the packing case disappeared from the garage. And then, of course, there's his background.'

'Eton and Christ Church, the Home Office, MI5 and the Travellers'.'

Rogers shrugged. 'Mr Stonehouse did a spell at the embassy in Budapest back in the Seventies. Assistant secretary, business attaché, one of those things. He made a lot of contacts which he was officially encouraged to keep up.'

'I thought Tommy was the one with contacts in Budapest.'

'That's how it looked but who knows? Maybe when Fernandez ran across Apple it was what you might call a happy accident.'

'Try telling that to Tommy now.'

The minute hand of the clock jerked forwards. An exasperated voice outside the door said, 'She's gone down to casualty. Don't ask me why.' Another voice said, 'The stupid bitch always gets it wrong.'

'What does the American say?' I asked. 'Langton Green, the one with the whisky face and the tassels on his shoes.'

Rogers sighed. 'I was never privileged to meet Mr Green. Mr Green doesn't figure on any of the lists. CIA, DEA, you name it, we've drawn a blank. But I suppose that's only to be expected in the circumstances.'

He got to his feet. His face was stern but not unfriendly. 'Loose ends don't appeal to me but what can we do?' he said. 'These are not matters any of us would necessarily want to enquire into further. As for yourself and your good wife, Mr Constantine: I don't foresee any charges. You'd plead self-defence, but frankly I don't think anyone would benefit if this case ever came to court.'

He paused at the door. Straight back, gimlet eye. 'Officially, this conversation never took place.'

'I've forgotten it already.'

No more squash. My right arm is permanently stiff, despite the physiotherapy in hospital and the set of exercises I solemnly run through every morning before breakfast. Lift, stretch, contract, stretch, swing.

The face I shave in the morning belongs to a hoodlum, the left eye stretched down to a long white scar across the cheek. Judy tries not to look but her eyes keep wandering back to it. We make love now with the lights out.

For a time, we talked about selling the house, getting out, starting over. But the market was still depressed and I wasn't sorry. The truth is, selling the place seemed a betrayal of my childhood, of my family who kept it going years after they could no longer afford to. In the end, we gave up pretending and brought in builders to convert the upper floors into studios, his and hers. No more commuting into town. No more separate lives. In due course, we will sell the old studios, but there's no hurry. The long financial drought that began with my father and lasted into my middle age has finally come to an end.

Thanks to Tommy.

My father would have hated the idea. I can imagine him shaking his head and saying, 'Not our kind of Jew.'

My father would have been wrong.

Judy and I are still trying to have a baby. So far without success. But the trying keeps us happy.

Once a month we drive down to Bournemouth and buy Aunt Rosie lunch at the Royal Bath.